I0690480

[KAGENT SERIES: #2]

TWISTPOINT

MARK SARNEY

TWISTPOINT (KAGENT SERIES: #2)
Copyright © 2014 by Great Star Publishing. All rights reserved.
First Print Edition: 2014

ISBN-10: 1-941188-03-6
ISBN-13: 978-1-941188-03-3

Cover and Formatting: Streetlight Graphics

TWISTPOINT (KAGENT SERIES: #2)

CHAPTER ONE

WHEN CRAIG LASSITER KNOCKED OVER Sudhur's market stall, he wanted to apologize to his friend and constituent, but he had a Chinese bounty hunter chasing him. And it was highly unlikely he would ever need Sudhur's vote again.

Craig dodged left through the crowded market, toward Muhammed's kabob-and-flapjack stand. He grabbed a stainless steel spatula out of the old man's hand as he ran by.

Muhammed smiled at Craig's antics, confused. "Mayor?"

Craig swiveled around and swatted away two plum-sized drones diving for his neck. The drones were studded with cameras, syringes, and zappers. They retreated out of reach and fell behind as he accelerated.

With his head turned to watch the drones, he plowed right into little Jagdish and his friends. They toppled over like empty trash cans.

Craig spun on one foot, flailing for balance, muttering, "Damn it, damn it, damn it. Sorry, kids."

As he spun, he saw the bounty hunter hustling through the crowd, his face shiny with sweat in the unforgiving midday sunshine. His pursuer was younger than Craig by three decades if he was a year. But the bounty hunter was dragging heavy body armor and a huge gun through the heat, while Craig only wore a thin shirt, shorts, and sandals.

The bounty hunter was blocked by the adults picking up Jagdish and friends, who were more indignant than injured. But as the only tall, pale, blond in town, Craig was easy to follow.

Friends, neighbors, and people who had voted for him watched in shock as the Mayor of Barabanki City ran pell-mell through the market, chased like a common thief by two drones and a one-man Chinese combat brigade.

"Behind you!" shouted Rajendra.

The drones approached from his left and right. He swatted at them again and they backed off. They could follow him around all day until he tired out. His lungs were burning, already.

He needed to get off the street, out of sight. He dodged around an old woman and knocked over a display of hats to block the path behind him.

"Victor, stop!" Fernando cried, grabbing the arm of the man he thought was Mayor Victor Champlain. "This must be a mistake."

Craig shook him off and kept running. There was no mistake. Craig had lived here under the name 'Victor Champlain' for over a decade. But now the game was up.

The buzz of a drone grew louder, nearer. It could zap him unconscious, tranquilize him, or maybe kill him on the spot. Did the bounty hunter want him dead or alive? Craig assumed the worst.

He dropped to his butt and whipped the spatula over his head. It connected with a satisfying crunch and thud. The drone spun away into a bush.

The bounty hunter fired his personal cannon into the air.

Before the gunshot's thunder stopped rolling, the crowd panicked, yelling, crying, shoving, pushing, and stepping on Craig.

He grabbed a hat that fell to the ground and bounced up to his feet. He covered his blond hair and followed the stampede down a side street, hoping to lose the drone in the crowd.

After running for a block, the crowd slowed and scattered. Other people came running out of shops and workplaces to see what had happened.

Craig reached the next corner and found himself at a residential cross street with a cafe on the corner. He stepped into the cafe, headed to the bathroom, and locked himself in.

He listened at the bathroom door, trying to get his heart rate and breathing under control. All he could hear was anxious commotion. Someone out there asked if it really was a gunshot and if anyone had called the police. After two minutes, he emerged and joined them in looking outside.

The police had just arrived in a three-man buggy. Craig didn't want to talk to them. He exited the cafe through a side door and walked down a side street.

He had practiced his escape for years. He had kept a cheap apartment under another name in case this happened, but it was on the far side of the market. He had to detour around it, go through the florist, and down an alley to Conroy's bistro.

But entering the florist would mean seeing Basu. Talking to her. They had done a stellar job avoiding each other since she ended their engagement.

He took a series of back alleys around the market to the street Basu's florist shop was on. A drone appeared ahead, at least twenty feet up, its lights blinking against the clear blue sky, scanning multiple streets at the same time. Its camera spotted him and it dove towards him.

Out of nowhere, a red-and-yellow soccer ball broadsided the drone in mid-air, knocking it into a wall. It fell into a muddy puddle in the street where it bubbled once and died. A kid cheered his kicking prowess. Craig hurried to the florist shop, but it was too late. Just as he reached the door, the bounty hunter sprinted around the corner toward him.

Oh, shit. Craig banged open the door to the flower shop and ran in.

The fragrant humidity coated him. Basu had always smelled so wonderful. He was drawing the bounty hunter right to her, but Craig didn't feel all that bad about it.

She was at the counter working on an arrangement and startled at the sight of him. For a brief moment, she looked happy to see him, like she always had. But when she saw his sweaty, panicked face her expression turned to concern. "Victor, what's wrong?" she asked in that low, sultry voice he adored.

"*Namaste*, sweetheart," he replied with a crooked grin as he ran past. He ran into the back, brushing past her new husband, who was confused. As Craig left, he could hear the bounty hunter opening the shop's front door.

He sprinted into the narrow alley behind the shop. He yanked open the back door to Conroy's. Conroy was slicing vegetables, unperturbed to see him.

Craig locked the back door behind him and clapped Conroy on the back. "It's time for me to leave."

Conroy looked at Craig and his face fell. "Ah, Vic. I'm so sorry."

Craig gripped the man's arm and nodded before ducking through a side door into the hallway that led to his second-floor apartment. Conroy went outside to wheel his dumpster to block the alley that Craig had come down. They rehearsed the plan dozens of times in the past.

Craig dashed up the stairs, fumbled with the lock, and finally burst inside. Nothing was moving in the apartment except for dust motes drifting in the windows' lazy sunbeams. He hadn't lived here since Basu dumped him. He grabbed his old beige rucksack from under the sink and was out the door in under twenty seconds.

He climbed the stairs to the roof. The sun seemed brighter and hotter up here. A drone buzzed in the distance, a black baseball of doom, and swung around towards him.

He wiped his brow and ran through the garden. The sticky leaves of the plants slapped against his bare legs as he powered through them. When he reached the roof's edge, he jumped.

He landed with a thud on the roof next door and fell into its thorny plants, getting scratched in a dozen places. Scrambling up, he sprinted across three more roofs in quick succession, the drone still in pursuit.

He saw the tiny blue Pradeshevy four-seater waiting by the curb. It was a distant descendant of a battery-operated cart, really. He slid down the fire escape to the street. Conroy must have alerted Svetanka; she waved wildly at him through the car window.

Craig ran for the passenger side and jumped in the narrow backseat without looking around. He was afraid of what he'd see coming after him.

"Drive, drive, drive!" he said, as he planted his face on the floorboard.

"We are headed to the train," Svetanka said, activating the nav.

The windshield cracked and a round zinged into the backseat above Craig's head. The sound of the gunshot followed. Svetanka shrieked and ducked.

The bounty hunter was ahead of them on the sidewalk, firing at the car. The car barreled into the right lane and turned right, away from the train station.

"What the hell are you doing?" Craig asked from the floor.

"Misdirection."

Craig dared a peek out the back window and saw the bounty hunter heading down an alley, presumably to cut them off.

"Are you hurt?" Craig asked.

Svetanka shook her head. "I'm fine. Are okay?"

Craig's middle-aged heart thumped away in his chest like a rabbit on a sugar high. "So far."

Before they reached the next intersection, Svetanka took the car off auto and spun the steering wheel. The Pradeshevy did a tight 180. It was headed in the opposite direction before Craig's stomach had finished whirling around.

Craig watched out the back window as the drone receded in the distance. They drove past Faizabad Road, against the afternoon traffic, and to the train station. Craig began to open the door, his bag in the other hand, but Svetanka swiveled around in the driver's seat and grabbed his arm.

"Basu is an idiot," she said and kissed him deeply on the mouth. "This was my only chance," she added with a sheepish grin.

Craig returned the grin with interest. "We'll always have Barabanki. You were a hell of a friend, Svet."

He hurried through the station, boarded the train to Lucknow and booked a flight out of the same city. He watched the platform to see if the bounty hunter boarded at the last second. As the train left the station, he sent the city Victor's resignation as Mayor. The train accelerated out of the station with no sign of the bounty hunter.

Craig admired Barabanki City, the verdant fields, and the mountains to the north as it all slid past. "It was a hell of a life."

Craig wasn't stupid, though. If there was one bounty hunter who had found him, there would be others. Lucknow was a big city with plenty of surveillance for bounty hunters to tap into. He needed more help to disappear again.

He made a call. It had to be early morning back home. It was answered on the third ring.

"Daniel Sloan? It's Craig Lassiter."

"Craig Lassiter? I thought you were dead years ago."

"Since Shanghai. I hid in India, made a life here. But a Chinese bounty hunter just found me. My old sins catching up with me. I need to get out of India, someplace safe. Can you help?"

Daniel sounded oddly pleased to hear this. "Are you interested in coming back?"

"The Stabilizer Alliance? Are you kidding me? I think the lifetime ban was for life, Daniel."

"Well, times change. Have you followed the news, lately?"

Craig grimaced. "A little. Sounds like you all have done fine since I left." It still stung a little, after all these years, that the Stabilizers had found success after his colossal Shanghai fuckup. It was as if he was a bad luck charm they had to lose before they could win.

"Not quite," Daniel said. "We hit a rough patch. I'm retired, but they really could use your help. That is, if you've learned from your mistakes."

Craig watched the topsoil farms zip by. They were farms that took garbage and feces and turned it into a critical import for offworld settlements. One man's shit may be turned into another's valuable lifeline, but Craig doubted he could ever be other than shit to the Alliance. He was an embarrassment, a cocky sonuvabitch who'd stretched the notion of nonviolence to its breaking point: using radioactive contamination of downtown Shanghai to render it uninhabitable. In retrospect, he was glad the Chinese had discovered the plot before he could execute it.

He shook his head. "I'm not that man, anymore. But I didn't think you all would ever take me back. I was just hoping you could pay for a plane ticket to the ass end of nowhere until I figured out where to hide next."

"Times change. I can probably get you a consulting contract with the Alliance," Daniel said. "If you're interested."

Craig had no idea what the hell anyone would want to pay him to consult on, but that was all happy talk and he didn't take it seriously. He just needed Daniel to give him a ticket and a place to stay back home. "Sure."

"I'll get you over here," his old friend promised.

"Thanks. That's...more than I expected," Craig said, relieved. He was headed home again, to the welcoming arms of the Stabilizer Alliance. What the fuck.

CHAPTER TWO

"THE STABILIZER ALLIANCE COULD BECOME immensely more dangerous than before," Nick Lincoln said to the camera. He stood in a teleconference cube, wearing a dark gray business suit.

He posted a line chart of Stabilizer Alliance activity levels during the last two years, since the crisis in Hamilton, Illinois. The line fell after their defeat in Hamilton, but had recovered to a stable level. A month ago, it had cratered to zero. The image appeared on the viewer of each leader of the Earth-spanning Burgess Consortium.

"But, if I may, Nick, this is only based on observable activity," Minister Seraprondi said. Every time Nick met with the leaders of the Burgess Consortium, she spoke first. And it was always critical. "Have you considered the possibility that they are conducting more subversive activities?"

"Terrorist activities. They are terrorists," stated General Burt Lasson, filling up his viewer's field of view.

Technically, the Stabilizers engaged in non-violent terrorism. But rather than argue, Nick said, "I know what you mean, General. But they are failing to terrorize anyone."

The General glared at him in disbelief.

Nick was used to the disbelief. It didn't shake his calm. Unfortunately, this rented tele-presentation room he was broadcasting from had blazing-hot lighting. Sweat trickled down his back under the heavy business suit. His armpits were peeling apart when he moved his arms. When he got sweaty, his unruly, spiky black hair became drenched and matted, and he looked desperate.

"Perhaps the Stabilizer Alliance isn't a threat, any longer," Nathan Li said in his gentle, delicate voice. "If they have become completely unsuccessful, perhaps they have given up trying to harm us."

Nick rolled his shoulders under his suit jacket and shook his head. "Organizational behavior research says this activity fall-off happens when an organization stops to reevaluate its purpose, change its personnel, and alter its capabilities."

"I created a threat index to measure how dangerous they are." He posted a graph of the threat index from 2307 forward in time. A blue line fell to zero on the threat axis by 2310. But a red line climbed sharply and reached 95% by 2312.

"Notice that in the next few years, the threat could increase or disappear. Which path occurs depends in part on what your Consortium does. The Alliance is at an impressionable point and you have a rare opportunity to influence it. You could push them toward the mutually beneficial outcome."

"We could?" Chair Hans Bechok echoed, incredulous. "How?"

General Lasson and Minister Seraprondi also looked skeptical.

Nick folded his hands together. "If you engage the Stabilizer Alliance as business partners, your residents get a slice of tranquility that the Alliance peddles and they benefit from your members' prosperity. Without enduring a costly ideological war that the Consortium may lose."

General Lasson waved his hand. "But we're already winning. Why change now?"

"Because the Stabilizer Alliance is regrouping and will become more dangerous," Nick replied. "Co-opting them is a cheaper, quicker path to victory. And the Consortium was founded to defend its member cities from the Alliance."

"How would we co-opt them?" Minister Seraprondi asked.

Nick posted a picture of a vacation resort. "Remember, I grew up in a Stabilizer Community. I know firsthand that these Communities struggle with employing their residents because they shun economic opportunities that come with offworld influences. They are hurting economically. The typical Stabilizer Community needs a perpetual subsidy to survive."

"The Consortium could partner with the Alliance to open Stabilizer resorts near your cities for your residents. This would hamstring their ability to finance terror activities, improve your citizens' mental health, and the Stabilizers would become dependent on the resort revenue."

"How do you know that?" Caracas Deputy Mayor Mac Nuviola asked. "Do you know the Alliance's financial situation?"

"No. This is based on deduction," Nick said. "The law of fundraising limits: An organization typically is raising all the money it can at the moment, unless grossly mismanaged."

"How is this a win for our member cities?" Minister Seraprondi asked.

"In addition to no more campaigns to crash them," Nick replied, "it could reduce your residents' stress levels, which are the highest in the solar system. Despite their economic stresses, the Stabilizers are almost as mentally well-off as offworlders." He posted a chart comparing mental health outcomes. "By turning the Stabilized lifestyle into a vacation experience, you would make it a place your residents like to visit, but not live in."

"Taken from a different perspective, what you are talking about here is melding these two cultures together." Nathan Li said, interlacing his fingers. "Using our members as the middle ground in which to tie together the offworld and Stabilizer lifestyles. While allowing each to flourish. Thus negating the Stabilizer need to be a threat."

Nick nodded. "I'm cribbing from offworld stream philosophy, which is actually compatible with the Stabilizer philosophy, but is more productive than the Consortium. We can take the best of both cultures, defuse the conflict, and improve both."

Nathan Li nodded. He seemed in favor.

"I don't understand," said General Lasson, throwing his hands up. "At the rate we are growing, their ability to threaten us will decline over time. While they navel-gaze, we can continue growing and strengthening our defenses. Have you factored that into these projections?"

Nick nodded. "Yes, but the Stabilizers know that they are losing if things continue. I think that's why they are navel-gazing. If you do nothing, they will take the more radical, destructive path. But we don't have long. Maybe six months at the outside."

Mac Nuviola leaned forward. "Why six months?"

"I wonder the same thing," Seraprondi added.

Nick replied, "It takes time to turn an organization in a different direction. Essentially, organizations have to progress through a grieving process. And if there are sweeping personnel changes, then it can take longer or shorter than a year for the organization to be functional again."

"Are these projections backed up by the work of other Kagents?" Minister Seraprondi asked. "I would like to know what validation you have done."

Nick shook his head. "I'd be happy to share that with you, but I'll just say that these projections are the cumulative work of all the Kagents. We don't have any models of the Stabilizers directly yet, though."

On each viewer, a different face scowled or frowned.

Deputy Mayor Nuviola scratched his forehead. "I have to tell you, Nick, there is a risk you haven't mentioned with your plan. What happens if our populations rub elbows with the Stabilizers and lose their work ethic?"

Nick said, "Your citizens are close to all-time highs for depression, stress, auto-immune diseases, and insomnia. Much higher than offworld societies. And yet, this chart I just put up shows that your productivity rates, innovation scores, living standards, and wealth are all below those offworld societies. What are you getting for all that anxiety?"

"You're comparing small offworld societies to billions of people on Earth, including millions who can't compete in the solar marketplace," Seraprondi replied.

Without taking his eyes off the screen, Nick subset the list of Consortium members to the ones with the highest productivity. Their mental illness indicators were above those of offworld societies, while their productivity and innovation scores were lower.

"You can't compete with offworld economies by becoming more stressed out, by working more. There is nothing superior about those offworlders; they just have better practices. And those practices could blunt the Stabilizers' attraction."

There was silence. "An interesting idea," Hans said in a guarded tone. He glanced at his colleagues' viewers. "Discussion?"

General Lasson cupped his hands together. "The Stabilizer Alliance is the enemy. Their threat is our reason for existence. Even making such an overture as this would be an admission of weakness."

"I agree with Burl," Abby Burgess said. "Let's not forget that these people are terrorists and they are not above using violence at times."

Nick forced himself not to frown. Abby, Juan's widow, was supposed to be one of his supporters.

Nathan Li stroked his bearded cheekbone with the back of his hand. "A win-win proposition is preferable, obviously. Co-opting them with our money seems feasible to me. This strategy is ingenious, Nick."

Mac Nuviola nodded emphatically in agreement.

Thank God for Nathan Li, thought Nick.

"But," Nathan continued, "our cultures have deeply-embedded notions about work and leisure. I am skeptical that we could orchestrate that. Or that we should even try."

Deputy Mayor Nuviola said, "We would need some confidence that the Stabilizers would be open to such an overture before we made it. We should send a low-level delegation to gauge their interest."

"Manipulating their internal decision making is black ops territory," General Lasson shot back in a low rumble, "which has its own risks. These are often hard to see until they cause a major problem."

Hans folded his hands. "The Consortium is still gaining members. We are finding our footing, focusing on how to defend ourselves from the Stabilizers. What I'm hearing from the Board is that we aren't ready to take the kinds of ambitious actions you propose, Nick. Your projections of the low-threat approach make more sense, based on what we've seen the last couple of years."

Nick nodded his head sadly. He had feared this. Show people a projection that confirmed their wishful thinking and it became impossible to talk them out of believing it. But he had to be honest, and show them the good and the bad. He tried to swallow his disappointment and not let it show.

"Well," Hans said with a plastic smile, "we must sign off and let Minister Seraprondi have a word with Nick." There were gracious smiles all around as the Board members thanked Nick and signed off.

Finally, it was just him and Minister Seraprondi. He gulped.

She smiled at him with brittle friendliness. "I have given you a hard time on occasion, but your work has been so important to us. We need 10 of you, especially given how fast the Consortium is growing."

That's wonderful, Nick thought. *I'll have to hire and train another Kagent.* His cash flow problems could be well on their way to becoming history.

The Indian woman continued, "We are forming our own group of about twenty analysts to collect and analyze our members' data. It is everything you had been doing for Juan. We will have to stop using external resources to help us, such as you."

Was she smiling because she had just gutted him? Shivers ran from his toes to the back of his skull.

But Serapondi smiled. "Oh, please understand: we want you to lead it."

17

Nick's eyebrows went up. "Hire me?" Something struck him funny about that. They had just shot down his proposal, but they wanted him to join them?

His brain froze for a good second or two before the implications rushed in. He would have to abandon his investments in a Kagent net for Earth. He would have to dump his other clients.

Seraprondi gave him her biggest smile ever. "Yes, we need you to spot security threats and conduct other data-driven intel activities. We want to monetize this aggregated data we are collecting. It would be a rich data source for marketing firms. While maintaining individuals' privacy, of course."

Nick grimaced. "The only way a Kagent can do that kind of work is to obtain a Warrant from a Kagent Privacy Council. I would have to quit being a Kagent. And drop all of my clients."

She didn't bat an eye. "I know, Nick. But your Kagent experience has prepared you for this position. You are ready for a bigger challenge."

He didn't want to quit. After years of being a bounty hunter, forced to curb-stomp privacy on a regular basis, being a Kagent was a dream-come-true.

But the prospect of struggling by himself on the sidelines while the Burgess Consortium blundered into an unnecessary fight with the Stabilizer Alliance made him sick. Shouldn't he sacrifice the Kagent dream to avoid the disaster he saw on the horizon? No, no, he would find another way. His instincts stood on their tiptoes and shouted at him. No. No. No.

"I'm sorry, I can't do it," he said.

For once, Minister Seraprondi didn't know what to say.

CHAPTER THREE

CRAIG HAD VISITED STABILIZER COMMUNITIES all over the world, but those of Northam and Europe had always struck him as the originals. For one, they were gated, contained places, with physical borders keeping the outside world away. For another, he had grown up in one and that meant that any close facsimile resembled his childhood home.

The taxi deposited him at the Community's entrance on a partly cloudy afternoon in early fall. No one traipsed around in a personal vehicle in a Stabilizer Community; traffic created noise and stress. You trammed or walked. And trams were for carting groceries, baggage, the immobile, or staying out of bad weather. And it wasn't raining, yet.

Craig walked, needing to burn off his nervousness. After almost two weeks of cautiously hopping across the planet to avoid detection, he needed daylight and exercise to readjust his internal clock.

He reached town center as the lunch rush emptied out of the cafes and restaurants. People stopped friends on the sidewalk and lingered. The town center was specifically designed to increase these happy accidents.

As a stranger, Craig maneuvered through the crowd without anyone recognizing him. He headed out to the residential neighborhoods that sprouted from the town center like broccoli florets from the stalk.

Neat, orderly houses stretched down the narrow residential streets. Stabilizer houses backed right up to the street, which were not more than utility alleys. The front of each house faced out on a common green that was bound together with sidewalks.

The houses themselves differed from the cookie-cutter designs elsewhere. They were designed to enhance community interaction, with the kitchen and porch facing the green, and the less-inhabited rooms in the back near the alley.

Craig had mixed feelings about this arrangement. As a kid, you could always see your friends outside, but as a teen, you felt like you were under the eyes of every suspicious adult. Teens took to hanging out alley-side and he had fallen into enough trouble 'off the green' that he had to leave home for a while.

Not that leaving his Stabilized Community had stopped him from falling into more trouble. It was just the way that his life had worked out. But now, here in the Carolinas, it felt like he was starting over.

The house he was looking for was halfway down the east side of Side Leaf Green. He knocked on the porch's screen door; there were no doorbells in a Community, because research pegged them as an annoyance and stress driver.

His old pal burst out of the front door, as if he had been hiding there waiting for him. God, Daniel had damn near gone gray since he had last seen him. Sure, it had been a decade plus since they had been forced to part ways, but his brain still carried an image of Daniel as he had looked on that final day in Shanghai.

"Craig, get in here," Daniel said and they embraced on the porch, gripping each other's upper arms to get a better look at the other. "You've jumped right into middle age, haven't you?"

"Me?" Craig said and laughed. He had hoped that the diet and sunshine of the subtropics would have slowed things down for him, but alas. "You look like an old retired bum."

"I am, now," his friend retorted and guided him into the house. It was a center hall colonial, with the kitchen on the left and the media room on the right. There were netpads scattered around the coffee table in the media room. A recent-model viewer hung down over the windows. On the viewer was a paused image of Daniel speaking, with a phony background behind him. He was wearing the same clothes he had on now: professor casual. He had been recording a lecture.

Daniel ducked into the kitchen and returned with old-fashioned coffee. Craig's was black; Daniel hadn't forgotten how he took it. "Semi-retired. I teach. Today's lecture-prep day, so I work at home. I hope you don't mind meeting here rather than at the office."

Craig waved away the concern. "It's great to finally see your house." There were pictures inside of two girls that he had never met. He had just stepped into his friend's private life in a way he never did when they served together. Heck, Daniel's youngest hadn't been born when the two of them had run for their lives after the Shanghai operation went tits up. Now, the girl looked to be about ten or eleven years old.

"Tell me about your wild life in India," Daniel said, easing himself onto the couch facing the viewer.

"Hot, peaceful, enriching."

"Have a family?"

Craig looked into his coffee mug, smiling through a bitter memory. "No, it never panned out, not like it did for you." He toasted Daniel with his mug and filled his mouth with hot coffee. The pain felt good. "So, how bad is it that you want to drag me back into the Alliance?" he asked.

Daniel frowned. "Very bad. Things went bad in Hamilton. I barely escaped and was slated to retire, anyway. Now the Board wants to liquidate Lobbying."

"No fucking way," Craig said.

Daniel continued, "The money types want to revisit our value propositions, as they put it. The very soul of the Alliance is up in the air. Which means our entire Stabilized way of life is at stake." He rubbed his hands together. "You need to get back in."

"With my past?" Craig asked. The last time the Stabilizer Alliance had done hardcore navel-gazing like that, it was because he'd screwed up Shanghai, at least in the Board's view. "I'm Lobbying's worst poster child."

"Until now," Daniel remarked sourly. He explained how his assistant for over a decade, Lisa Radisson, had turned out to be an offworld spy who had lied to him, had a hand in the violence that erupted in Hamilton, and had personally killed a Kagent. Just mentioning it aged him a decade.

"I'm sorry about that. But how do I help in a fight over Lobbying?" Craig asked.

Daniel shrugged. "You'll have to re-establish your credibility, of course. The Alliance can't be picky, anyway. The Burgess Consortium is adding members by the dozen, preparing themselves against our next move. If we give up, or even dither too long, the Alliance will lose all the progress we made after Shanghai."

"I know. We're slowly losing, already," Craig said. "You know that offworld developers even made it out to the sticks in India? In Barabanki, we rebuffed them the first couple of times, but the neighboring villages eventually took their money. The material living standards increased; the livability standards fucking tanked. We signed a contract with the Alliance, but that will only slow the damage."

Daniel scratched the back of his head, like in the old days, when he would rake his scalp while he racked his brain. "They asked me to find a consultant to work on the Lobbying problem. They have a caretaker running Lobbying now, Mandy DeCasas, but she won't do a single thing unless the Board tells her so."

Craig smirked. "So, you want to run an op against the Board?" The audacity of doing something like this made him a little giddy. The Alliance had pioneered the methods of nonviolent terror, stealth influencing, and subtle coercion. Some would call these advanced psychological tactics, organizational maneuvering,

22

or office politics elevated to a high art form. He thought of it as twisting other people's minds.

He and Daniel had run all kinds of ops against communities they were trying to crash or lobbying to adopt a Stabilized way of life. Play on an elected official's fears, gin up red herrings to influence a group, intimidate a reporter with the threat of outing a personal scandal, wield groupthink like a finely-honed weapon. They had done it all.

Until Shanghai, when Craig had gotten desperate, and stupid, over Daniel's wiser objections. There was something about having his hands on lightly radioactive material that he couldn't resist the temptation to use.

But these twisting techniques had never been used within the organization.

"Yes," Daniel said with a sly grin, "we have several friends on the Board but not enough. Without any Lobbying experience, the Board will be unaware that they've been played."

"You're still a slick operator, old man," Craig said. Shoot, the two of them, together again, twisting people into doing their bidding unwittingly. This could be fun.

"No terror tactics. No viruses, no radioactive anything, no demonstrations that go out of control. Got it?" Daniel asked.

Craig grinned. "It'll be good to get back into the old techniques. Work people at the retail level, one by one. Like we were trained to do."

"You won't have much in resources, other than your consultant fee and expenses," Daniel said in a low tone. "You'll be on your own."

"On my own? What about you?"

Daniel shook his head. "No, I'm out, retired. I'm still tainted by the Hamilton fiasco and Lisa Radisson. I can only help from afar."

"That sucks about half the fun out of it right there."

Daniel shrugged. "I know, but you need to be operating from a clean slate. You can't be linked to me or anyone else currently in

Lobbying. You're the experienced old hand who can come back in and evaluate the situation objectively."

"While secretly pushing our ulterior agenda," Craig added. "Okay, so what's my playbook?"

CHAPTER FOUR

IT WAS A COLD, MISERABLE walk home through the bustling streets of Hamilton, Illinois. The temperature hovered just above freezing and an icy rain pelted Nick like the sky was mad at him. He stopped for neon chili takeout, the latest crazy from the Southam zones.

The rain stopped as he carried the chili home to the rooftop apartment he shared with Pam Sullivan, his girlfriend and fellow Kagent. Her specialty was business negotiation and she was in her third year of serving as the City of Hamilton's Trade Representative.

He and Pam lived in a converted rooftop greenhouse in the neighborhood that contained the swankiest restaurants and offworld boutiques. It was the closest analog to the communities where Pam she had grown up on Tessa, or Mars, as most Earthers still called it. Pam had filled the greenhouse with plants when she moved in, and green fronds, bamboo, giant green leaves strained against the glass roof.

The apartments's warmth and humidity washed over Nick like a steam bath when he stepped inside. The smell of jasmine, moist dirt, and roses chased the chill out of his sinuses.

Pam was working in the front room. She turned and arched her eyebrow in a silent inquiry.

"I've had an interestingly bad day," Nick replied as he took off his coat. He explained how he lost his biggest client and turned down a job offer.

Pam blinked a few times. Then she walked over and pulled him into a hug. Nick held her tight, closed his eyes, and inhaled the scent of her dark hair. He tried to grab a moment where his stumbling Kagent business was not foremost in his mind.

Pam locked her arms around his waist and looked at him. She had these dark eyes that he felt like he could tuck his soul into. But lately, he had a harder time looking into them. He had tried running a Kagent business for over two years now and he had felt like a failure every step of the way. Pam couldn't be so blinded by love that she didn't realize the same, could she?

"Let's eat. You'll feel better," she said, opening the chili cartons.

Some enterprising jungle farmers had created these fluorescent-colored peppers that had become a thing this winter. It made the chili glow and provided a lot of spice.

It also gave him and Pam something to chat about while they ate. As a rule, Pam didn't talk about work during meals. At first, he hated that because he had another Kagent sitting across from him but couldn't talk shop with her. But these days, it made meals a refreshing respite from the growing gloom that covered his work like a bad smell. But dinner only lasted so long, and as Pam handed him cartons to wash out and throw in the recycling, she said, "You were tempted to take the Burgess offer, weren't you?"

"Yes, of course," he said. "But taking that job is too much like a bounty hunter. Plus, I couldn't take any other clients. It means quitting as a Kagent. I couldn't do that even if it means I go bankrupt."

"That doesn't have to happen. My offer still stands," Pam reminded him. The moment she left the Trade Rep job, she would have enough business that her consulting income and her client list would keep him afloat.

Nick sighed. "I don't want you to leave prematurely to rescue me." He worried that mixing business into their relationship would be disastrous for both his business and their relationship.

"This is a bigger issue than whether you can run a Kagent consulting business on your own," Pam said. "You're trying to establish the Kagent profession on Earth. Singlehandedly. You have been pouring all of your revenue into a Kagent net to rival the BHN. You can't do that alone. Offworld, we would organize a consortium to raise the capital and build the infrastructure for an entire Kagent net."

Nick stewed rather than answer. He was feeling several things all at once: anger, shame, relief, and hope. There just weren't words to say it all.

Pam tilted her head to the side. "You don't want to be dependent on me, is that it?" There was ice in her voice, the same ice that always threatened to slice right through his jugular when they argued.

"Yes," Nick said. "Yes, that's part of it. We live in your apartment. I landed some of my contracts because of your help. I want us to be equals."

She folded her arms. "We won't be equals in everything all the time. We need to help each other out, sometimes. You're exaggerating just to feel worse about yourself."

Nick shook his head. "My corporate contracts jumped 20% after we attended the Civic Center gala three months ago and business types saw me on your arm."

"I've used you as an incentive to seal deals for the city, too," Pam countered. "I want to help you out. Not just because of us but because you're trying to do something for all Kagents, down here and offworld."

Nick groused like a pouting toddler, "I don't want you to see me as your employee."

"Haha, don't be a pissy little dickstool." She kissed him on the cheek.

Nick brought the plates to the sink. Her sink. "I can't fail at this. Not this. Being a shitty bounty hunter was okay because I was only in it for BHN access. But not this." He turned and looked at her. "I need to be a successful Kagent."

"Do you think your role in averting the crashpoint here was a fluke?" Pam began scrubbing. "You're a good Kagent, but you're a business virgin, okay? You have to fail to figure out what works."

She rubbed his arm. "That's what those who succeed in business do: They keep trying, keep learning, keep adapting as things change. It took me four times to get my consulting business running when I started out. And I was consulting people about business!"

Nick chuckled. "I've rebooted my business plan only twice. At first, I went for building the Kagent Earth net as fast as I could. When I burned through money too fast, I switched to building a positive cash flow. Now that has turned to shit though."

"And taking the Burgess job would solve those problems?" Pam's voice dripped with skepticism.

He shook his head. "No, it would mean the business had failed. I just couldn't let that happen. Not yet."

"What, then?" Pam asked gently. Despite her soft tone, she definitely wanted to know. Suddenly, he felt like a houseguest who had overstayed his welcome.

Nick replied, "I'm going to stick with it. Teach me how to run this business so I can continue being a Kagent. It's always darkest before dawn, right?"

"Or it's because you're dead. Sometimes, it's hard to tell," Pam suggested with an arched, mocking eyebrow.

He sighed. "A lot of my potential clients held off because the Kagent net on Earth wasn't big enough." He began scrubbing the plates in bubbly brown water with fizzing, gritty soap that tickled his skin.

Pam tossed her hair back with her hand. Her lips sealed in a thin line; she was irritated. He must not be understanding something. "Can you speed up the development of the Kagent net? Are you open to bringing in other investors? More help building it?"

Nick handed her a dish for drying. "You mean terrestrial investors? Other Kagents?"

"Not me, no. I'm barred from investing while I work for the city," Pam said. "I meant finding other investors. Other Kagents. The mistake you are about to make, again, Mr. Lincoln, is assuming you have to do it all yourself. Every start-up has people with different strengths. The technical genius may not be the best salesperson. The finance whiz may be lousy at logistics. If you create a firm or a consortium of firms, you can find partners to handle functions that you don't know."

It clicked in Nick's head. "My aunt Kelly already is an expert at Earth data collection. She and you have connections with offworld Kagents. We would need someone to manage the data and security."

"And you need to see Meredith, Nick. You need her help. She does the same kind of Kagent work you do. I can't really help you much there. And, Meredith needs our help too."

He had promised Meredith Radisson, the widow of his Kagent mentor Bridge Radisson, to visit her and learn from her. "I will, at some point."

Pam huffed. "Nick, it's been two years."

His eyes shot over to a messy painting stuck to the glass wall in his tiny workspace. His niece Sally was four years old, and he hadn't seen her in eighteen months. It seemed like she had just been born last week. If he went to Tessa, there was a good chance he would be disowned and would never see her again.

Pam followed his gaze. "You can't live your life in fear of your family's travel restrictions. Millions of people cross from one planetary system to another each year and return home."

Nick nodded. His parents had all but disowned him over a three-day trip to the Moon. Sally's mother, Nick's sister Dez, let her stay in touch with Nick for now, because Sally was too young to know why everyone avoided Uncle Nick. He still thought he could salvage the situation. But jetting off to Tessa would kill those chances. The prospect of losing all contact with his parents, Dez, and Sally tore at him like falling through a thorny rosebush.

"I'll go," he blurted. "I want to meet your parents and Meredith. You think I would squirrel out of that?"

Pam rubbed his cheek. "I would rather you keep trying than give up and become miserable."

He smiled. "Thank you. But I can't take failing like this for much longer. I feel like I'm letting you down, my parents, the entire Kagent industry."

Pam snorted. "No one expects that much out of you or anyone else." She sent a financial chart to a nearby viewer. "Our combined cash flow is still positive."

"Yes, but time is running out to take advantage of the Stabilizers' navel-gazing," Nick said. "If I try salvaging my business, I'd have to let that go."

She regarded him coolly. "You really think there's a way to twist the Stabilizers to take the more enlightened path? Cross has rechecked those projections?"

"Cross reruns the projections every hour to capture any new info. There hasn't been any change in weeks," Nick said.

As a general rule, Cross, Nick's female AI assistant, was not active in the apartment or around Pam. Pam and Cross didn't get along. There was some kind of coworker-girlfriend tension there that Nick didn't understand.

"I suppose I could snap my fingers and get the Burgess people to reconsider my boyfriend's contract," Pam said, tapping her finger on her cheek thoughtfully.

Nick folded his arms. "Your smartass tone suggests I should give up on taking advantage of this Stabilizer twistpoint. But you don't want to say it like, you know, an adult would."

"You must be rubbing off on me," Pam replied.

"I dry-hump you when you're sleeping," Nick shot back.

"Like a dog, figures. Anyway, I don't see how you are in a position to pursue that twistpoint right now," Pam said. "You couldn't even 'twist' the Burgess people to extend your contract."

Nick pulled the plug on the sink and watched the fizzing broth drain away. Much like the opportunity to turn the Stabilizers away from a mutually destructive strategy.

Pam took hold of his chin and guided his gaze back to her. "You always put yourself second. For all the right reasons, but still, you keep finding new reasons. You don't have to do that to yourself."

She was right, of course. Somehow, offworld Kagents pranced from one glorious assignment to another, their eyes twinkling in self-fulfilled ecstasy, while he beat his head against a locked doorknob. Maybe he was his own worst enemy.

"Aren't you supposed to save me from myself?" he asked, half-seriously.

Pam thrust her hip to one side and looked him up and down in disgust. "Hell, no. You're a grown adult. Besides, I like your panicked-squirrel routine. It's cute."

He reached over and kissed her on the lips and she sent him over to his workspace. Fall down, get back up, she meant.

Cross was less supportive. [YOU ARE AN IDIOT,] she texted across his viewer. [The Burgess contract was the majority of your cash flow. You only have enough savings left to operate for a few more months. Here's how your business will likely end.] Cross posted a short-term projection of his balance sheet.

[It's either this or starve, Cross,] Nick texted back.

[It's a good thing I don't need to eat.]

Unfortunately, the Kagent nets didn't model how to keep a Kagent business running on a place like Earth. Nick would have to figure something out fast or he would have to actually call Rotty's. Or beg Abby to have the Burgess Consortium take him back.

Nick reviewed his latest data purchases for the Earth Kagent net. He had a copy of the inventory database from a hardware retail chain in the Southeast, the finances of an East Coast network of health clinics, and the entire corporate data platform of a pet supply wholesaler.

Another few pieces of the puzzle. He thanked all three companies for letting him buy access and offered to discount his standard analysis package: scan for security vulnerabilities, data errors, and any cross-tabulations they might want. Since these entities had just sold him a copy of their data or outright access, they were predisposed to have him see what was lurking in there.

Nick called these jobs "data hustles." They were a low-revenue market niche that bounty hunters ignored. Rather than predict future shoplifters from a Rotty's convenience store, bounty hunters only caught shoplifters after the fact. Since most of Rotty's products were eaten or used immediately after they were stolen, this didn't help.

Nick discovered falsified purchasing, three instances of stolen fish food, and projected an upcoming surge in indigent patients at the health clinics. Good, that would keep those businesses coming back for more of his analysis.

[Let me see the revenue projections for doing this work,] he texted Cross, so Pam wouldn't hear.

Cross displayed the new graph. Nick's business financials didn't look any better. His business was sprinting in a race it was doomed to lose.

CHAPTER FIVE

DANIEL HANDED HIM A NETPAD with a list of the six Stabilizer Alliance Board members. Each one was labeled as a friend or foe.

"Salvador March? From my hometown?" Craig laughed. "We grew up together. How the hell did he get on the Board? He's not rich!"

Daniel didn't laugh. "Five years ago, there was an investigative journo who made a pile of money exposing lousy conditions in our poorest Communities. The donors were upset, recruitment cratered, and people even left. Your friend Sal had been warning the Board for over a decade about the situation. The donors wanted to make sure the Board had a voice like his."

Craig shook his head. He hadn't seen Sal for years before Shanghai. He had a hard time picturing his childhood pal rubbing elbows with the rich and privileged. "You labeled him a foe? Last I knew, his primary concern was recruiting burned-out buzzers."

Daniel nodded. "He is not a friend of Lobbying."

That actually sounded like Sal, too. Growing up in South Haven together, just east of Baton Rouge, Craig and Sal saw plenty of poverty and hard living. Sal had decided when they were teens that he would dedicate himself to improving conditions for people, both materially and spiritually. Craig had to screw around for a while before figuring out what he wanted to do.

"If you think he'll change his mind just because it's me asking, you're dead wrong," Craig said.

"No," Daniel said. "But I thought you would have the best chance to persuade him."

Craig grunted. "He knew I was a slick bastard twenty years before you did. I tried to talk him out of the priesthood and look how well that went." He noticed the concerned look on Daniel's face. "Don't sweat it, if I can find something mutually beneficial, he'll listen. That's how I got him laid before he went off to the seminary." He held up his hands innocently. "What?!?"

Daniel looked sheepish. "I just remembered what you tried to pull at my bachelor party."

Craig laughed. "Most guys would have enjoyed a gel-fueled sex club on their last night of freedom. Anyway, who else is on the Board?"

He paged through the list of Board members on the netpad, none of whom he knew. A rich philanthropist, a business owner, an entertainment mogul, a cutthroat tycoon, and another philanthropist.

Daniel highlighted one name. "The Chairwoman, Penny Andrews, is your client. You'll be her consultant to the Board, hired by her with the consent of the other Board members. But you really work for her, to research the situation and report on possible strategies."

Craig skimmed the personality profiles, the areas of agreement and disagreement, and the members' positions on a number of Stabilizer issues. "So, what kind of op are we running on them?"

"The playbook is wide open," Daniel said with a grin. "Your only constraints are keeping your ulterior motives hidden and obeying the Alliance's ethical guidelines, of course."

Craig held up his hands. "Of course, of course."

"Also, no bounty hunter profiles of the Board members. They are all highly protective of their privacy. They have alerts on any searches of them in the bounty hunter databases. Even Alliance HQ doesn't know who the Board members are."

Craig shook his head. "You know we can't twist people if we don't have a psyche workup on each one and how they interact with one another. Unless y'all came up with some fancy new methods while I was in India."

Daniel gave him a hard look. Something Craig had said reminded the old warrior about Hamilton—he could see it in his eyes. "We didn't. Just the old-fashioned tools, these days. But most of these folks are known well enough in the public arena that whatever you can dig up yourself should be plenty."

Craig refused to stumble around blind without proper intel. He just had to find a discreet bounty hunter. Daniel wouldn't know. But he nodded his agreement and Daniel continued. "Your real problem is time. They are debating whether the Lobbying's strategy has failed and if it's outlived its usefulness. Short-term, I'd recommend issue-framing, choice architecture, a stall-for-analysis maneuver to buy time, too. If you have to, use de-urgency moves on our allies who want to force the issue before you're ready."

Daniel ticked off the next item on his fingers. "Medium-term, deal with the business types' profit interests, because they started this re-examination to buff the Alliance balance sheet. Remember, the playbook is wide open. Long-term—and by that, I mean a few months—map the Board's group dynamics, find leverage, and hit those twistpoints."

"And, somehow, not let them catch on that I'm puppetizing them?" Craig shook his head. "They know about these tactics, some of them helped develop them. They're going to see this coming a mile away."

Daniel leaned back on the couch, picking lint off his sport coat. "The target never sees it coming if we've done our homework. They are as blind to their own blind spots and pressure points as anyone else. What do you think?"

Craig wasn't so sure. The old playbook wasn't old to him; he'd been using it all along in India; it's how he became mayor. He looked at the list of Board members again. There was a difference between running an op on unsuspecting locals and running an op against Cooper Mangold, who practically wrote the playbook when he helped found the Alliance. Jesus. It would be a hell of a challenge. "I'll do it. But you already knew that, didn't you?"

"Of course. Ms. Andrews can tell you how to work the other Board members. Talk with her first," Daniel said. "It's the closest that we'll get to a psyche workup on the others."

Craig thumbed through the list of Board members. They were scattered all over the globe. He would have to meet each one in person, he guessed, to gain their trust, hear their take on the situation, and build a repertoire that would help him twist them when the time came. "This sure beats wasting away in India, or hanging around here, seeing which of my relatives are still alive," Craig said.

Daniel frowned. "You are going to visit the family, aren't you? You haven't been back since before your dad passed."

Craig waved a hand. "I'll visit my mother, sure." It had been over two years since they had exchanged a message, though.

Daniel handed over a netpad and access to an expense account. "Expense accounts can be used for visiting family; that hasn't changed. You've been away a long time."

Craig chewed the inside of his cheek. "Everyone but my mother will lose interest when they figure out I don't have any money."

Daniel grimaced, but before he could say anything, his daughters opened the door, back from school. It was like a loud pink firecracker went off: backpacks scattered to the corners, followed by jackets amid a steady stream of garbled pleas for attention.

Daniel introduced the girls to Craig. The older one eyed Craig warily while the younger one pumped his hand enthusiastically. They were nice kids and Daniel was a good poppa, buzzing around the kitchen to get the girls a snack.

The house began to buzz with that hustle that irritated Craig on some level. Daniel would be distracted with his daughters; it was time for Craig to leave.

Daniel walked him to the front door. Craig shook his hand. "Are you really going to sit this out?"

Daniel jerked his head in the direction of the two sisters squawking at one another at the kitchen table. "Timing's not good for me. Besides, the Alliance and I are on a break—they really don't want me around."

Craig shook his head. That he, the disgraced, loose cannon, was virtually back in the Alliance while Daniel, the goody-goody, was virtually exiled was strange.

He began the long walk back to the tram stop. The temperature had dropped and chilly weather wasn't his thing. He patted the netpad in his pocket, eager to tackle the challenge of twisting the organization that had disowned him. But first, he had to get this family visit out of the way first or every Alliance person he met would badger the hell out of him about it.

CHAPTER SIX

THE FIRST TIME HE HAD met Nick Lincoln, Eldred Borbola had been full of confidence. He had ambushed Nick on the Moon, and had kept Nick's head spinning with his superior knowledge and tech all through the Hamilton crisis.

Now he felt twitchy about encountering Nick again. He wasn't used to needing help or having to ask for it, and the mere concept made him feel weak and inadequate. And having to ask this homegrown Kagent made it worse.

The candlelit bistro named the Canary Soup Shoppe looked like a romantic dinner spot to him. But Nick had picked this place and arranged for a table in the back dining room. Borbola's drones verified that the entrances were easily watched and their voices wouldn't carry far.

When Nick sat down he looked stiff and sour. He didn't trust Borbola, and for good reason: Borbola had lied to him frequently. But it had been so worth it each time, so entertaining. Borbola considered it an unavoidable cost of being himself.

"Eldred, it's been a long time," Nick said with a deadpan expression. He looked at the menu pad and then set it back down. "You running a drone patrol in here?"

"Of course," Borbola said. "Didn't I teach you to keep a perimeter up at all times?"

Nick frowned. "The city banned unapproved offworld drones. Especially after your little demo of them here."

Borbola chuckled. It had been awesome to send tens of thousands of gnat-sized drones sweeping through the Hamilton streets like a biblical plague. They had choked and shocked dozens of Dragoon contract security troopers who were trying to conquer the city.

Instead of getting the key to the city and a big fat thank you, though, the city ordered Borbola to leave. The media had spun his drone attack as a horror show and a violation of privacy, decency, and everything good. The City Council banned the use of small, gnat-sized drones within city limits.

"I recall saving your life with those drones," Borbola replied. "I also see that you have your own drone patrol running. As you should."

"The city gave me permission when I asked nicely and promised to keep it discreet. So, what do you want?"

Borbola wiped the smile off his face. "I wanted to apologize for what has happened between us, Nick. I've treated you badly. And you were right about the Stabilizers. I should have trusted you."

Nick blinked in surprise. "Was I actually right about something? And you're admitting it? I'm feeling faint."

Borbola continued, "Screw you. I've learned a lot the last two years. Tracked down some leads and hounded some Dragoons."

"Destroyed the Dragoons is more like it," Nick said. "And I cheered when it happened."

After running the Dragoons out of Hamilton, Borbola and his affiliates and helpers had continued to assault and embarrass the contract security outfit. The Dragoons had lost half their contracts and their stock's share price had plummeted. They had fallen to the point where he had lost much of the enjoyment he used to feel trying to ruin them.

Yeah, Borbola thought, *he doesn't trust me at all.* "It only led me to realize that the Dragoons were a symptom, not a threat. I've become more and more concerned with the Stabilizers. In part because I can't seem to learn anything about them."

Borbola's bounty hunting business was built on him knowing

what others didn't, often by any means necessary. That approach had driven him out of the Kagents years ago, but it had kept him rolling in money as an independent bounty hunter. When you got used to omniscience, feeling ignorant itched like an eyelash scratching your eyeball.

Nick thumbed his order into the menu. "The Stabilizers have been quiet, lately. A lot of people think they aren't a threat."

"Yes. I heard you lost your contract with the Burgess Consortium because they thought you had become Chicken Little."

Nick glared at him, confirming it. "I'm not discussing my clients with you."

Borbola held up his hands. "That's fine. I'm here because I was wondering if you and I could work together on figuring out the Stabilizers. I do think they are a threat."

Nick's jaw dropped. "Work together? Wait, why do you think the Stabilizers are a threat?"

Borbola smiled. "I have a small merry band of sources and helpers. Remember Jerry Craftchek, the Dragoon weasel who tried to start the civil war here?"

Nick nodded. "I do tend to remember people who try to kill me or Pam."

"How is Pam?" Borbola asked, leaning back in his chair. He remembered too late that this was another sore point on the trust issue. "Are you two still together?"

"She hasn't wised up yet," Nick said. "She hasn't figured out that I'm a total failure."

Borbola laughed. "She's smarter than you think. She knows we're all failures, but she still likes you. Anyway, Jerry works for me now, off and on, running down loose ends. Now, you may think that means I've been hearing all kinds of troubling things. But the problem is, no one has heard anything at all about the Stabilizers."

Nick nodded. "I've had the same problem. I don't have a Warrant to do a full profile. The models show the Stabilizers either are a huge threat, or no threat at all. But you could investigate them in ways that I can't."

Borbola held up his hands. "I've tried. They mask their Communities from surveillance. They even blind overhead satellites from the ground. I can't even tell who's coming or going. I can't even figure out who is bankrolling them. The BHN is near useless because they use secure darknets."

"Well, why don't you just hack them?" Nick asked.

They both laughed. It was an old bounty hunter joke. Amoebas were so clueless about modern network security that they thought you just had to select 'hack' from a pull-down menu. The reality was that network security had become a never-ending battle between hacker and sentinel Simons. No bounty hunter bothered with that—they usually had all the data they needed from the BHN.

"I thought we could help each other out," Borbola said as the food arrived. Nick had a steaming bowl of pea soup while Borbola had three appetizers. They split a carafe of distilled water, but neither one had opted for gels. "I can keep probing them like a bounty hunter; you keep working the Kagent angle. We share notes."

They ate in silence for several minutes. Borbola finished his spinach side salad and Nick dug a sizable hole in the soup. Nick finally said, "Tell me why you're interested in the Stabilizers when I can't convince anyone to give them more than a glance."

Nick wanted to know Borbola's motivations. The trust issue combined with his own mysterious nature. Borbola chased down the last bite of his stuffed mushrooms with a mouthful of water. "Any organization that is a black box reminds me of the Dragoons, and has people like Lisa Radisson worries the hell out of me."

Nick teared up for a moment and tried to clear his throat. He took a long drink of water and dried his eyes. Lisa had killed her own stepfather, and Nick's mentor, Bridge. Borbola had heard that Nick had been present at the fatal family showdown.

"Sorry," Nick said, his voice filed down into gruff tones.

He's such a softy, Borbola thought. *Nick only knew Bridge for a*

41

few weeks, at best. Borbola had known Bridge for over a decade and never felt half as emotional about the old man.

He was much more upset that the Stabilizers' rapid success in crashing cities across Earth had been fueled by Lisa's theft of Kagent forecasts. The more he learned about how close the Stabilizers had come to crashing Hamilton, the more concerned about them he had become.

Nick shook his head. "I have a Kagent Warrant on Lisa. I have a way to spot her when she uses disguises and dead spots in surveillance. If she appeared in any city on the BHN or Kagent surveillance, I would know. But there's been no sign of her for two years now. Her trail is totally cold." He twirled his soup spoon. "Given how tightly hidden the Alliance is, I think she taught it how to avoid Kagent surveillance, too."

"Really? Shit. She could be the key to cracking open the Stabilizers then," Borbola wondered. He grinned. "Have you been doing all your searching virtually? You have? You need to go pound some pavement, Nick. Think like a bounty hunter. Occam's Razor says she's hiding some place you haven't looked, yet. You have to talk to people where she may have dropped off the grid. Depopulated mountainous regions, the Amish."

Nick mulled that over. His eyes went wide. "Inside Stabilizer Communities?"

Borbola shrugged. "Maybe. Go hit the ground in those Communities, spread some drones out, and look for her. By yourself though. I'm banned from all Communities because of some, uh, reasons." He smiled mischievously.

"That could take a year," Nick said. "But the Alliance is regrouping now, and it'll be back on its feet in a few more months. Right now it's soul-searching. I think we can convince it to pursue a non-destructive path."

"Convince? You mean twist them, trick them into becoming less dangerous." Borbola couldn't picture the Stabilizers becoming soft and cuddly. "The annoying, dangerous assholes who have protested in the streets and taken over liftports for decades?" He bit off a chunk of potato skin and pushed the cheesy bacon goodness around in his mouth. "With human weapons of high destruction floating around, like Lisa. And you want to convince them to drop all of that?"

"I want to convince the Alliance that it can succeed without the dangerous tactics. Something mutually beneficial."

Nick knew more than he let on, Borbola thought. The certainty with which Nick had just said that was based on something. Could he be right to some degree? If the Alliance was having an internal fight like Nick said, maybe all they needed to do was help the sane side win. But what would that entail? Borbola had no idea. He held up a mostly eaten potato skin. "I think you have some crazy ideas. But I can work with you despite that."

"I don't trust you, Eldred. But I can work with you despite that. We agree to share any information about the Alliance. Nothing more and nothing less."

Borbola had multiple game pieces in motion, all in interlocking and interrelated moves to free Earth from offworld influence. The Stabilizer question mark made those moves impossible.

For the first time, Borbola wondered if maybe he would get played by Nick this time around. But the only way to learn anything more about the Alliance was to play ball with this spiky-haired punk. Borbola smiled and shook Nick's hand. "Deal."

"Great." Nick tossed his napkin on the table and stood up. "Now pay for this; you're richer than God."

CHAPTER SEVEN

CRAIG SLIPPED IN AND OUT of his mother's assisted living building during a weekday, when his brother and sister-in-law would not be around. His mother was older and more fragile, but it was a good visit. He promised to come by regularly and insisted on sending her money, once he was paid.

And then he slinked off, tracking down his old friend Sal to an East Baton Rouge parish council meeting. He took a taxi into the city and endured a full body search in the fortified ring around the parish government center.

He loitered in the lobby, waiting for the meeting to end. Whenever someone exited the council chamber, an auditory furball of anger and tension boiled out of the room behind them.

He didn't have to ask what the council meeting was about—he knew that somehow, the Stabilizer Community was about to get screwed and Father Salvador March was fighting a losing battle on its behalf. Sal always inserted himself into delicate situations like this, a one-man savior crusading to right wrongs for Stabilizers everywhere.

Craig busied himself studying the publicly-available information about the other board members. Some were famous, some were unknowns, but all were wealthy. When the meeting broke up, he was reading another puff piece on the tycoon Cooper Mangold that was probably crafted by Mangold's PR people at GoldLand Entertainment.

A steady stream of happy and aggrieved faces paraded past Craig, but no Sal. He was probably jawing at a councilman or calming someone on the losing side.

Five minutes passed.

Craig tried another search for material about the elusive Haruka Gallardo when a final clump of people left the council chamber. The last one out of the room was a familiar face.

"Father March, as I live and breath," Craig said, letting his hometown accent pour forth thick and rich.

"Good God, Craig Lassiter?" The portly man jerked around and wrapped Craig in a bear hug. "It's so good to see you again, man! Another lost soul finds his way home. Where have you been the last twenty years?"

"Traveling the Orient, learning the mystic arts from yogis and Tibetan monks," Craig replied with a wink and a grin as they shook hands vigorously.

"Have you been by your folks' place, yet?"

Craig acted shocked. "You think I'd come running to see some pudgy *padre* before I saw my own kin? Goddamn, who do you think I am?"

"Blasphemer heading for hellfire and damnation, naturally," Sal laughed.

"Can I tear you away from this for a few minutes?" Craig asked. "Official business."

Sal led the way outside, away from prying ears.

The raw Louisiana winter had a chilly bite to it. Sal kept carrying his coat and smirked as Craig tugged his jacket closed. It was just the two of them strolling the streets, like when they were kids.

"So, you still priesting?"

"Oh, yeah. Ministering to the buzzers in New York Jersey and the saved here at home. The Church lets me work part-time for the Alliance as long as I do real work in my parish." Sal looked at him. "What have you been up to?"

"I may be the Board's new consultant," Craig replied. "I have to interview with Penny Andrews."

Sal furrowed his considerable eyebrows. "She did mention a consultant might be coming around, talking to us. I expected she would find someone respectable, professional."

"Rumor is that one may be too high-priced, so they're looking at me, instead," Craig said, spreading his arms. He explained his mission to evaluate the Alliance's strategy. "Anything you can tell me before I meet with her?"

"I've tried to stay out of the Board's arguments," Sal said. "My only concern is that we do right by our own folks."

Craig nodded. Sal hadn't changed a bit in decades, other than to gain weight and lose hair. "So, how did you get on the Board?"

Sal shrugged. "Someone thought the Board needed a token regular guy to counter all those rich bastards. I couldn't say no."

"Good to see the Board has a moral center." Craig patted his friend on the shoulder.

"Eh, not much good that's done. The Board is pretty split on what path to take. This Radisson woman managed to do all kinds of wrong in our name. We may have to shut down Lobbying, Craig," Sal said, looking worried.

"It's okay. I can be an open-minded consultant now, evaluating all the possibilities, right?"

Sal chuckled, unsure whether to believe him. "I can't see a reason to keep Lobbying," he added, searching Craig's face for a reaction.

"Well, that won't answer the central question—what should the Alliance be doing? Has the goal changed? The strategy? Or maybe just the tactics?"

Sal shook his head. "Nice dodge. I hope you have a plan, or something. We've been lost since the Hamilton op failed. Conditions across the Communities took a hit. Recruitment is down. The Alliance's wealthy benefactors have signaled that they're feeling less generous. This whole thing could unravel pretty quickly."

Craig sniffed. His nose was running in the cold, dry air. "What do you want the Alliance to do, Sal? Tell me your Stabilizer dream."

Sal smiled. "Communities spread across the world, with living standards and clout equal to the richest buzzopolises. A waiting list to move in. Billions of peaceful, content people living lives of their own choosing, with meaning and dignity. And, of course, more Catholics."

"Of course," Craig agreed with a wave of his hand. "How do you think we do that?"

Sal threw his hands up. "Beats the devil out of me. I've got buzzers in Brooklyn who are burnt out, but don't want a crappy life in a rundown Community. And I got people in our Communities here facing a huge increase in their water bills while their work hours get cut. Both groups think that at least the crazy buzzer lifestyle means you can pay your bills. You tell me how to do it, because honestly, I'm too busy hanging on for dear life."

"Whatever I come up with has to be acceptable to enough of the Board," Craig noted. "But if that were easy, you would have already found it."

Sal nodded. "I'd rather support the Communities than fund half-cocked political crusades against the rich buzzers. And the business types want the Alliance to make a profit. Or clear the way for them to make their own profits. It looks like we're getting out of the stealthy political stuff."

Craig raised an eyebrow. "You think the other Board members want Lobbying to disappear?"

"They're clueless about the moral dimensions of the Alliance's existence. They'd shut the Communities and Lobbying and just use the Alliance as an interest group to front for their businesses. None of them have ever been working class, you know? At best, some of them view this as a charity."

Craig nodded. He shouldn't have been surprised that Sal was opposed to the Lobbying efforts. He was surprised that Lobbying being doomed was a foregone conclusion and Sal was sweating how the Communities would fare in a shakeup.

"Look, old friend, I have a date with a confessional and a lot of sinners," Sal said. "If you need anything, just let me know. But you know where I'm coming from. I haven't changed since I talked you into joining the Alliance."

A taxi drove up and stopped in front of them. Sal's name was blinking for attention on its rooftop display. Craig pumped his friend's hand again and they hugged. Sal climbed into the taxi and tossed his unused coat on the seat. The taxi zipped away, leaving Craig shivering in the cold.

CHAPTER EIGHT

AFTER MEETING BORBOLA, NICK WENT home and fidgeted for two hours. He paced around the living room, letting his fingertips graze the plants that never seemed to be outside arm's reach.

Pam sat on the couch and ignored his pacing until she turned off her netpad. "What's wrong?"

Nick explained what he and Borbola had discussed.

"What is he playing at, trying to get you to go tour Stabbie Communities?" she asked, perplexed. "Is it a trap?"

Nick shook his head. "I don't think so. He's really as much at a loss as I am. He sent me a ton of data and intel he's gathered; Cross is incorporating it now."

Pam raised an eyebrow. "I'm surprised. What else?"

He rubbed his lower lip with a knuckle. "He thinks Lisa is hiding in a Community, that I need to search for her on foot using my. Leave the drones behind in each Community to spot her, if need be. I think I can do it."

Pam folded her arms. "What about going to see Meredith?" *And meet my parents,* she didn't add..

Nick looked down. He wanted to say this wouldn't take long, but he still wasn't confident he would actually find Lisa in a Stabilizer Community. She could be living on another continent. "I'm not trying to put that off. But the clock is ticking on this. I just need to do a quick visit to each one."

Pam returned to her book, fuming.

Cross signaled Nick that she had new projections ready. She posted 14 tables and charts that took different approaches to detecting Stabilizer activities. It was like watching the ocean waves to learn what a squid was doing deep underwater. It was crappy, irritating, and inexact, but it was the best that Nick had at the moment.

The first chart was a distribution of outcome certainty. The Kagent models that projected Stabilizer activities each provided a range of outcomes that Cross grouped into similar categories: from the Alliance giving up, to turning into a military force, to becoming a real estate investment trust. Most of them had low scores on an uncertainty index that had evolved over the centuries from the confidence interval and various statistical tests.

Low certainty score really damaged his case at the Burgess briefing, he felt. The two major groups of outcomes, dangerous and benign, each measured under the standard certainty minimum: 55%. Every outcome category peaked in the low thirties.

Nick had hoped that Borbola's intel would have boosted the low certainty scores for a few categories. He rubbed his face in frustration when he saw the certainties from before Borbola's intel compared to the current ones. It was a minor improvement, a few points at most.

Nick scratched his elbow. "These models are just not sophisticated enough. Let's dig into the details of what he found."

Cross texted. [Borbola isolated the number of potential Stabilizer flights into Orlando; the Alliance's headquarters are in Celebration. He subtracted from the total number of executive jets flying in and out of Orlando those that belong to GoldLand Entertainment and other corporations, or are otherwise known in the BHN. The remainder must be Stabilizer flights. He's also tracked those plane IDs to other airports around the continent.]

"Brilliant," Nick said. Sharing intel with Borbola might not have been a bad idea, after all. The Alliance bought stuff like everyone else. If he could isolate their shadow purchases, with trends and patterns, he could see the logistical underside of the Alliance. And the logistics could indicate what they were doing. "We can use this technique to discover their other activities. Cross, track all the purchases in the Orlando zone to purchasers in the BHN. Then highlight the remainder; those are Stabilizers. Show me trends in the shadow purchasing over the last few years. Are they buying more towels or less?"

[Look at this:] Cross posted a graph showing a pronounced spike in probable Stabilizer purchases 3 months after Lisa Radisson went into hiding. The purchases were clustered around unusual spikes in the home organization, moving container categories. Storage containers and unassembled boxes. People getting ready to move house.

"I think this could be a side effect of a leadership shakeup," he said. "Certainty score?"

[Over 95%. What we have is a shadow image of economic activity by the Stabilizers' headquarters.]

She posted 16 graphics of shadow spending trends. Nick chose overall spending, which was down since Hamilton had failed to crash two years ago. But to its left was spending on items related to the Celebration Headquarters resort's upkeep: Those had climbed.

Nick flipped through all of the graphics. This could be a sneaky way in to the inner workings of the Alliance. It was shadows on the wall kind of thing, but it still told him something.

"Are you going to eat dinner?" Pam asked from the kitchen.

"Yeah." Nick turned back to the viewer. [See if you can build a model of their activity based on these shadow purchases. And feed it back to the Kagent nets, let them play with it.]

He walked over and kissed Pam. "I'm making progress."

After a dinner of assorted vegetables in a spicy ranchero sauce, and a small seafood side dish, Nick cleaned the kitchen and returned to his workstation. He inserted his earpiece so Cross could talk instead of taking up viewer real estate with text messages. He dove into the transportation comparison charts. Rail, car, tax, shuttles,

51

air travel, orbital traffic. He could isolate Stabilizer usage of each, but it didn't tell him much at first glance.

He flipped the charts this way and that, scrutinizing the significance tests and confidence intervals. He tossed out the insignificant results and asked for deeper breakouts where there were noticeable trends, then studied the significance diagnostics and repeated the process.

"There was a notable drop in executive jets arrivals and departures to the Orlando airport after Hamilton," Nick observed. "The number hasn't recovered, either. This may not tell us who runs the Alliance, but they either started flying public flights or they are not meeting in Celebration as much."

"Should I query who has stopped flying in?" Cross asked.

"No," Nick replied. "Not without a Warrant. But Borbola doesn't have those restrictions, does he?"

"Are there any ethical problems with having an amoral bounty hunter do work you are barred from, and then you using that information to secure a Warrant?" Cross asked.

"You're right. Tell Borbola that he should only communicate to me what the results are, not how he got them."

"That's not what I meant," Cross said.

Nick sighed. "A man tells a Kagent that his neighbor is building a bomb. The neighbor only knows this because he secretly tapes his neighbor taking a shower every day. Does the Kagent act on it?"

"He should do his own investigation and secure the Warrant through legitimate means," Cross said.

"You're thinking too much like a lawyer," Nick chided her. In some ways, that's what Cross was. She had originally been developed to refine cross examinations in criminal trials. "He's still using the fruits of that spying to investigate someone he normally wouldn't. Is that right?"

"Could he then organize a team of voyeurs to skirt the Kagent privacy protections?" Cross asked.

Nick shrugged. "If he wasn't breaking the local privacy laws.

As long as he didn't abuse the Kagent nets, then it's not a Kagent violation. The spirit and intent of the Kagent privacy protections are to prevent abuse of the massive amount of personal and private data stored in the Kagent nets."

"I thought the Kagents were the guardians of privacy," Cross retorted.

"We are," Nick said. "I would bust a Kagent who used voyeurs like that. He probably ought not to be a Kagent if he's so willing to pry into people's personal lives. This is different: I'm investigating a shadowy organization that wants to destroy civilization."

"The ends justify the means?"

Nick rolled his eyes. "Okay, now you've spun off into hair-splitting. I'm not violating any person's privacy; I'm trying to crack into the darknets of an organization that every Kagent is trying to defeat."

"But that won't help you find Lisa," Cross pointed out.

"No, I have to visit those Communities. We know, roughly, who Lisa has worked with in her Stabilizer campaigns. It would be easiest for her to set up a new life where people didn't know her. Can we get a list of priority Communities to check based on that?"

On a map of NorthAm, Cross highlighted the Communities that Stabilizers seen with Lisa had not been spotted near on the BHN since the Hamilton crisis. They dotted the map from north of Vancouver to the Arizona Territory, and over to the East Coast cities.

Nick said, "If she is still working for the Alliance, she's probably right in Celebration. But if not, she's on her own and wouldn't want to be spotted by her old comrades."

"But she's a master of disguise," Cross replied.

"Nobody wants to live their life in disguise. And one that fools coworkers and friends long-term? The chance of discovery would be too high. The fear of discovery would be too stressful. Better to bug out to a Community where no one knows her."

Nick looked at the map. "I don't have enough drones to drop a full complement, and hidden recharging stations, in each Community.

It would take me a year to see all those Communities. If I order more drones, I can't finance the Earth Kagent net."

Cross said, "If you find Lisa, the Privacy Council will pay you a reward and expenses."

"That's a big if," Nick said.

"Looks like you're not the only one traveling," Pam said, putting her hand on his shoulder. "The Consortium asked me to join a delegation to Celebration, Florida for exploratory talks with the Alliance about a business partnership. So, you'll need to buy the drones if you want me to put eyes and ears in Stabilizer HQ."

Nick smiled. "Does this mean I don't get blamed for delaying our trip to Tessa?"

Pam slapped him on the butt and walked away. "No, you're the one that gave the Consortium the idea in the first place. It's getting late, by the way."

Nick was surprised; it felt like dinner was twenty minutes ago. He had been in a stream-state for hours. "It's like falling asleep. I never realize when it's happening."

"Your biochem telltales indicate that you're tired," Cross noted. "You need to let your subconscious chew on all of this. When I don't push you to take a break, your intuition operates 43% slower."

He stepped away from the viewer. "Fair enough. This has been good: we have a way to indirectly see the Alliance's economic activities. And Pam may not kill me for going on a road trip after Lisa."

CHAPTER NINE

CRAIG STOOD IN HIS NEW suit on a windy street in New York Jersey and marveled at how much he hated the city. Its blinding glitz, relentless pace, and fabulous cheesecake. Its buzz enthralled and irritated him simultaneously. He talked faster, ate faster, walked faster, and loathed himself and the world faster.

To think he and Danny had relished this scene when they were younger and had failed to crash this metropolis. Back then, it had felt good to be on the move, driving change, away from the solid boredom of their home Communities. They had been young and stupid men.

Penny Andrews had an office on the 30th floor of the Empire State Building II. While her secret identity was chairwoman of the Stabilizer Board, she was known to the world as an heiress with a full-time career in giving away the family fortune. Daniel had said she was picky, highly-opinionated, and sharp as a tack.

On the 30th floor, behind a door labeled The Andrews Charitable Funds, sat a young Asian man named Frank. Frank didn't talk much: He checked Craig's ID and wordlessly ushered him into a spacious conference room. He poured him a steaming cup of tea and disappeared. *Nice chatting with you, Frank.*

Penny swooped in a moment later, carrying a netpad, and poured her own cup of tea. She was a small, stocky blonde woman in her sixties, sporting pearls, a peach pantsuit, and a large diamond brooch. Her hair color stretched from auburn to blonde with a shimmer of reddish highlights. It looked more expensive than his entire personal net worth.

"Craig Lassiter, well-met," she said in a clipped British accent.

He stood to shake her hand, but she headed to the other side of the desk and sat down. Craig sat back down slowly.

"I trust India is the same as it always is," she said.

"It wasn't the quiet oasis I'd hoped," he replied. "Eventually, the bloody offworlders showed up and began turning people into brainless buzzers in flashy suits."

Penny chuckled. "Matching my mannerisms and speech patterns? Bravo. I find myself liking you for reasons I suspect are entirely of your creation."

Craig allowed himself a smile. He adopted strangers' speech patterns, mannerisms, energy level, and facial expressions to build a rapport with them. He was barely conscious of it, anymore.

"During your time on the subcontinent, the Alliance has lost its way," she said. "It's not only Lobbying. We're re-examining our business practices, our values, our mission. We're soul-searching to the point of paralysis."

An icy fear gripped Craig's shoulder blades and slid down his spine. She meant the whole damn Alliance was unraveling. He nodded. "Which means the Alliance would take several steps backward."

"Quite. I can't snap my fingers and make the other Board members come to Jesus, so to speak. I need a consultant who can give things a good scrub and help set things right."

She glanced at her netpad. "Daniel vouched for you. He said you are highly perceptive, good with people. And he called you a very good puppeteer. I hope that is some kind of compliment."

Craig smiled wryly. "He means I adapt my approach, find and pull strings on people without them knowing. He and I used to do this all the time; it's the heart of Lobbying. We would find a situation's pressure points and then gently, painlessly apply pressure to convince a city to knife itself in the belly."

She put the netpad down. "That may be. But Lobbying violated our core principles in Hamilton and put the entire organization at risk. Several Board members want to close it." She raised an eyebrow. "Bringing you in has its own risks. I'm sure they will remember your little trouble in China. Can you address those concerns?"

Craig nodded. This interview was more of an interrogation than anything friendly. He tilted his head forward to appear more competent and lowered his voice to a sober octave. "Yes, I made a terrible mistake, which I am still regretting. I'm committed to the Alliance's values and using only our proven, nonviolent methods. The ones that let you twist a targeted group to think that your idea was their own in the first place."

Penny nodded. "I want you to use those methods on the Board. I understand that this sounds unorthodox, but it's necessary to preserve the Alliance's work. Can you do that, Mr. Lassiter?"

Craig reached for his tea cup. "Without my knowing more about the Board, it would be foolish to agree at this point, don't you think?" He sipped his tea.

"Some members want to work with the Burgess Consortium rather than fight it. They smell money and talk about donors' return on investment, and the Alliance's financial health. They want to drop expenses and boost revenue, which is sensible for a business. But not for the Alliance." She tilted her head. "Your job would be to talk them out of it while appearing to conduct an impartial assessment. How would you go about accomplishing that?"

Craig rubbed his hands. "I'd map out how the Board members interact, as well as how you all work with the operating divisions. I'd need an insider to brief me on the members' personalities, goals, how they interact. And then I would have to meet with each Board member, under the guise of collecting information for my evaluation. But I would be nudging them towards where you want them to be."

Penny looked down at her hands, the disappointment etched in the worry lines on her face. *Here it comes,* Craig thought. *The strings, the limitations, the other shoe with a steel toe falling on my head.*

"Board meetings are limited to principals and are never recorded," she said. "Information and access are highly compartmentalized. In fact, officially, you will be a consultant to the acting head of Lobbying, Mandy DeCasas. She will be your boss, nominally, but I want you to report to me regularly."

"Understood," Craig said with a grin. In some way, all employees ran an op against their bosses, currying favor, proving their worth, and avoiding pitfalls and land mines in the bosses' psyches. He didn't care who his boss was.

"I really do want you to assist her getting Lobbying properly sorted. But I'm afraid you won't have much to work with. Without the Kagent projections, that group is strategically and tactically lost, I'm afraid."

"No matter how fancy Kagents seem, predicting the future is impossible," Craig said with a dismissive hand wave. "I know plenty of market analysts, weather forecasters, oceanographers, and demographers. None of them felt comfortable making anything other than the broadest, vaguest extrapolations of observed data into the future. And they all pray that no one asks for their track record."

Penny raised an eyebrow. "To the contrary, my sources say the Kagent's own predictions were key to stopping us in Hamilton."

"If they could predict the future, why didn't they come after us before, when cities were falling, one after another?" Craig chuckled. "These offworlders were clueless all those years and then stumbled around when they noticed the threat. Daniel said the Alliance modified its strategy several times during the Hamilton campaign. How come the predictions didn't tell Lobbying what to anticipate from the beginning?"

Penny was quiet for a moment. "Interesting. Regardless, Lobbying needs to be rebuilt. If you can make it successful without those projections, you'll have my full support. Are you with us?"

Craig beamed. Until meeting Penny, he was treating this as a paycheck, something to tide him over until he got his feet back under him. But after hearing the situation in more depth, he was surprised to find himself committed to the cause again. "Absolutely."

She stood and extended her hand. "Welcome back to the Stabilizer Alliance. Good luck."

Craig spent the rest of the day setting up appointments with the other Board members and finding a place to stay overnight. He didn't want to leave the city until he was sure his expense account was functional. He had made that mistake in rural Massachusetts when he was in his twenties and ended up sleeping in an abandoned bus in a cornfield.

He found the cheapest, no-frills hotel room he could in Brooklyn and settled in for the night. He took a basement room because the dazzling brilliance and noise of the New York Jersey night scene just gave him a headache. He preferred to stare at real brick.

He showered and began to shave. With the faucet running, he thought he heard a voice. It sounded like someone said, "Great view in here" from inside the room. He turned off his razor to listen more better.

Maybe the hotel had a porn AI that thought a single, middle-aged man was an easy mark late at night. But he had turned off the viewers on each wall.

He ducked his head out of the bathroom, adrenaline shooting through each limb. Was he a sitting duck for robbers down here? It was the cheapest room in the hotel, with minimal housekeeping, and they charged for electric. Maybe security was an option he had to pay extra for.

There was a tall, dark-skinned man in a business suit sitting in the guest chair, grinning at him.

Craig opted for a growling bark. "Who the hell are you?"

"Eldred Borbola. You're the one who wanted to talk to me."

God. Relief rippled through Craig's body. "I'm not dressed for a business meeting," he said, keeping the command tone to his voice. "And it's late."

"I wanted to talk now." Borbola crossed his legs, getting comfortable. "So, speak."

Craig didn't hesitate. He had put the word out that he wanted to meet Borbola, but he had no reason to expect that the bounty hunter would agree to it.

He pulled on a clean, plain t-shirt from his luggage. "I wanted to contact you, but you were impossible to find." Actually, it was impossible to contact the notorious, independent bounty hunter. Other bounty hunters wouldn't help. Borbola had hundreds of possible profiles, spread across the nets, many of them fueled by poorly-researched media accounts and half-assed action feature films. It annoyed Craig because he was used to knowing the other party in every situation.

Borbola's grin grew wider. "I know. That's why I came to you."

"Okay. I'm a consultant who needs information about his clients. But any information you find needs to be held strictly confidential." When Borbola simply nodded, Craig continued, "I mean that no one can know about this job, about me, or about what you find. You can't profit from this information in any other way."

Borbola dipped his head again. "That will cost you extra, but I'll do it."

They agreed to a contract and Craig showed Borbola the list of Board members. The bounty hunter ran them through the public nets. "You could profile these people for a lot less than you're paying me."

"Yes," Craig answered. "But I doubt people as rich and powerful as these have much on the public nets or your bounty hunter databases. This will probably take original, sophisticated surveillance. Like what you gathered on the Dragoon leadership."

The bounty hunter consulted his netpad. "You know about that, huh? Interesting that I have very little on you for the last two decades. The Stabilizer Communities are offline, huh?"

Craig nodded.

"You were a Stabilizer a long time ago," Borbola noted. "I can tell that because your childhood records are missing, which only happens in Louisiana if you grew up in a Community. Are you still connected with them?" The bounty hunter looked at his netpad. "That looks like a yes to me."

Craig scowled. "I didn't say anything, smart guy."

"I read your vitals." Borbola looked up at him. "These people keep a low profile on the nets. Profiling them will cost you some serious freight."

Craig spread his hands. "I have an expense account."

"Good. Here's the other thing. I get enough work now that I don't need to take jobs I don't want. The Stabilizers freak me out a little. Too secretive, too hard to get a fix on."

Craig smirked. "Your reputation is that you're heartless, ruthless, amoral, and highly successful. You took down the Dragoons, cracked their corporate nets wide open."

Borbola rolled his eyes. "I may have. But the media likes to exaggerate. The thing is I'm not sure working for the Stabilizers fits into my moral portfolio. You are working for them, aren't you?" He waggled the netpad.

Was this bounty hunter playing hard to get? His "moral portfolio"? Craig shook his head.

"So you are working for them. You may as well tell me the truth," Borbola said.

Craig sat down at the end of his bed to be eye to eye with Borbola. "Look, I want to return the Alliance to its core values: non-violence, no offworld interference. Just slowing things down some, to protect our way of life —"

"— I'm going to go ahead and cut off your bullshit right there. I was in Hamilton last year. The Stabilizers were just as much of a threat as the Dragoons. I don't want to help you take a second shot at an apocalypse."

"Apocalypse? I don't know what you're talking about. I'm trying to help the Alliance move on from offworlder-caused mistakes made in Hamilton. But I have to convince people internally, first. And to do that, I need to know them very well, without them knowing that I've learned much about them. That's what I'm paying a premium for."

Borbola tightened his eyes. "What are you afraid of?"

Craig sank his chin to his fists. "That we'll lose heart and give up, because it's more profitable and easier."

Borbola leaned forward, mimicking Craig's posture. "Okay. So, who are these people to the Alliance?"

Craig held Borbola's gaze for a few long moments. "Let's say they are important."

Borbola thought about it. "Okay, I'll take it. But if you're wrong about these people, and the Alliance, I'll make you pay non-monetarily. You got it?"

Craig grinned. "Absolutely, cowboy. I'm just a consultant. And don't you forget that this is all strictly confidential."

Borbola stood. "I heard you the first two times. I'll be in touch." He walked out.

Craig finished shaving. He hated putting a scruffy cheek on his pillow. He killed the lights and plunged into bed in complete darkness and silence. "Jesus, even bounty hunters need a sales pitch, these days."

CHAPTER TEN

PAM FLEW TO ORLANDO WEARING an archaic three-piece wool pantsuit that itched the whole flight. The gray wool was too rough. It felt heavy and the fit was much worse than offworld clothes.

Pam didn't like disguising herself. Like the wool suit, the persona of an Earth-born member of the Burgess Consortium negotiation team fit her poorly. Or maybe it was because she was on a secret mission.

Despite the Burgess Consortium canceling his contract, it had adopted Nick's idea to try working together with the Stabilizer Alliance. Preliminary talks with the Stabbies about a partnership to provide stress-free lodging for vacationing 'buzzers' had led to this preliminary step.

Both sides were meeting at the Stabilizer Alliance headquarters in Celebration, Florida to discuss how a joint real estate venture could be structured. The Burgess Consortium had asked Pam, as Hamilton's Trade Representative, to help with the negotiations. She wasn't sure what her value add would be; typically, she estimated how both sides could reach an agreement based on knowing their goals, negotiating styles, personalities and constraints.

The flight landed and after she reclaimed her bag, she searched the mammoth Orlando airport for a shuttle to Celebration. Down two levels and past the GoldLand section, she found a line of pastel pink Rolling Fortresses bound for Celebration that were loading up tourists and business types like her.

The last seat available in the Fortress was next to a family with a girl about four years old and a boy about eight. The kids bounced in their seats and asked the taxi's Simon how long it would take, which the Simon patiently answered. The boy and the girl were intensely cute, aware that they were performing for Pam and the other passengers.

There were two kinds of childless adult travelers, Pam had concluded: those who abhorred children and those who enjoyed them. Pam was the latter and couldn't help beaming at the kids. "Where are you from?" she asked the boy.

"Charlotte, Carolina," he said, as his sister flopped in his lap and he held onto her so she wouldn't slide to the floor.

"We got a great deal through our Community," his mom added.

"That's great," Pam replied, trying to sustain her enthusiasm. "I'm here on business, but I've heard good things about it as a resort."

"I want to go to the pool!" The girl sat back in her seat. The cab eased into traffic and the mom snapped her daughter into the foldout child seat.

It was easy to forget, only two years after Hamilton, that entire swaths of the Stabilizer Alliance, especially its real estate and resort businesses, were benign operations. Nick wanted to take her for a visit to his home Community, but they just hadn't had the time. Nick believed seeing a Community up close would erode her caustic opinion of the Alliance. *You can talk to them,* Nick insisted, *make deals with them and build things with them; they can be a force for good.*

Pam needed a lot of convincing.

The taxi's happy scene made Pam question whether her view was skewed. Nick's instincts were rarely wrong, even if they made things worse before they got better. Maybe her perception was colored and biased by the combination of other things going wrong. Nick's side of the business was sagging. His fervent belief that he could redeem the Stabilizers and their own relationship troubles all probably played a part.

The convoy of pink taxis rumbled down elevated highways past large lakes with still, silver water. Dense, bright-green tropical flora grew right up to and over the fluorescent yellow guardrails. Viewers dropped down from the Fortress' roof and a narrative began playing about Celebration.

"The Stabilizer Alliance rescued Celebration from a swampy, watery grave," it began. It was in a jokey manner, aimed at the kids. "For centuries, the region hosted millions of tourists a year, until the floods came in 2220."

Old video clips of the floods showed the neat 20th century houses floating away and a close-up of soggy Mickey Mouse ears among the debris.

"Much of the area turned into a brackish swamp. The amusement parks closed in quick succession. Then the monsoons came for twenty years and washed the golf courses away, making dads everywhere very, very sad." A young girl onscreen hugged her dad, both of them in rain gear during a downpour.

The video showed the remains of Celebration's town center, the docks smashed by debris, the buildings marred by streaks of mud. "But the people of Celebration refused to give up. They rebuilt the city, improving on Walt Disney's original design and taking into account the new environmental conditions."

The video showed a montage of shots of the city under construction, ultimately morphing into a recent snapshot. It turned into a Stabilizer ad from then on. Designed for family, with kids in mind. The premiere Stabilizer Community had been rebuilt as a modern take on the hanging gardens of Babylon. The office buildings melted into the tall rainforest that covered the city.

"And now, look at our city," the recording said.

The kids next to Pam gasped when Celebration came into view in the distance, like they were completing a religious pilgrimage. The brightly-colored city towered over a small sea dotted with green islands and white watercraft. Highway 4 served as a bridge over the little lakes and swampy vegetation surrounding the other sides of Celebration.

The recording continued, "Our workers live here in the community, so they are deeply invested in our success. Our customer satisfaction rivals GoldLand's Disney parks."

Pam tuned out the Stabbie propaganda. The cab dropped everyone at Celebration's front entrance off Route 417. It looked like the secured entrance that Nick said was at each Community. But it reminded her of the entrance gates to an amusement park.

Pam wished her taxi mates a fun vacation and entered Celebration without a fuss. She transferred to a tram that took her to the town center. The New Bohemian Hotel sat on the shore of the vast lake that the floods had created from Lake Evalyn and Lake Rianhard.

The air felt like the steamy inside of her greenhouse apartment but with a breeze. The sweat pooled in her lower back, but she blamed it on the pantsuit that felt like a constrictive wool blanket.

She checked in, went to her room, showered, and changed into a casual outfit. The agenda was light this afternoon as the Burgess folks arrived and got settled. She had some time before the first event started.

She admired the view out the room window: A vast, shimmering lake stretched to the southern horizon like a placid sheet of glass. There were half-a-dozen sailboats cutting through that glass and an 18-hole golf course that jutted into the lake like a massive green pier.

She sighed, resigned to get to work, and unpacked the bomb hidden in her luggage.

CHAPTER ELEVEN

DAVID POOLE. THE REAL ESTATE magnate was one of the Board members most interested in killing the Alliance's Lobbying arm. He was a small-bore thinker and had a limited worldview focused on profits, probably shaped by growing up in war-torn but highly entrepreneurial Houston. Or so said the dossier prepared by Borbola.

Craig had no trouble meeting with Poole; the business tycoon didn't keep a schedule, apparently. His assistant told Craig to come to Stabilizer headquarters in Celebration, Florida and they would fit him in. And since Craig was working for the Alliance again, Poole's people set him up in one of their condos by the lake and charged the Alliance.

Craig dropped his bag in the minimally-furnished condo and savored the view out the sliding glass door of the twinkling lake on a sunny, breezy winter day.

He would have time to wander around later. He walked to the Pooled Developments office in one of the office buildings in the town center. An assistant escorted Craig to an unlabeled wood door at the end of an empty hallway. Craig couldn't help but be amused.

"He thinks executive suites are a waste of money. It's all about the square footage," the assistant explained in a whisper.

Hmmm… Borbola hadn't mentioned that. But the publicly-available pictures of Poole showed a hard-to-read guy who kept his eyes half-lidded out of either disinterest or boredom, or both. He reminded Craig of a car salesman he knew once.

The door opened and Dave Poole stuck his head out. "Craig, come on in." After they shook hands, Poole sized him up and said, "Let's do this on the golf course." He said it like he was showing off property to a prospective buyer around.

"You come down here a lot?" Craig asked.

Poole dropped a straw hat on his fat, bald head. "It depends on business." They left the building and rode to the golf course in a powder blue golf cart. Poole spoke in long, slow drawls about Celebration real estate, the selling points of the golf course, and customer demand for premium vacation space. He was pitching Craig on the business merits of a different strategy for the Alliance, without saying so directly. Craig said little, but dropped his eyelids and dug around for his old bayou accent.

The golf course extended out over Celebration Lake. A full 18 holes, clubhouse, and surrounding lawns all stood on a series of pilings 50 feet above the water. Just as Poole had described on the way over.

"We built this golf course after the first one flooded," Poole explained. "This entire thing is supported on carbon nano-tube pilings. Won't rust in a thousand years. You golf, Craig?"

"I've hit some balls."

"I do all my business on a golf course, if I can," Poole explained. "You learn a lot about a man when you see him golf. How he approaches problems, how he deals with adversity, how he handles success."

"Of course," Craig said. "After a man hits that ball, his face is stripped of all the pretending." He paraphrased a quote from the autobiography of one of Poole's favorite golfers.

That prompted a smile. "Exactly."

Poole had his own clubs, of course, and he lent Craig a set from the pro shop. There must always be a steady breeze blowing this high up, Craig thought when they set up at the first tee.

His golf skills had never amounted to something that could have rusted from disuse. If Poole had some golf-proficiency requirement to do business with him, then Craig was about to waste his time.

Poole led off with a wimpy low little drive that looked like he was trying to skip a stone across water. He watched the ball come to rest about two hundred yards away. "Huh," was all he said.

Craig stepped up to the tee and took a tremendous whack at the ball. He hit it into the wind, expecting the wind to push the ball to the right into a gentle fade.

The ball continued right into the wind and plonked into the lake.

"Do you yell 'fore' to the boaters when that happens?" Craig asked with a sheepish grin.

Poole rubbed his chin and smiled broadly. "Nah. If they're dumb enough to be close, it's their problem. You want to take a mulligan?"

The way Poole smiled, it was clear to Craig that he expected to win. "What would that tell you about me?" Craig asked.

Poole thought it over for a second. "Are you playing by my rules or your rules?"

"I don't make the rules," Craig said. "I play within the rules I'm dealt."

"Two-shot penalty and ignore the wind. It gusts and you can't count on it. That's why I hit lower."

Craig lined up another shot and drilled it high where the wind tossed it into the rough, but it was fifty feet ahead of Poole's ball.

They jumped in the cart and motored towards Poole's ball.

"So the cease-fire is holding, I hear," Craig said.

Poole's expression didn't change. "It always does, until it doesn't."

"Reminds me of the days I wore a uniform," Craig said. "Things were clearer. We had a clear mission, we were part of a cause."

"You realize that the Alliance has changed since you were around," Poole said. "Hamilton was a big lesson. I never was sold on Lobbying having a worthwhile return on investment."

"It all depends on what the Alliance's goal is," Craig said.

Poole regarded him coolly. "I'm sure Penny told you that the Board is debating that very issue."

"Yes. That's why you want me to see if Lobbying is worth keeping."

They reached the ball, Poole eased out with a club in hand, and hit the ball. The ball rolled up to the lip of the green.

"I'm plain with people about where I stand, Craig," Poole said when he restarted the cart. "I've had it with these expensive fights with the buzzers and offworlders. Kagents showed up in Hamilton and to me, that was a warning. We do not want to bring offworld power down on us. The whole cause will be lost."

"Are the Kagents that much of a threat?" Craig asked.

Poole floored it and the cart arrived at Craig's ball in a few seconds. "When Lobbying goes too far. I've gone up against businesses that Kagents advise and it's nearly always a losing proposition."

Poole jerked a thumb toward the shore. "My people are talking to the Burgess Consortium people today about a partnership on vacation resorts. From what I heard, the Consortium is advised by Kagents. So, I expect that they won't be easy to roll in the negotiation. But the opportunity is too good to pass up. We'll be much more financially stable."

"I thought the Kagents were statisticians," Craig said.

Poole shrugged. "Doesn't matter. They make accurate projections of business conditions and you don't want them advising the other side of the table in a business deal, let me tell you. If the Kagents are telling the Burgess people to do business with us, that's a real good sign."

Craig swallowed. Poole might be reassured that these Burgess buzzers wanted to do business with the Alliance, but Craig worried. Was Poole the weak link that would allow the offworlders to nullify the Alliance? Or was that paranoid thinking?

Poole interpreted his silence as disagreement. "Let's be hard-headed about reality here. We can't pacify the entire planet. We have to live with the buzzers down here. The way I see it, the money play is finding a way to take advantage of their wealth."

Craig selected a driver. "That seems to be the crux of the Board's disagreement. Make the best of the circumstances, or fight them."

His shot was still twenty feet shy of the green. It took another shot to make it there. Poole chipped in his ball in two strokes, but Craig whacked away until he ended up with a nasty seven on the hole.

"Just knocking the rust off," Craig explained with a big grin.

Poole laughed, happy that he was far ahead. Craig was going to keep it that way.

"Let me tell you," Poole said as they arrived at the third hole, "a consultant needs to be neutral and impartial." He sent the ball over a hundred yards up a dogleg. "I was a consultant back in the day. It's a young man's con game. I used it to launch myself into the manufactured housing industry. What's your angle?"

"Repaying my debt to the organization," Craig said. "I'm not proud of the things I did in Lobbying when I was younger."

Poole turned his half-lidded gaze out to the lake. "So, if we eliminate Lobbying, how would you handle that?"

"I've been out of that racket for over a decade, so I have no dog in this fight. Eliminating Lobbying for Hamilton could hurt the Alliance if it still needs those capabilities. Or it could be the first step toward a much stronger strategic position. It depends on whether doing so is consistent with the Board's goals."

Craig sliced the ball and it rolled up against the fence that kept golfers from falling into the lake.

"Figuring out the rules as you play?" Poole said. "Smart man."

"Thanks."

They climbed into the golf cart and scooted toward Craig's ball. Craig hit it onto the green.

Poole nodded. "In my view, the Alliance needs to face reality and deal with the world we live in. Otherwise, the Communities get picked off one by one as the buzzers continue to spread around them. Pooled Developments is not only a financier of the Alliance, it's a firewall. Our economic power is what keeps us safe."

Poole selected a wedge, and popped his ball up and onto the green. Most of this game was riding in golf carts, which gave them plenty of time to talk.

"Over three-quarters of our Communities have waiting lists. The number of poor souls trying to escape the buzzers keeps growing. The further we expand our lifestyle product, the more economic power we gain and the stronger we are."

Craig remarked, "Move slower, but more sure-footed, and build off successes to keep the money flowing. I understand." He deliberately used Poole's own language from an interview with a business magazine five years ago.

Craig let that remark echo for a while, until they were ready to tee up on the ninth hole. Craig fell further behind Poole, but then began to close the gap. Mimicking body language wasn't only ingratiating. It helped to poach a better player's golf swing.

"Lassiter, you know, you're all right. You're persistent and adaptable. Even with lousy clubs like those shovels you got there."

Craig took that as an opening. "The Board wants Lobbying to help market the residential side. Is that your idea?"

Poole nodded. "Lobbying needs to pull its own weight if it wants to stay around. It's the Communities that are the front line in our fight with the buzzers, not street protesters."

Craig drew a battered putter from his bag to finish the hole. The cup was on the side of a gentle incline. He squatted down to pretend to examine the shot. He stood and positioned himself.

"Mr. Poole, that doesn't seem sufficient to me," he said, looking down at the ball. "You could go hire a real marketing firm to do that. For Lobbying to be worth sticking around, its expertise could be used to help the Communities."

He tapped the ball too hard and it rolled past the cup and down the hill. "Tricky hole," he muttered.

Poole didn't notice that his lead grew. He blinked. "Help? Like what?"

"Favorable zoning, reduced hours at competing stores outside a

Community, slower traffic speeds at night, a whole bunch of things," Craig replied. "Lobbying could boost the Communities' financial position, which they need. It would be a lot more constructive than tearing down big cities. Cities that happen to be some of your most lucrative clients." Craig's ball was directly downhill of the cup. He lined up and gave it a small whack that sent it racing uphill to plunk inside the cup.

"I like the way you think," Poole said. His phone buzzed and he looked at it. "Damn. I need to get back to the office. Listen, you finish out the course, on me. It was good talking with you; I like the direction you're heading." He shook hands with Craig and zipped off in the golf cart.

Craig squinted at the sunny sky. "I don't mind if I do," he said and began whistling to himself.

CHAPTER TWELVE

THE BOMB WAS DISGUISED AS a sanitary napkin. The puffy yellow package actually contained thousands of offworld drones, each smaller than a gnat. This bomb didn't explode though; it released the drones a few at a time.

'Bomb' may have been too strong a word for the device, but it was the reactionary Earthers' fault. When the Hamilton City Council banned unlicensed offworld drones, Councilor Geoff Starke had called them "plague bombs of offworld killer drones." The name had stuck with the media.

Pam turned the sanitary napkin over. The bomb was an offworld invention courtesy of Meredith's folks. A Tessan engineer had slimmed down the gnat-sized surveillance drone to pack more of them into a tiny space. What Borbola had needed a canister for during the battle in Hamilton two years ago had been miniaturized.

The bomb distributed enough drones to create a thorough surveillance grid across a specified area. The spy—in this case Nick—could remotely control the drones after deployment to maximize intel by moving them to more valuable locations. All Pam had to do was walk around and let the drones drift away.

Nick was busy looking for Lisa Radisson in other Stabilized communities. That search had interfered with his attempt to break through the Stabbie darknets and figure them out. The bomb was his way of trying to do both things at once. Pam feared he wouldn't do either thing very well.

A legitimate visit to Celebration was too good an opportunity to pass up. Pam could deploy the bomb and let Nick spy on the Stabbies in their Celebration Community at the least. He hoped in doing so that he could catch Lisa here, too.

Pam slipped the bomb into the bottom of her handbag. The handbag had a small hole that the drones could fall out of without anyone noticing. She had a small remote in the pocket of her shorts that would control their release.

The optimal way to distribute the drones was at night, under cover of darkness, when no one could see gnats very well. But Pam and the rest of the Burgess team were scheduled to do a guided tour of Celebration later in the afternoon. She figured she would spread the drones around town and then let Nick or Cross maneuver them into key positions.

The tour began at the town center, a series of quaint 19th century-style buildings down the street from her hotel. Pam reunited with the Burgess team. Macario Nuviola, deputy mayor of Caracas, was leading the delegation, which mainly consisted of number crunchers and development experts from Consortium members.

The tour guide was an older guy named Jim who seemed like the easy-going type who whistled a tune everywhere he went. He took them through the residential areas and explained how they designed social spaces and social-engineered residents' lives for maximum tranquility and happiness.

Pam drifted to the back of the group and released drones at infrequent intervals. She didn't plan to drop many in the residential areas; she just wanted to see if it worked. She checked behind her a few times and didn't spot a single one. It occurred to her that she didn't know if that was good or bad.

The tour arrived at Celebration's amusement park just as an afternoon thunderstorm began. The tour took cover in a pavilion as the rain crashed down and the skies flashed and rumbled.

Could the drones survive a heavy downpour? They were supposed to mimic insects, but did real gnats seek shelter from heavy rain?

The rain stopped just as quickly as it started and Jim cracked a joke about rapidly changing weather. But the air seemed twice as muggy, and the number crunchers were looking even more uncomfortable in their polo shirts and pants.

Jim took them back to town center and to a five-story office building. The Stabilizer Alliance headquarters. The delegation had to pass through security, including a metal detector and a bag search. The drones didn't have enough metal to set off the detector, but that didn't stop adrenaline from fizzing into Pam's veins.

A guard went through her handbag. She couldn't resist watching him do it. He used a small rod to shove the contents around, peering into the corners, looking under the yellow maxi pad. Pam hoped that no drones reacted. If one of them flitted out of the bag into his face, she would be caught.

Although time stretched out for Pam, it really only took two seconds. He was done and waved her on.

Jim led them down a hallway decorated with posters that told the inspiring story of the first Stabilizer Community. The story was a series of pictures showing a couple dozen intrepid people looking for a saner way of life and spreading their cause around the planet.

Jim launched into a cute anecdote about the rebuilding of Celebration after the floods. People on Earth seemed to have tons of these 'storms do such weird things' stories. You'd think that after centuries of climate change, they would have become accustomed to super-powered storm systems wreaking weird, random effects on them.

Pam couldn't help thinking that it was somewhere in these plain-looking offices that people plotted a civil war in Hamilton, riots in Atlanta, and chaos in countless other zones. One person had set a giant stuffed animal on top of their cube. It was strange. Nick had a point that these 'Stabbies' were regular people like anyone else.

She felt guilty for a few seconds, but then tapped the remote to launch more drones. Hopefully they weren't doing anything that could attract attention. Sure, Florida was lousy with insects but not inside a climate-controlled office building. She was just waiting for someone to notice gnats hovering around her handbag.

She did a quick glance over her shoulder to make sure she wasn't leaving a trail of gray gnats floating behind her. She didn't see anything, not even on the carpet.

She began to feel relieved and elated. Nick might find himself listening in on some telling conversations. This was the closest that Jim would take them to any sensitive areas. But Nick could maneuver the drones where he wanted later.

Jim moseyed into a conference room where the Pooled staff were waiting. It was clear from the clutter that the staff had worked out of this room. An interesting datapoint.

The Pooled staff were nearly all young men, wearing perfectly-pressed casual shirts with not a hair out of place. Pam carefully observed each one of them, their body language, how they reacted to Jim, each other, and the Burgess delegation. Without much information about Stabilizer negotiators, this was one of her best chances to collect first impressions.

These guys treated Jim like a client rather than a boss. They had a feral gleam Pam had seen a million times in Hamilton or offworld, but it surprised her here. Striving to get rich was not something a Stabbie was supposed to do.

They reminded her of the Burgess team but were more shark-like. They were eyeing the team, not like you would size up a competitor, but how you would size up dinner. Or an easy mark if you were a con artist. Yes, they looked like con artists to her.

One of the sharks shook her hand and looked down past her elbow. He looked back up at her carefully. "What's that? I'm sorry."

"What's wrong?" Pam blurted, turning around like there was a caterpillar climbing her back.

But the Pooled guy was looking down at the floor near her handbag.

"Oh, I thought I saw a mosquito near you," the man said, puzzled.

CHAPTER THIRTEEN

DOWN THE HIGHWAY FROM CELEBRATION was the college campus-like headquarters of GoldLand Entertainment. GoldLand's corporate headquarters was a village of one and two-story buildings clustered on a few streets, surrounded by rolling lawns of brilliant green tropical grass.

It was hidden away from the surrounding amusement parks and resorts behind thick foliage, walls of living bamboo, and multiple security checkpoints that scrutinized Craig's credentials.

Signs along the road into town told the story of how Cooper Mangold had rebuilt the hometown of his distant childhood and turned it into a living, breathing community that ran a massive, solar system-spanning conglomerate.

The last sign claimed that the Stabilizer Alliance had used GoldLand's headquarters as a prototype for their earliest Communities. As Craig drew closer to the village, he saw the similarities. Clustering employment in one location, forcing people to commingle when they were coming and going, using architecture to foster a tight-knit community.

The main street consisted of 22nd century-style shops and eateries, constructed out of the faux-natural materials that were the rage then. Cooper Mangold clung to his childhood and had the money to make everyone else cling to it, as well.

Each shop was actually an exhibit center for a particular operating division or entertainment line. News nets sizzled and flashed inside a shop made entirely out of quartz. The amusement park division was in a sandstone office building with concept art for a new park in Brazil displayed along the sidewalk. Ads for the movie studios' latest releases played on the marquee of a bark-covered movie theater.

Old-fashioned digital street signs, from the days of manually-driven cars, pointed to where the various headquarters departments were located. Marketing was in a dry cleaners. Corporate Overhead was in an apartment building that looked like it was chiseled out of a cliff. Human Capital was in a court building made of concrete sculpted to look like seashell.

The executive suite was in an old-fashioned rescue station tucked between a seafood restaurant covered in fish scales and a jewelry shop made out of crystal. The rescue station had an actual ambulance, EMT crotch-rocket, security cruiser, and a fire truck parked inside its garage.

Craig was directed upstairs by an EMT washing the fire truck. The second floor looked like a fancy hotel conference suite with thick carpeting and walls of ash-colored granite.

"Craig Lassiter, come on in!" Cooper Mangold called through an open double door to his office. He had a bright, white grin and a head of thick black hair.

As Craig drew closer, he saw that Cooper was a lot older than he appeared from a distance. The jet-black hair was dyed and he'd clearly had skin tightening done on his face. He had to have thirty years on Craig. That made sense, because Cooper Mangold had played the genial, middle-aged uncle for most of Craig's lifetime.

"Good to finally meet you," Cooper said. "Call me Coop."

Craig mirrored Coop's high energy level. "It's an honor to meet you. You've been a role model for me."

The old man laughed and escorted him deeper into the large office. He directed Craig to stand with him against a fancy backdrop of an old fashioned bookshelf filled with paper tomes. He shook Craig's hand as a camera hanging from the ceiling took their picture.

"We'll get you a copy of that for your glory wall," Cooper said with a wink. He motioned to two people who walked in and stood off to the side. "This is my assistant Arianna and my chief attorney Heinz."

Craig shook their hands and they all sat in chairs arrayed around a table made of varnished driftwood.

"So, you are the consultant who will sort out what the Alliance wants and how to do it," Cooper said. His voice dripped with genial derision.

Craig wasn't surprised. When he'd learned who was on the Board, he realized that this man would be his primary obstacle. When Penny told him that Cooper was one of the Alliance's original founders, he knew he needed a special strategy to deal with him.

There would be no selling or twisting this guy. The best he could do was get along with him, maybe bond with him, and figure out how best to deal with him later.

"I'm only here to help," Craig said. "But first I want to listen and learn."

Cooper nodded. "I agreed with Penny that you are the right man for the job. I didn't want a pack of bright-eyed virgins whose only job experience came out of their orientation packets."

Craig laughed out loud. This is not the genial uncle he remembered. He liked this man a lot more.

Cooper sat back and crossed one leg over the other. "When we started the Alliance, I was the only business guy in the group. The rest were researchers or true believers. Lobbying was my idea, stolen from corporate espionage techniques I used to take over half-a-dozen other companies. But we have discovered the limits of its use. The crashpoint strategy failed and Lobbying is a liability."

Craig nodded. "Everything should be on the table. The key question, it seems, is what helps support the Alliance mission?"

"Yes, exactly. We're at a turning point. We need to plan long-term change. Low risk and high probability of success. I hoped to see the Alliance triumph, but that's not in the cards. I've made my peace with that. That's why I'm open to a deal with the Burgess Consortium."

Craig nodded again. "How do you see us pushing back against the offworlders and their fans down here?"

"The smart man knows when to say he doesn't know." Cooper grinned.

"I don't think there will be any fast and easy solutions," Craig said, matching Cooper's jovial-but-helpless tone.

The two men laughed.

Coop leaned forward. "This Board is heavily divided on direction: stopping the buzzers or profiting off them. There's a risk that the Alliance could break up because of this. And that would be the end of any efforts to stop the spread of the buzzers. The main reason I wanted a fellow like you on the job was to keep the Alliance together and moving toward long term goals. If you can do that," the old man paused and smiled, "I would be deeply indebted to you."

Craig understood.

"Now, if you'll excuse me," Cooper stood up slowly, with support from Heinz. "I have some amusement park numbers from the Middle East to look over."

Craig returned to Celebration by late afternoon. He was itching to take a walk and let his mind chew on the interview. He hit the streets looking for an early dinner.

He found an Asian cafe that Daniel had recommended. Craig was just as adventurous with food as Daniel was a wuss. He was the only customer at the sushi bar. The chef pointed to a digital menu behind them.

Craig smiled and shook his head. "Treat me like a native," he said, letting his Creole accent seep in to his voice. "Give me the hottest wasabi you got."

The chef did. And the fire in Craig's mouth kicked his brain into gear. He began to see how he could avoid upsetting good old Coop. Keep the Alliance together. Long-term goals. He shoveled steamed brown rice into his mouth to quench some of the sting. He began making notes on his netpad.

CHAPTER FOURTEEN

PAM WAS CAUGHT. SHE WHIPPED her head around to look for the bug behind her. For a second, she saw the glint of a gnat at knee height. But it was swallowed up by the multicolored carpet.

She had no idea what the laws were here in Stabbie central for illicit spying or planting surveillance devices. Especially by an offworlder. Would anyone be able to help her?

Disasters flashed through her mind. The Burgess negotiation would end before it began. Nick's effort to redeem the Stabbies would die. No one would ever trust her again; her career would be over. She should never have volunteered to do this for Nick.

"Are you sure?" She jumped back. "I hate flies."

The guy frowned and squinted at the carpet. "I don't know. I thought I did. It looked like a mosquito or something smaller."

They both looked at the carpet.

He frowned and lowered his voice. "I'm sorry. My mistake." He turned on his feral gleam and she realized she had attracted the bed-hopper. There was always one in a business negotiation who tried to scope out the opposition from the crotch upward. She smiled back at him and they hung together for the rest of the tour, sparing the other women from him.

With the drone forgotten, Pam decided to hold off on dispersing drones inside a well-lit building. Or in daylight. She would wait until nightfall.

The sun was setting over the lake when the tour wrapped up.

Pam suspected it was a deliberate move by Jim to show off a brilliant fuchsia sunset. He was selling them on the Alliance delivering a unique experience. Everyone oohed and aahhed and took pictures.

The Burgess team returned to the hotel to prepare for the evening reception. Pam slipped away to the lakefront. It was dark enough now that she could distribute the rest of the drones without too many worries.

She watched the daylight ebb with gawkers gathered along the boardwalk. There were a lot of couples. She wished Nick were there. They hadn't had a vacation—or a break, really—since they had met. Both had been too busy.

She called him and he picked up instantly. "I was thinking about you," she said.

"Same here. I'm getting an amazing view of the bottom of your purse right now. Just kidding, I'm so happy you got drones inside their headquarters."

He had stomped all over the moment. Pam said, "I learned that spreading them in broad daylight is not the best idea."

Nick sucked in a breath. "Are you okay?"

"Yes," she said in an icy tone.

Nick replied, "I'm getting great intel from the ones you already deployed. It's amazing. Thanks so much for doing this."

"Yay. I'm waiting for dusk and then will finish up. I was calling you, idiot, to share this moment." She sent him a video feed.

"I'm sorry. It's gorgeous," Nick replied.

They both watched the sky for another minute. The boardwalk's lights turned on.

"Okay, back to work. Love you," Pam said and hung up.

She turned away from the lake to head west toward an open air food court and shops. She bumped into a man as she pocketed her netpad.

"Excuse me," said the man. He had been staring intently at his own netpad. "I should have watched where I was going. Got this picture of the sunset," he held up the netpad so she could see.

"Me, too," Pam said with a polite smile.

The man looked around. "We're the only people out here who aren't with someone." It could have sounded like a pick-up line, but it sounded wistful to Pam.

"I'm here on business," she replied with a shrug.

"Me, too." He extended a hand. "Craig Lassiter, strategic vision consultant."

"Pam Monroe, commercial real estate."

"Good to meet you, Pam." He smiled under a pair of dazzling blue eyes. With his formal shirt open at the neck, she imagined that he scooped up tipsy middle-aged divorcees by the dozen. And maybe some of the soon-to-be-divorced, as well. "You buying or selling office buildings?"

Had he picked her out, or was this actually an accident? Either way, she was amused but not at all interested. Lassiter's presence just emphasized how far away Nick was, touring some Community a couple of time zones away.

"Leasing, too. Plus resorts and hotels. I'm seeing how the Stabilizers handle things. Who's strategic vision needs fixing?"

"Stabilized Communities."

Alarm bells went off in Pam's head. Was this actual spying, developing a contact and getting an inside look at the Alliance? "They seem to have things well in hand here." She pointed at the illuminated ferris wheel in the amusement park.

Craig gave a small grin. "It's really a routine check-up rather than fixing. Executives like to stamp their fingerprints on things and pay me a healthy hourly rate to make the stamp."

"Nice," Pam replied lightly and pushed away from the boardwalk's old-fashioned wooden railing. "I have a business meeting to go to. See you around."

"Yes, I hope so," he said with a small, leering grin.

She smiled and walked away, dropping drones along the entire length of the Lake Evalyn boardwalk.

She turned towards the open-air restaurants and shops. It was dark, noisy, and crowded enough that she wasn't worried about anyone spotting a pseudo-gnat. She dropped the rest near the hotel and Alliance headquarters, hoping that the next downpour wouldn't wash them down the sewer.

CHAPTER FIFTEEN

HOME HAD NEVER LOOKED SO familiar or felt so strange. Nick's taxi passed the green-and-white gates welcoming him to Wertzville Community, established 2247. Maybe it felt strange because he was coming home with far less than good intentions.

There had been a heavy shower on the ride in from Harrisburg proper, but the sun had begun to peek through the thick, gray clouds. The taxi dropped him off at the line of check-in stations that processed visitors and residents to the Community. The chill of the cold, damp air went right through his jacket.

The first time he had approached a Community check-in station a few weeks ago, at the Whistler Community north of Vancouver, he had been scared out of his mind. He feared that the Alliance had added him to the blocked list after Hamilton, or that they would search his luggage and find the drones. But his record on the Stabilizer darknet still listed him as a resident in good standing and they welcomed him warmly.

After that, it had become a routine. Nick entered a Community, scouted a hidden power outlet for the drones' charge station, and launched several thousand drones to look for Lisa. As he worked his way down the Pacific coast and into the Rocky Mountains, he spent less and less time in each Community. Three weeks ago, he had managed to get in and out of four Communities in a day around Salt Lake City. He had found an outdoor power outlet behind a maintenance shack that turned out to be in the same location in every Community.

He had plenty of time in airports and during taxi rides to analyze the vast amount of footage that these drones were sending in. So far, there had not been a single sign of Lisa. And the hoped-for side benefit of learning about how the Alliance functioned hadn't materialized. The Communities were just not involved with those activities.

Only the drones that Pam had deployed in Celebration had returned any useful intel. Nick had been building a picture of how the headquarters operations were structured and who staffed what. But it was still mostly incomplete.

The man at the check-in station brought up Nick's file before he even reached the window. "It's good to see you back home, Nick," the man said. Nick had never seen him before but no matter. It was all about community here, right?

Nick gritted his teeth and smiled his way through the process of obtaining an updated visitor tag. The guy wanted to know when Nick would move back and Nick joked that he must have talked to his mother. "I'm just visiting for now," he said.

For the umpteenth time this week, he wished he could wrap his hands around the Stabilizer darknets. Instead, he would have to settle for drone surveillance. Darknets were for residents only.

He had been to two dozen Stabilizer communities in the last two weeks and he naturally fell into comparing stores, landscaping, and architecture. Instead of the Stabilizers' gated community concept producing generic copies, each community was noticeably different on the surface. Local architecture, regional tastes, and personal touches made each one unique. Except for the electrical outlet on the maintenance shack near the center of town where his drone recharger went.

Nick launched his drones without thinking about it consciously. It had become second nature to him. By the time he boarded the tram to Millers Gap, the northwestern village where his family lived, his drones had spread out to the community's far corners. Stabilized Communities' traffic patterns and general layout were highly similar. Cross had run the same search grid method on each one: Focus on females in public spaces. The majority of the drones would cover the more densely packed areas of the town center and the village greens. The rest randomly traveled the residential streets and industrial areas. Because it was too cold for insects to be buzzing about, they were running on a stealth profile to stay out of sight.

In less than two days, Nick's drones would tag and identify over eighty-five percent of the adult women in the community. About half of the potentials the drones spotted had no prior entry on the BHN or the Kagent nets; they existed solely in the Stabilizer darknets, beyond Nick's reach. Each one had to be scrutinized more closely, even if that meant a woman found herself brushing away a gnat.

When Nick stepped off the tram at the Millers Gap village green, he immediately noticed the changes since his last visit. A Rotty's convenience store had opened—with limited operating hours, of course. A glassware boutique had closed and been replaced by a fabrication shop. Someone had restarted the weekend flea market on the village green. Change happened slowly here compared to the big cities.

He walked into the residential areas he knew by heart. A house had been repainted here, a new porch added there, but it was still the same otherwise.

He passed the street where his parents lived. He headed for his sister's house and picked up the pace as the cold bit past his jacket's insulation.

No one was about. It was too chilly and damp, a late winter's day, and Friday afternoon to boot. Few Community residents worked on Fridays. Even though few people were outside, Nick stuck with the deserted back alleys rather than the open green spaces that the houses fronted on. The access alleys always felt a little more urban to him, a little more real than the sprawling, green, well-manicured lawns that the houses shared.

His sister Dez, her husband Jay, and their daughter Sally lived in a two-story Cape Cod at the end of a street. His brother-in-law Jay was in the garage, rummaging around in the back with fishing poles. Despite his breath coming out in white gusts, the man only had on a sweatshirt and jeans.

"Hey, bro," Jay said nonchalantly, as if chagrined that he had to be social. It occurred to Nick that Jay may have chosen to hang out in the garage to miss Nick coming in the front.

"Jay, how're you doing?" Nick couldn't help feeling a bit excited to see a relative, any relative. He pulled Jay into a brief upper-chest man-hug.

"Going fishing tomorrow," Jay said.

Nick nodded, hoping he wouldn't have to turn down an invite that neither one of them wanted him to take. But Jay stayed silent; Nick would be responsible for keeping any conversation afloat here. They had never been real close, going all the way back to grade school, when Jay was a wrestler and Nick was the scrawny geek looking for the exits in gym class. Best to move right along. "Girls are inside, right? Okay, I'll catch up with you later."

Jay grunted.

Nick came through the interior door, surprising his sister Desiree in the kitchen. She did a double take and then turned to hug him, carrot peeler in hand.

"Oh, I thought you were Jay," she said. "So, the trip was okay?"

"It was fine," Nick replied, thinking about the Privacy Council Warrant and his drones flying loose in the town. He shook his head. "I got Sally a gift, if that is okay."

Dez looked puzzled and dried her hands on a striped dish towel. "What is it?"

Nick pulled it from his bag. "It's from offworld."

Dez looked mesmerized. "Uh, Nick, I don't know if that's really appropriate here. Don't get me wrong—she'll love it, you know," she said. "But she'll show it to everyone and I don't know. Having something like that around." She looked at him, hoping he would understand and take it back.

Nick understood perfectly. It was the same thing his parents had done to him. Hide what the world offered outside their little gated town. "But I'm the uncle who goes to exotic places. It's my thing. I want her to have something that will remind her of me."

He could tell from her look that Dez thought that was the problem right there. "You're putting me in a tough spot," she whined. Nick loved it when she whined because it meant he would get his way.

He put the gift back in his bag and grinned evilly. "The real thing is ten times better." He only needed a couple of seconds of Dez's darkest look before he looked around the kitchen. "So, where is she? It's very, very quiet in here."

"Ms. Big Ears? She's in the other room. Spying on us," Dez said loudly.

Sally, so much bigger than Nick remembered her being, stepped around the corner. She was four years old with straight, light-brown hair and green, mischievous eyes. "I know when you're talking about me, Mommy."

His niece. Nick knelt down to Sally's eye level. "Do you remember who I am?"

Sally nodded. "You're Uncle Nick, but I call you Stinky."

"Sally...." her mother warned.

"I've actually been called worse, Sally, so that's okay," Nick replied.

"Uncle Stinky is invited to my show, in there," Sally continued, pointing to the living room.

"Can you show me where to put my bag?" Nick asked. Sally led him upstairs to the guest bedroom and gave him a tour of the room; the bed, the closet, the bathroom and the night light. The location of the night light was very important to Sally.

"I got you a gift from my travels," Nick said.

"What are 'travels'?" Sally said while she peeked into the dark guest closet.

"Oh, well, I live in Hamilton, Illinois and for my job sometimes I go far away from home. Other cities, even into outer space."

"Outer space?" Sally said and laughed. "Silly, you can't live in outer space. There's no air."

"Well, inside a space ship, there is air. And there are other planets, with cities and towns just like this one." Nick pulled a snow globe out of his bag and handed it to her. Inside it was Concordia, as it looked under the city tent. If you shook it, the globe filled with bright morning light and tiny plants wriggled to life along the streets. The globe darkened as night fell and the buildings lit up randomly. All the while, tiny air taxis flew around randomly.

"It is so pretty! Thank you, Uncle Nick! Are there princesses there?"

Nick smiled. "All of the girls there are princesses. They wear these big cloaks, which are kind of capes." He showed her how to shake the globe and a baby-tooth-filled smile broke out.

"Mommy, look what Uncle Nick got me!" she ran out to the hallway, holding the globe in one hand, its weight bending her wrist.

"That is a very nice gift. Also delicate," Dez yelled back, not bothering to look at it. "How about you keep it in your room?"

She looked down at her bent wrist, shook the globe again and marched off to her room. Nick returned to his room and dumped most of his equipment on the bed—except his netpad, of course.

"Cross, give me a beep if you find anything," he said as he placed his smartshades on a wooden dresser.

"Who are you talking to, Uncle Nick?" Sally asked from the hallway.

"Sorry, it was a phone call," he replied. "Now where is this show I heard about?"

She bounced down the stairs ahead of him, yammering away about the dance number, the talking puppets part, and where Uncle Stinky got to sit.

"Hey, Dez, you're not going to miss this show, are you?" He asked his sister in the kitchen.

"I caught two performances earlier today," she said from the kitchen, "and they were wonderful."

He stuck his head in the kitchen. "Oh, does it get better the second time?"

Dez stuck out her tongue at him.

"Now, Uncle Stinky, don't argue with Mommy. Come sit down, right there, while I start the music." Sally fussed with her kid netpad and music started to play. Nick suddenly wished he was wearing his smartshades, because he wanted to record this for Pam.

CHAPTER SIXTEEN

WHEN THE CAPTAIN OF THE sub-orbital flight announced that they would land in Shanghai in a few minutes, Craig took a deep breath. He flipped on the view from the plane's nose-cam and watched skyscrapers grow in size as the plane decelerated. A half-dozen more had sprouted since Craig had last been here and tried to destroy the city.

He exhaled slowly. It was the last patch of Earth he had ever thought he would return to.

Borbola had confirmed that the city had dropped any warrants against him years ago and even showed him on the BHN to prove it. Shanghai was part of the Burgess Consortium now and from the looks of Craig's fellow passengers, they let anyone in.

The city officials didn't give him a second glance as he breezed through Customs. He exited the terminal into a chilly, sunny morning. The trees had fuzzy halos of green leaf buds.

There was a black limousine waiting for him, with a chauffeur holding a netpad with 'Lassiter' in big print. Inside, on the bench on the far side of the limo was a woman in her fifties with shoulder-length black hair and an Asian face. Her keen gaze went right through Craig. He doubted anyone could hide much from her.

She smiled from her lips all the way up. "Craig? I'm Haruka Gallardo. Pleased to meet you."

"The pleasure is all mine," Craig said, shaking her hand.

She was widowed, childless, and hailed from an immensely

wealthy family with businesses circling the Pacific rim. The Gallardos were one of the Alliance's biggest contributors. Borbola's profile of Haruka showed her listed in Shanghai, Singapore, and Manila tax records as the primary trustee of several large trusts. She handled the family's charitable giving, officially. Beyond that, the family was careful to keep information about itself scarce on the BHN. But she also sat on the Alliance board.

"Would you like something to drink?" she asked.

He accepted a bottle of iced green tea and stretched out on the bench. "You have a real driver?" he asked, thumbing over his shoulder at the front seat where the chauffeur was sitting. Buzzer cities like Shanghai had turned their streets over to robotic drivers, throwing thousands of taxi, bus, and truck drivers out of work. More efficiency, faster pace of life, and entirely less human.

"A chauffeur can do more than turn a steering wheel," Haruka said.

"Where are we going?" Craig asked.

"YuYuan Gardens," she said. "It's a tourist attraction."

Craig looked out the window. "Somehow, I missed it when I was last here." The protests here were particularly violent during the Lobbying effort; the police had an extra special problem with marches in the streets. Craig watched the streets of Shanghai slide by outside the window. "I'm surprised I could come back."

She nodded. "It took some convincing of the Mayor and law enforcement. Luckily for you, it's a really old warrant and word of what you tried to do didn't become public knowledge."

That made Craig uneasy. The greatest mistake of his life, erased by wealth, power, and influence? "First, the Alliance forgives and now Shanghai. You went to all that trouble so I could consult for the Alliance?"

"Yes," Haruka said. "Because Penny asked me. We have our differences, but we both feel the Alliance is in trouble. She said it was *bloody* critical to recruit you."

Craig took a quick pull on the iced tea. She watched him closely, sitting tensed on her seat. He straightened up his posture to mimic hers. "Please tell me how to repay that debt."

"Start by telling me what you did in exile," she replied.

It was an odd request, but he didn't mind. "I traveled around northern India. Didn't like any of the cities I stopped in. Eventually, I settled in Guna, a little town south of New Delhi. Took the simplest job I could, a dishwasher."

"Were you punishing yourself?" she asked, appraising him. She was testing him in some way.

"At first, I just wanted to hide. This city sent bounty hunters after me and I had a couple of close calls in New Delhi, Jaipur, and Mumbai. When I realized they weren't bothering with rural areas without satellite coverage, I went there. Made a life for myself."

"Do you have a family?" Haruka asked.

He smiled. "No. But not for lack of trying. When the developers came sniffing around, I got into local politics in Barabanki to fight them off. Until the bounty hunters caught up with me."

"A regular Jean Valjean," Haruka joked. Craig didn't catch the reference and she let it drop.

Based on her profile, he pegged her for the Dave Poole side of the Board that wanted to accommodate the offworlders. But there was something about her that hinted that her mind could be open. She wasn't a blind follower.

"How did you get on the Board?" he asked.

She said, "My family runs its businesses as non-profits and the proceeds go to charity, which we have a lot of influence over."

Craig wagged his finger at her. "Wait a second. How much of those donations go to making sure the offworlders don't take your market share? Fess up now, Ms. Gallardo."

She smiled. "Guilty as charged. We're protecting a way of life, based on family, community, and jobs to support them. Protecting future generations."

"How many nieces and nephews do you have?" Craig sensed an opening.

"Over two dozen, and counting." When Craig's eyes bugged out, she added, "I have eight siblings."

"But no kids of your own?" He already knew the answer, but had to ask.

"Well, none that I know of," she said with a grin.

"Doesn't sound like you have a very Stabilized lifestyle," Craig chided her. "Tsk, tsk, tsk."

Haruka crossed one leg over the other and hugged her knee. "Should there be a purity test to participate in the Alliance?"

Craig grinned. "No, I wouldn't pass it. And I'm anything but pure."

She laughed, her eyes twinkling. "My father thinks I need to work hard enough to make up for the children I didn't have. I handle emergencies. I'm also the aunt to confide in."

Craig nodded. "Because you're the cool aunt who won't rat them out to their parents, right?"

"No," Haruka, said with a salacious grin, "because whatever trouble they get into, I probably did worse at their age."

Craig raised his eyebrows.

"Oh, look, here we are."

The car stopped at what used to be the northeastern corner of the garden. Craig and Haruka got out and the limo rolled away.

The Gardens were a green oasis that had expanded eastward over the centuries until the Exquisite Jade was at the center and pompous skyscrapers surrounded the borders.

As they walked into the park, the fresh smell of tree pollen replaced the metal tang of the city. The city's cacophony of sounds also receded a little, replaced by bird chirps and water burbling. *They must have used trees or walls to dampen incoming sound waves,* Craig thought. The Chinese knew how to make calming, soothing, and restorative spaces.

An orbital transport rumbled by overhead. Craig frowned, the tranquil moment blasted away. The garden was just a mirage to cover the sad truth that the city was hooked on a faster pace of life.

They walked down a stone path, past a dozen middle-aged men

doing Tai Chi in a tree-covered plaza. The park had meandering waterways, thick with green vegetation, and long, green lawns where children chased kites and each other.

"From an Alliance perspective, tell me what all of this makes you think," Haruka said.

Dark thoughts crowded into Craig's mind, not fooled by the outdoor frivolity. "This is where buzzers go to escape stress. It's an exhaust port that keeps the buzzer ecosystem from exploding."

Haruka shook her head. "That is outdated thinking. The buzzers would just leave town before they blew up."

He had the sense that he might have failed a test. Maybe she wanted to see if his perspective was still mired in Lobbying.

She swept her arm to take in the entire garden. "Meanwhile, a much more workable tactic could be right in front of us. There is an opportunity here. Can you see it?"

He saw people enjoying the sun and the promise of spring. But that was it. He smiled and held up his hands.

"Your brain is still stuck in Lobbying. Think as if you came from somewhere else in the organization."

They followed the crowds into the Garden. Haruka turned left, across a pedestrian boulevard and toward the newer gardens, which were beyond a large stone wall. Craig noted a small plaque by the arched entrance. It said that this exhibit was thanks to donations of the Gallardo Family Trusts.

Maybe she was showing off. Maybe she wanted to test his art appreciation or knowledge of botany. Craig had to be ready for anything if he wasn't going to let her down again. And he felt like his job hung in the balance if he didn't meet her approval.

"Are these your favorite gardens, by chance?" Craig said, pointing to the plaque.

She leaned in close to him and he caught the scent of something pleasant, like lilacs. "These gardens are an experiment," she said.

They stepped under a stone archway and onto a broad green

lawn that ran 40 meters to a line of evergreens. Dirt paths cut through the evergreens to four separate gardens.

The further they walked in, the sounds of traffic, orbital transports overhead, and nearby trains disappeared. All Craig could hear was leaves rustling and water gurgling from a stream that cut across the grass lawn.

"It's so quiet," he whispered.

"Sound dampening technology," she whispered back.

Knee-high red pagodas dotted the field, all the way to a towering line of evergreens. Visitors milled around from one to another, admiring the flower boxes outside the windows and gawking at the ornate, sculpted roofs.

They took the path to the left. The sound of running water grew louder, mixed with splashing and the squeal of happy children.

The daylight faded as they walked down into a dimly-lit observation room that was surrounded by an aquarium tank. Fish and turtles swam overhead and all around, past brightly-colored plant life and around pink coral. The only light came refracted through the water, making wavy blue impressions on the calm faces of the people watching on benches and seats.

Craig said, "It's kind of hypnotic."

Haruka nodded and walked up a ramp to the next garden, a humid greenhouse of tropical plants and cackling birds. The aquarium surface served as a pond. A number of couples cuddled on the short tropical grass. Craig breathed in a wet, tangy, fruity smell.

The next garden was a fake cave, with delicate, transparent stalagmites that were back-lit in a slowly-changing constellation of colors. An apparatus connected to a thin sheet of stalagmites played a tune, sounding like a flute.

People sat, watching the colors change, or watching water drip into a small pool. These were relaxation spaces. Buzzers ate this stuff up, Craig remembered. You could forget for a moment that you weren't in an actual underground cavern.

The final garden was one big pit of soft white sand, bordered by round white walls that rose about 12 feet, Craig guessed. Despite all the years in India, he never understood metrics. Two old men with simple rakes made designs in the sand. A Zen garden. Or a mandala. But this one let people walk through the sand, disturbing the patterns and making new ones.

Haruka had been watching his reaction to each garden. He tried to look neutral, but his initial opinion hadn't changed. At best, this was a nice resting place; at worst, it enabled the buzzers to avoid burnout to keep them and the city moving at a toxic pace. "It's gorgeous," he said.

They passed back under the stone arch and returned to the tourist-infested madness of the older sections of YuYuan Gardens.

Haruka held up her netpad for Craig to see. "The archway records biometrics of each visitor when they enter and when they leave. We compare their emotional and physical states to see how much this has relaxed them."

Craig nodded. "And they're more relaxed, of course. How could they not be?"

"We get a hundred requests a year to build a resort based on these gardens," she mentioned off-hand.

If she thought there was a business opportunity here, he didn't see it. "If you charged admission, it'd be cheaper for them to swallow some anti-stress gels."

If Haruka was surprised by his reaction, she gave no sign of it. "That remains to be seen," she said. "Let's go to the Tea House."

CHAPTER SEVENTEEN

JAY RESURFACED IN THE HOUSE around dinner time and said little while he ate Dez's pot roast. He grunted in appreciation at Nick's story about what life was like in other Communities.

After he was done eating, he avoided Nick. He had to wash up, he had to check the bait, he just had to be in a room that Nick was not.

Sally went to bed after announcing that she had to think about whether Uncle Stinky would be allowed to escort her to the wildlife preserve tomorrow.

"I don't know if I like you," she concluded. "You seem nice, but Mommy and Daddy say you're stinky."

Nick laughed out loud.

"We most certainly do not," Dez said, aghast. "Time for bed."

Dez continued to reprimand her daughter as she marched her upstairs. It wasn't more than fifteen seconds later that they began arguing loudly about what pajamas Sally would wear.

Jay and Nick sat in the living room, the awkwardness snowballing. Nick tried to think of some common person or thing they had from high school days that he could ask, but his mind had gone spectacularly blank.

"Kids," Jay finally muttered, shaking his head. He then grabbed at his netpad and mumbled an excuse, "Lazy asses don't want to get out of bed until noon unless I make them quit the pub early."

Dez came back downstairs with a load of laundry, looking

defeated and apologetic. Nick followed her to the washing room in the back of the house by the garage.

"How are the parents?" he asked.

"Haven't heard from them much, huh?" Dez said as she tossed in dirty clothes.

Nick shook his head. He was tempted to ask if they ever talked about him, but he feared the answer.

"You were the one who made these choices, kid," his sister said.

Nick began to fold clothes she yanked from the dryer. Incorrectly, as it turned out, when his sister glared at him and refolded them.

"Do they know that I'm here?"

Dez tried folding a pair of Jay's pants that looked like they had never seen a washer. Paint blotches, grease stains, and an assortment of other discolorations had accrued on the tough material. She settled for bending them in half. "No." She looked at Nick carefully. "They'll find out, I'm sure, from Ms. Mouth upstairs. Are you sure you can handle her by yourself tomorrow? I'm happy to come along," she said half-heartedly.

Nick could tell she wanted to him to say no. She had a rare afternoon off from Sally patrol, but she was still a mother. She worried.

"If I can handle politicians and bloodthirsty clients, I can handle a four-year-old," Nick said, puffing out his chest. "At least for a few hours."

Dez laughed and became serious. "Just don't lose her, please."

"I'm a trained expert in not losing people."

Dez smiled. "How is the girlfriend?"

"Well, she's good, but I don't know about the relationship. We may be headed in separate directions; she's successful."

"Too bad," Dez noted. "Because if you settled down, changed some diapers, paid a mortgage, it could help with Ma. Even if you don't live close to here." She was talking about reconciling with their parents. Maybe with her and Jay, as well.

"Sally's a great kid. I want to be in her life. She's almost enough to make me want to move back. Almost."

"You can't put us between you and them," Dez shook her head. "We're not taking sides."

"I don't want you to take sides. I just want us to be normal, where you don't have to hide my visit."

Dez picked lint off of her pant leg. "Sally has been excited all week about your visit. She did mention something to Pop and he took it in stride. But I'll hear about it."

Nick shrugged glumly. "Is it so bad that they don't want you to let Sally see me?"

Dez nodded.

"Hell of a family," Nick said.

"Maybe you should think about staying away for a while after this trip. Just to avoid trouble, until Ma and Pop come around."

Nick didn't need his smartshades to tell that his sister was trying to ease him into a painful place. A place where he wouldn't see his niece grow up. Where she wouldn't hear about him or about his unusual life.

As he followed her back to the front of the house, his netpad buzzed. It was a special buzz Cross used to get his attention. He looked at the message. Cross needed to talk to him urgently.

He slid the netpad back in his pocket. "Look, not a lot is going well right now. I need to see all of you. I want to see Sally grow up. Is that not as important as keeping the parents fully satisfied with you?"

The answer was clearly yes, but Dez bit her lip and patted him on the shoulder. It was a 'you will get over it' pat that he remembered from when she comforted him about skinned knees and unrequited crushes. Dez said goodnight and went upstairs.

Nick sat in the quiet family room for a few minutes. He was jealous of what Dez had here. Every bit of it, down to the knick knacks on the fireplace mantle. The casual disorder of a house lived in, with Sally's toys barely contained in a corner, the family photos lining the stenciled wall, the tasteless-but-comfortable plaid furnishings. A life.

Cross buzzed again. Nick went upstairs to his room and donned his smartshades.

[The drones need to recharge,] Cross texted.

Of course. Nick had forgotten about that. He cracked the window open and a gray cloud blew in with the cold night air. They slipped into their home base and the charge light turned on.

[There are 12 women here who match Lisa's general description. Three of them could be possibilities.]

Nick texted back, [Okay, we've seen this before, though. And facial recog didn't make a Lisa ID? Let me see their pictures.] Defeating facial ID software was not very difficult, despite centuries of refining facial recog techniques.

All of the women looked a little like Lisa, but none of the pictures were good enough to tell. They were all taken late in the day in bad light.

[Keep me posted. I'm taking Sally to the preserve tomorrow. Goodnight.]

Nick undressed and crawled into bed. Was it silly to expect any different from his sister? He had been surprised that she had agreed to let him come for the weekend in the first place. She had a soft spot for him, always had. But that soft spot could disappear.

He resolved to enjoy tomorrow with his niece, and for once, not worry about the future.

CHAPTER EIGHTEEN

AT THE GARDEN'S CENTER, A long, quiet line of people blocked Craig and Haruka from an elaborate tea house that looked like it was floating on a lake.

"This line is to see the Exquisite Jade," Haruka said.

They shuffled past the line. From what Craig could see, the Exquisite Jade was an ugly, craggy, gray rock, not green in the least, and not worth waiting in line for. It looked like the remnant of a meteorite that had mostly melted on reentry. But he did snap a picture of the tea house to prove to Daniel that he had actually returned to Shanghai.

"How are you feeling right now?" she asked as they entered a noisier section, full of tourists.

"Many people come here to wait in that line, or stand by it. The city thought that expanding the gardens would meet that need, but people still keep coming to visit the Exquisite Jade."

"I don't like crowds much." The quietness of the Gallardo garden experience was a soothing balm compared to the cacophony around them.

They shouldered through the crowd on the zigzag bridge across the water to the Tea House. Once inside, they were shown upstairs to a private dining room.

A young, serious kid served them tea in an ancient iron teapot.

Craig regarded the steaming liquid. "*Salud*," he said, clinking his porcelain tea cup against hers.

"To finding a way forward," Haruka added.

Indeed, he thought. He sipped the tea, relishing the heat on his tongue. "Your relaxation garden," he said. "Explain to me what your idea is there. You'll have to excuse my thick-headedness."

Haruka downed the rest of her tea. "You think that offworld culture is irresistible. That the only way to stop its spread is to stomp it out all across the planet."

Craig nodded. "I haven't seen evidence that proves otherwise."

Haruka poured another cup of tea for herself. "But the Stabilized pace of life has its own attraction. Many of the people who live in a city like this haven't experienced it. If they did, they may move away from the buzzer life."

Craig shook his head. "In Lobbying, we called those spa conversions. A day at the spa and a buzzer would throw away his money, possessions, and social status for a healthier life. It hardly ever happens and usually doesn't last."

Haruka didn't like that answer one bit. "Our fallback plan is to publish research on the data we've collected at the archway. But I can see you're not impressed with that, either."

"There are conflicting studies," Craig replied. Scientific research was just another propaganda tool to him, regardless of the academic field. If you beat the data long enough, you could make it sing your tune.

"You just don't believe that a nicer pace of life is better," Haruka said. "We're dangling a better life in front of these folks. They come out feeling refreshed, calm, and centered. The contrast with their day-to-day life is extreme.

"They begin to crave it. We're tracking repeat visits and the number of repeat visits increases over a year, three years, five years. There's a long-term effect."

"That's a really long-term plan," Craig said dubiously.

Haruka smiled. "We're planting seeds, right in the heart of the most hectic cities and zones. We're building three more gardens in Los Angeles and two in New York Jersey."

"We're going after their vacation dollars, too. Relaxation parks, Stabilizer spas. Tranquil housing projects. Some of these investments will pay off slowly but more surely than Lobbying's political stunts and public relations campaigns."

"And if you can't counter the power of money and materialism?" Craig asked.

Haruka's eyes flashed. "The Communities are failing. They lose money and residents every year. It's not just Lobbying that is in trouble."

She was hinting about a totally different way to approach the conflict. She wanted to see if he could understand very different alternatives to the Alliance's standard strategy.

He nodded. "You think we should use a multi-pronged approach, a mix of short-term, long-term, and very, very long-term strategies. An eclectic approach."

Haruka replied, "Maybe Dave Poole has a good thought here and Penny or Ciebrian has another over there. I don't see why one ideological position has to dominate."

Craig smiled as he drank his tea. "Because resources are limited. That's where the fights start."

"That's a failure of vision," Haruka said. "Here's how my family's business model works: We use our profit centers, run very much like offworld enterprises, to finance our Stabilizer-related activities."

"You use the buzzers to finance their own redemption," Craig remarked.

She nodded. "Combine the economic strength of offworld business to carve out Stabilized spaces here and to push back against offworld culture. Use their economic strength to fight their culture. Imagine what the Alliance could do with that strategy."

Craig wanted to be cynical, but he found himself believing her. The Alliance had been crashing cities in hopes that a fake change of heart would become real if it happened repeatedly. They had disregarded the option of trying to actually change those hearts.

It was inherently defeatist thinking, predicated on being unable to save their way of life without Lobbying's subtle terror techniques.

He raised an eyebrow. "You sound better qualified to do my job than I do. And I mean that as a compliment."

Haruka held up a hand. "Craig, please, I'm just a snotty rich bitch. I have grandiose ideas, but I don't know how to implement them." She laughed. "The rest of the Board considers me a dabbler in the real world. And they're probably right."

Craig leaned forward. "You've done more strategic thinking than the rest of the Alliance has done in decades. I know that sounds like bullshit, but it isn't."

"I believe you, Mr. Lassiter."

"A minute ago, I thought the Alliance doing business with the Burgess Consortium was a horrible idea. But now, I'm not sure."

Haruka fiddled with a spoon. "If we can leverage their money to further our own aims, why not?"

"But here's my problem: What if doing so strengthens them and spreads the offworld buzzer culture even further?"

She reached over and clasped his hand in hers. "Which is more attractive? The buzzer life or the Stabilized one?"

Growing up, he was sure it was the buzzer life, because living in the Community was so boring and constrained. But a relatively tranquil life in India had been rich and fulfilling. He was ready to fight for that life.

Her hand lingered on his. "My family became rich poisoning ourselves in the buzzer world and causing ourselves a lot of pain. My grandparents re-oriented the businesses—our entire lives—to find tranquility and shun the buzz."

Craig shifted in his seat and looked down at his tea cup. Tea leaf debris floated in the bottom until he stirred it up. "I used to feel that the buzzer culture was an unavoidable lure that needed to be driven out of existence, but now I know that won't happen. I'm not so sure about your idea, either."

"Good! Certainty is not a virtue." Haruka waved her hand in

circles. "The ones who feel the strongest know the least. I will get a call from one group saying that the loss of ocean reefs will doom the planet, while another claims that the world will end unless we feed hungry children. In my opinion, passion should stay in the bedroom."

Craig laughed.

"Oh, did I embarrass you?" She smirked at him. "Too bad. That must be my saucy Latina side."

Craig looked at her for a long second. "I'm not embarrassed."

She patted his hand. "Good. Don't want to damage the psyche of the man who could save the Alliance."

Before the pleasant moment could disappear, he asked, "Given your flexibility, what do you think about Lobbying?"

"It has failed numerous times, nearly brought the entire Alliance down, twice," Haruka said. "For the resources it consumes, we could have a legitimate Lobbying effort to blunt the buzzer culture in the political arena."

"I understand," Craig said. More relaxation gardens, she probably meant. "So, Lobbying doesn't necessarily play a useful role in a multi-pronged approach? I'm looking for a solution that would unite the Board members around taking action."

"Can Lobbying find a way to actually change hearts and minds? I heavily doubt it, I'm afraid. An organizational culture of cloak and dagger is not needed where the Alliance is going. This argument has been going on among the Board for decades, I've heard."

Perpetual arguing on the Board? During his earlier stint in the Alliance, it seemed like the Board spoke with a single voice. But now all he saw was a Board that was irrevocably split.

He smiled wryly. "My charm must not be what it once was."

She shook her head. "No, you are plenty charming." She batted her eyelashes at him. "But you're just a handsome terrorist. And I'm only saying that because I'm a straightforward bitch."

He chuckled and squeezed her hand. "Sounds like my type. Let me prove it by asking you to dinner."

She withdrew her hand and returned to fiddling with her spoon. "I'm not sure that would be appropriate, Mr. Lassiter. A potential conflict of interest," she added in a high-pitched voice.

Craig grinned. "Not if we always disagree on Alliance business," he pointed out.

She laughed. And Craig ended up staying with her in Shanghai's finest hotel suite for the next two days.

CHAPTER NINETEEN

NICK WOKE UP BEFORE DEZ and Sally and made them breakfast while wearing his smartshades. Cooking was easy with Cross posting overlays and spoon-feeding recipes and steps.

"What are you doing, Uncle Stinky?" Sally said when she came downstairs, shaking the snow globe.

"'Uncle Stinky,' I like that," Cross said out loud.

Sally stopped rubbing her eyes and looked around the kitchen. "Who said that?"

"Oh, that's my Simon," Nick said. "My artificial intelligence partner. Her name is Cross and she lives on the net. Cross, say hi to my niece Sally."

"Hi. Can I call your uncle 'Stinky,' too?" Cross asked.

Sally giggled.

"I tell your uncle what to do and he does it, just like a robot. Want to see?"

Sally nodded. "Yes, yes."

"Flip the pancakes, Stinky, before they burn," Cross said in a stern tone.

Nick rolled his eyes, but saw that Cross was right. He flipped the pancakes. "Is your Mom going to wake up soon? These pancakes are almost ready."

Sally nodded and ran upstairs. "Mom! Uncle Nick is making pancakes. And there's a girl downstairs with him!"

Dez appeared in the kitchen less than a minute later in her robe. "What was she talking about?"

"Me, Mrs. Grounds. I am a Simon named 'Cross' and without me, your brother would have burned your house down by now."

"I can believe that," Dez said, digging through the fridge for milk. She poured a glass for Sally and found some caff gels for herself. "He tried to cook hot dogs in the fireplace when he was a kid. Remember that, Nick?"

"Ooh, collecting embarrassing stories about him is a hobby of mine," Cross said.

"Pancakes are ready, Sally," Nick called out in a hurry.

Dez smirked. "Does my brother drag you around everywhere, Ms. Cross?"

"He couldn't function without me."

"Are you Stinky's girlfriend?" Sally asked.

"No, and Cross has to go away now," Nick said. He shut off the netpad.

"Bye, Cross!"

The three of them sped through breakfast. Jay had left before even Nick woke up. Dez claimed that he didn't need much sleep and wanted to get fishing as early as possible. Nick suspected that Jay just wanted out of the house.

Leaving the house with Sally was a complicated affair. Dez gave him the appropriate documentation that he wasn't kidnapping Sally, plus some snacks, plus extra gloves for hands that sometimes got wet, plus some back-up diapers and clothes in case of accidents—she's only four—and oh, you're sure you can handle this, little brother? It took cajoling and reassuring by both Sally and Nick before Dez let them leave.

The second the two of them left the house, Sally's little paw firmly gripped by his, Nick activated his drones. Most of the drones spread out over the Community to form a surveillance grid. A handful zipped away to track down the possible Lisa suspects and get a better read on them.

111

And two dozen were assigned to Sally duty. Half-a-dozen hovered over her in a circular air patrol. Nick ran threat assessment programs continuously: kidnappers, loose pets, motorized traffic, cracks in the sidewalk. He was not losing his only niece.

They trammed to the Community gate and caught a taxi out to the wildlife preserve. Yes, into the outside world; Sally was excited.

The wildlife preserve was a combination kid's playground, petting zoo, and research center. Nick had gone there dozens of times as a kid. Kids and animals could run free at this place.

Sally wanted to go to the playground first. The playground was actually a city block-sized jumble of sand pits, moon bounces, cargo nets, and mounds of brightly colored play equipment.

Sally looked it over like an expert playground connoisseur making a careful evaluation. Like she had a fun index that scored slides, ladders, and climbing structures.

She announced the order in which she wanted to play, which included the moon bounce twice, skipping the cargo nets, and an extended session of throwing foam blocks at Uncle Stinky.

They spent the morning there. She asked if Nick and her Mom came here when they were kids. Nick said he had been here so many times a goat learned to say his name. She didn't believe him.

Nick scored major points by letting her eat an ice cream bar and three cookies for lunch. Uncle's prerogative, he declared.

They went off to tour the petting zoo. Cross took a ton of stills of Sally feeding sheep, petting rabbits, and pointing at goats. She made Nick feed a horse that she was too afraid to get near.

After the petting zoo was the monkey habitat. One chimp was screeching the whole time, but the rest quietly played or ate. Sally grew cautious and withdrawn. Maybe monkeys were scary.

Nick patted her head. "Do you want to leave?"

"My stomach hurts," she mumbled and then projectile-vomited onto the asphalt in front of them.

The monkeys turned around at the sound of liquid splashing.

The loud chimp chittered and applauded. The others whooped and some beat on the glass.

Nick comforted her as much as he could and guided her to a nearby bench.

"Mean monkeys," she grumbled. "That's not nice!"

"Are you okay? We can go home if you don't feel good," Nick smoothed the hair on the forehead, checking for a fever. There wasn't any.

The loud chimp kept laughing. A maintenance worker arrived to clean up Sally's mess.

"You're a bad monkey," she yelled at the chimp.

Nick felt guilty about letting her eat all that junk at lunch, but she seemed to have bounced back. "We should probably head back to your house," he suggested. The sun was sliding toward the horizon.

Sally burst into tears.

The drones jumped into action on their patrol and Cross began listing possible reasons. Nick ignored all of that. "What's wrong?"

"I'm cold and tired. But I want to see more animals!"

Dez had said something about the dangers of missing nap time, but Nick had not paid it much attention at the time.

He rustled Sally's hair. "We can come back some other time, when that monkey isn't so mean."

"I'm telling Mom about that monkey," Sally replied darkly. And then she was okay with leaving.

It was twilight when they reached the Community gate. Sally snuggled up to Nick by the time they reached their stop. He carried her to the tram. She was tired when they still had a five-block walk back to her house.

She flung her arms up. "Will you carry me, Uncle Nick? I'm so tired."

"Uh, I'll try." He doubted his arms could last the distance. He hurried, bypassing crowds on the pedestrian street, his muscles beginning to ache. A crowd was pouring out of one of the bigger commercial buildings. The village movie theater. Blocking his way and slowing him down.

"I'm hungry," Sally said into his shoulder.

"Okay, honey." Dez's house had never seemed this far away. His arms and back went from groaning to yelling by the time he reached the Grounds' front door.

Dez and Jay were sitting in the front room, trying to look like they had been doing something other than waiting anxiously for Nick and Sally to come home.

"Mommy, Daddy," Sally said cheerfully and ran into her father's arms, "I ate cookies for lunch and then I threw up!"

Dez and Jay shot angry looks Nick's way.

Sally slipped out of her father's arms and ran down the hall to the bathroom, but she stopped and turned around. "Don't yell at Uncle Nick, I tricked him into letting me eat cookies."

"I didn't see it coming at all," Nick added.

"What did she do to you, bro?" Jay said, amused, looking for physical damage on Nick.

"She asked with that cute little face." Nick shook his head sadly. "What could I do?"

Dez sighed. The back doorbell rang. Dinner in a box had arrived, a Lincoln family tradition. Fast food franchises had a rotating menu of sample platters that offered the appearance of variety. When they were kids, Nick and Dez would fight over who got stuck with the vegetables and who had the most mini twice-baked potatoes. Two franchises sat right outside Wertzville to handle the surge of orders that came in every night.

Dez cooks about as much as Ma, Nick noted, while Pam cooked all the time and had been teaching Nick. Apparently, you could process your own meals from raw food stock—who knew?

He monopolized the fruit cup and the mini-avocado tacos, and pretended to steal Sally's cheesy breadsticks, which she giggled at. When she offered one to him, he accepted it only in exchange for her taking one of his fruit cups, so he didn't get a case of the fruit burpies.

"There's no such thing as fruit burpies, Uncle Nick." She shook her head. "Are you coming to dinner tomorrow at Nana and Papa's?"

Dez took that moment to begin clearing the table. Jay grinned at his daughter and said, "We'll just have to see."

Nick swallowed, looked at Jay, and turned to Sally. "Sorry, but I have to leave before then. It's okay. Will you give Nana and Papa hugs for me?"

Sally looked from her father to her uncle and saw that something else was going on. Before she could ask, Dez shooed her off to bed.

"What time are you leaving tomorrow?" Jay asked.

Nick replied, "Before dinner." Then he excused himself and went to his room to recover. He slipped his smartshades on before he closed the door.

"Anything to report?" he asked Cross.

[Same possibilities but no facial matches.]

Nick sighed. He was leaving tomorrow and he was out of Communities to search. He would have to go back to Hamilton and face Pam. She wanted to go to Tessa and Nick wouldn't have any more excuses. *So, tomorrow may really be the last day I see Sally,* he thought.

CHAPTER TWENTY

NICK WOKE AFTER A FITFUL sleep, obsessing over whether Lisa was here in Wertzville or if he had simply imagined seeing her. In the pre-dawn gloom, he packed his things and launched most of his drones to blanket the Stabilizer community.

Over a breakfast of egg sandwiches, Sally insisted that Nick take her to her Sunday playground session. Dez and Jay were going to a brunch at Mantle's restaurant in the town center and would catch up with them later.

It was a sunny, chilly morning, just on the edge of needing a hat and gloves. A dozen kids were already there, running around the red and yellow play structures, the younger ones wearing safety helmets.

Sally saw several pals from preschool and told Nick to stay with the parents at the playground's perimeter. He pulled out his netpad to ward off the chatty mother who was working her away around the circle of parents.

His drones had spread slowly throughout the Community, using the wind, gliding to conserve power and extend their range. He kept a couple close by, circling high above Sally so he never lost track of her in the maelstrom of kids that ebbed and flowed around the play structures.

The playground session broke up at 11 and Sally found Nick. "I want to talk to your friend Cross," she said as they began walking.

"We have to go meet your mom and dad at the town center," he replied.

"Is that a long way?"

"Yes. We have to go from the village center to the town center, where the tall buildings are. Are you cold?"

Sally shook her head no.

It would be a decent walk, but no longer than waiting for the tram to carry them the same distance. Nick considered how he could add to his total of cool uncle points. "Let's play a game on the way there. Hold your hand out. Take your glove off."

He slipped his smartshades on and took manual control of the surveillance drones circling meters above Sally's head. He could try to hide his gear around her, but if he found the drones fun, why wouldn't she? He wanted to be the fun uncle. God knew how she compared him to her other uncles, Jay's shaggy, unemployed brothers who lived in log cabins deep in abandoned state parks.

The drones landed on her outstretched hand.

"That tickles," she said. "What are they?"

Nick set the drones to fly in circles perpendicular to one another like a gyroscope. They landed back on her hand. "My tiny flying cameras. They help me and Cross look after you, so you don't get lost. Here, take a look." he handed her the smartshades. "Cross, set to a kid interface."

Sally had to hold the smartshades so they wouldn't slide off her little nose. She laughed when she saw the video feeds coming from the drones in her hand. She made a series of faces, moving her hand closer to and farther from her face, to watch herself zoom in and out.

Nick beamed. "You wear the shades and this earpiece. I'll hide and you keep seeing if you can find me."

It took Sally a few minutes to master controlling the drones with the simplified voice commands that Cross fed her. Nick hid among the trees down the road and Sally sent the drones chasing after him. She laughed as he swatted at them in the seemingly-empty air. Sometimes, he could see his drones following him, in his peripheral vision.

When he peeked around a tree, he saw that Sally had stopped walking. When she saw him, she ran over and took off the smartshades. "Miss Cross told me to go get you."

Nick slipped the smartshades on and popped the ear bud in. Cross was flashing text and saying something in a sickly sweet voice. His old interface snapped into place and he was looking at a video feed of Lisa Radisson boarding a tram headed towards the Wertzville town center. She was in the northwestern village of Glendale.

He and Sally were too far from a tram stop. He'd have to run into the town center to catch Lisa before she exited the tram and disappeared again. But Sally's little legs wouldn't carry her that distance. He couldn't leave her though.

He would just have to let Lisa go. Or hope the drones could track her until he could dump Sally on her parents. But he had searched for Lisa for two years, through countless cities and Communities. She was the missing key. He couldn't let her slip away.

He looked down at Sally, who was clapping her hands as Cross kept her occupied by flying the drones in intricate patterns over her head. They buzzed her forehead and she squealed and jumped up to catch them.

[What are you going to do? Lisa will be outside of drone sensor range soon.]

Nick checked his drone reserves. He could protect Sally, himself, and take down a dozen Lisa Radissons. His niece wouldn't be in an iota of danger if she came along. In fact, she'd be safer than she had been the whole time Lisa had been in Wertzville. Was Lisa here to come after his family? What if she slipped away and came back to hurt them? He had to apprehend her now while he knew where she was.

[I can't arrest Lisa in front of Sally,] Nick texted Cross with small movements of his fingers. How traumatizing would it be if her uncle got in a fight with another adult? Or arrested someone? Or if Lisa pulled out a gun? Sally was too young to see that kind of thing and it was too dangerous. No, she couldn't be nearby.

[There's no time to get her parents or your parents to pick her up,] Cross noted. [And you can't leave a child that young by herself unsupervised.]

What did unsupervised really mean though? [I could park drones over Sally, and we could both watch her while I grab Lisa.] That prospect seemed unsatisfying for some reason, but Nick didn't have a lot of experience with kids, so he couldn't nail down why.

Cross replied, [You shouldn't be distracted by Sally when you face Lisa. Think about what Dez would worry about.] Cross directed the drones towards two rabbits hiding in the underbrush, but visible on infrared, and Sally chased after, which caused the rabbits to bolt.

"Uncle Nick! Bunnies!"

"Don't scare the little bunnies," Nick replied. He sighed. [She'd worry that an adult would come by and wonder where Sally's irresponsible parents were. Or worry that an adult would kidnap her. Or worry that Sally would run into the street or get hurt somehow.] The drones couldn't restrain her physically, short of rendering her unconscious.

Nick texted Cross, [I'm going to put Sally some place nearby to Lisa, but safe. You and I will watch her with drones like a sheepdog would watch a kid, you know, corral her from wandering off, while I go deal with Lisa.]

[And if she tries to run in the street?] Cross asked.

"I don't know. Use the drones to go up her nose, or tickle her ears, or block her way. The drones can provide better protection than if she ran out of my reach. Come on, let's coax her into coming along."

A dozen drones moved another meter out of Sally's reach. She grinned and lunged for them, but they retreated a meter. She walked after them and they backed up past Nick. She ran and they kept pace, staying just out of her reach.

[You really don't know anything about children,] Cross texted.

[Thanks,] Nick replied and hurried after Sally, on the way to Lisa.

Nick ran the last hundred meters to the town center's tram stop despite feeling a cold tear in his windpipe. His lungs felt half their normal size. He was overdue for some hands-on-knees panting and gasping. Maybe even some dry heaves.

Sally was further ahead, still grabbing at the drones. He had started off planning to let her win the race, but once she had a lead, he couldn't catch up.

Nick texted Dez about turning over Sally earlier than planned, but his sister didn't respond. He was stuck with Sally, and for the first time, he was unhappy about it.

He had no idea how grabbing Lisa would turn out. And he couldn't forget how his last meeting with her had ended in bloodshed. If she carried another EMP bomb in her shoe, she could fry all of his fancy toys, leaving him and Sally defenseless. What would he do then, wrestle her to the ground?

The tram was already empty when Sally and then Nick caught sight of it. Some passengers were headed for the parking lots at Wertzville's south entrance, and the rest were spreading out into the town's side streets.

The drones spotted Lisa walking to the parking lots. Damn. That meant Nick had no time to mess around, or to stash Sally somewhere safe. Once Lisa took a car out of here, his probability of losing her would jump above 87%. Lisa was also with two women, which complicated things.

[The other women are local residents,] Cross reported. [Tammy and Jess. Almost no records on either. They probably grew up here.]

Sally took off running and disappeared into the tram crowd. Nick switched over to the feed from her drones while pushing the Lisa feed off to the periphery.

The two feeds overlapped and then became identical. Oh, God. Nick ran after Sally, while powering up his drone reserves.

Lisa Radisson bent down to Sally's level and smiled. "Hello, dear. Are you lost?"

CHAPTER TWENTY-ONE

"NO," SALLY GROUNDS SAID. "I'M with my uncle."

Lisa Radisson looked up and saw Nick running up to them. She stood up quickly and her eyes blazed. "Nick, you came back. And you brought your niece?" Lisa shook her head.

"We were at the playground," he replied. "This is my hometown. What are you doing here?"

Lisa just stared at him.

"Is this that old boyfriend, Anne?" asked one woman standing next to Lisa. Her loud tone was more of a warning to him than an actual question to Lisa.

"Tammy, Jess, this is Nick," Lisa said with a touch of bitterness. "The old boyfriend."

The other two women tensed up and so did Sally. Lisa must have told them some bad boyfriend tale in case he ever showed up. In his own hometown. The fact that she chose to hide here meant that she had profiled him, right down to the relatively small chance he would ever search for her here, given his family troubles.

Cross was having all of his drones converge on Nick's location at maximum speed. He had enough drones to take out Lisa and the two women, if they intervened.

Lisa glanced up at the growing dark swarm of gnats a meter above her head and then down at Sally. She squatted down to the little girl's level. "I actually know your uncle, but I haven't seen him in a while. Isn't that funny?"

Sally noticed the drones gathering meters over Lisa's head and froze in place, uncertain what was happening.

"What's wrong with you?" Jess said. "Using a child to help stalk an old girlfriend."

"Kids and dogs are a great way to meet girls," Nick countered with a wheeze. He closed the distance between him and Sally. "Her name is not Anne. It's Lisa Radisson. She was born offworld. She's wanted by several authorities."

[She's powering up a weapon,] Cross ran across the bottom of Nick's smartshades.

"Maybe I should call security," Jess said.

Actually, he didn't want any attention from the Wertzville cops. It was possible they would side with Lisa, an official resident, while he would be viewed as an outsider. Stabilizer Communities had banned surveillance devices like drones and smartshades. He had the feeling that waving around arrest warrants from Hamilton and Mars would not help him. He shrugged nonchalantly. "I grew up here. I probably went to high school with the local cops."

"Your uncle is right," Lisa said to Sally, "I need to talk to him alone, okay?" She sent her back towards Nick. Sally looked uncomfortable and about ready to cry.

"Sally," Nick said, "Ms. Cross can start walking back home with you. I'll catch up in a minute. Okay?"

Sally nodded. He gave her a hug and sent her after a hundred drones, which danced ahead of her.

All three adults waited for Sally to round the corner. Lisa and her friends ran in the opposite direction.

Nick sent the drone swarm after them and walked, his lungs still feeling raw. It was Sunday and Lisa and her friends had two blocks of closed stores before they could reach the parking lots. And then there would be no question of cover until they got in a car or building.

[She has a gun.] Cross displayed an infrared feed that picked up power signatures warming up in a shoulder holster, Lisa's purse, and right ankle. Wonderful.

Tammy gestured frantically at an enclosed vending kiosk, but Lisa kept running. She knew the drones could penetrate a closed glass door.

The women reached the end of the block, with a sea of parked cars ahead of them. Nick formed a wall of drones to block their way. Lisa pulled a gun from her purse.

Jess walked straight into the drone wall and was zapped multiple times. She crumpled to her knees and then flopped down to the asphalt. Tammy shrank back from the drones.

Tammy began hyperventilating and shaking. Poor thing—she had no idea what was going on. Nick sent in a dozen sedative drones and she dropped next to her friend.

Nick continued approaching Lisa, watching his other drones escort Sally further away.

Lisa raised two weapons at him. It reminded him of the last time they had met. "What, no guns? You've really become a Kagent, Nick."

Nick grinned and pulled out his stunstick, a gleaming chrome penis. It used to belong to his mentor, Lisa's stepfather, Bridge Radisson. When Lisa had shot her stepfather, the dying man's last act was to save Nick by sedating him with that same stunstick. It had been in the dark, thank goodness, so Nick didn't have the visual memory of getting leg-humped by a robot's dong.

"That won't stop a bullet, Nick," she said.

"The penis is mightier than the semi-automatic," he replied, "because it's enough of a distraction to coat your arm in drones. So, put the gun down or I'll do it for you."

She hesitated a second and Nick activated the drones on her wrists and elbows. Her arms spasmed as the drones zapped the nerves. Both guns clattered to the sidewalk.

He approached her and sprayed her numb wrists with a thick, purple stream of Bondcuff. It hardened like a spider web around her wrists. He marched her back to the tram stop. There were taxis parked there; shopping outside the community was a major cash cow for the taxi companies.

"I thought you were never coming back here," Lisa said. "Your parents thought the same."

Nick smiled. "I know, but I have to keep trying. Especially when I run into so many good friends when I visit."

"You're gloating," Lisa said.

"Yes."

"Stop," said a mechanically-amplified voice. Nick and Lisa turned to see a brown Stabilizer security car pull up to the curb, its orange lights flashing.

Two security officers exited the car and approached them with weapons drawn. "What are you doing with our resident, Mr. Lincoln?"

"Lisa Radisson is wanted in several other cities and offworld for major crimes. I have several warrants giving me permission to apprehend her." Cross squirted the Warrants to the netpad cuff on the cop's uniform.

The cop glanced at the warrants. "She's a resident of this Community, but you are not."

"I was born here. I grew up here; she grew up offworld," Nick countered.

The guards were unimpressed. They were reading his file in the Stabilizer darknet. "You're not really welcomed here, are you Nick?"

"My niece wanted to see me," he stated between clenched teeth.

"You can't apprehend her. There's no criminal accusation in our systems."

Lisa glanced at Nick, but he was too busy thinking about his options here. He wasn't in a rush to leave, but he feared dealing with the Wertzville cops get involved would somehow end with Lisa walking free.

[Your sister called and is quite angry. Sally and I have been trying to explain. We need your help.]

"Lay your weapons on the ground, Mr. Lincoln," the cop said.

Nick pulled Bridge's old stunstick out and carefully and slowly laid it on the sidewalk. Both cops eyes followed his every move in detail. He stood slowly, raising his hands.

"What the hell is that?" asked one of the cops, right as the drones landed on his face and neck.

"It's the only weapon I have," Nick said.

Lisa shook her head. "He's lying. Look above you!"

Both men spasmed and toppled over. The exhausted drones, flying like drunken bees, returned to the charge cartridge on Nick's belt.

Lisa choked on a laugh. "They'll ban you for life for doing that," she said. "You idiot."

He slid his stunstick back inside his jacket. He hoped not, but he knew she was right. He was surprised they hadn't barred him from entering in the first place. The Stabilizer darknets were not well-integrated, at least when it came to the residential and terrorism wings of the organization.

He hustled Lisa to a waiting taxi as more sirens pierced the air in the distance. The cops must have had biosign trackers and dispatch knew instantly that officers were down. They probably had seen everything from the cops' shoulder cam footage. They would come after Nick, not Lisa.

"Cross, I want to talk to Sally, and then recover the drones," Nick said as he shoved Lisa inside the taxi. On his smartshades, he saw two dozen drones gather by Sally's ear. Dez looked furious.

"Sally, it's Uncle Nick. I have to arrest this woman you found, and take her away. She could have hurt you and your parents. I've so sorry I have to leave."

"When are you coming back?" Sally said.

"Are you talking to him?" Dez asked. "Sally, let me talk to him."

Nick swallowed. "I don't know girl, I don't know. It may be a long time."

Cross began flashing warnings that Nick would lose the drones unless he recovered them now.

"Sally, tell your mother, I'll call her later. And I'm really sorry, but I have to make sure you and her and everyone else stays safe."

Cross pulled all the drones back at maximum speed.

Nick told the taxi's nav program to drive to the Harrisburg airport. The taxi eased away from the curb at normal speed, which was just really irritating. Nick cracked the window so the drones could get in. Cross had calculated that they would just reach the taxi as it left Wertzville.

While Lisa fumed and looked out the other window, Nick composed a lengthy message to Dez. As the taxi crossed the river into Harrisburg, Cross showed Nick that he had been officially exiled from all Stabilizer Communities. At least he grabbed what he had gone there for. But all it took was a single thought about Sally, and whether he would ever see her again, and his eyes welled up and he sniffled.

Lisa fished a tissue out of her purse and handed it to him. The feeling in her hands must have returned. "You should have tried to catch me outside the Community borders."

Nick wiped his eyes, a sharp retort on his tongue, but instead he bit it back and watched the Susquehanna River roll by. "I couldn't risk you getting away again." He looked at her.

Lisa shook her head. "So, you got me. I'm not talking. Just throw me in some dungeon and collect your reward, bounty hunter. I'm not saying anything unless you take me back to Tessa yourself."

"Me?" Nick said. "Why?"

She looked at him coldly. "You afraid of going offworld?"

Nick shook his head. "No. But you aren't in a position to make demands. And Hamilton, among others, will prosecute you for a number of crimes. You'll never get out of jail."

Lisa smiled evilly. "I know that. But I also know you desperately need me to talk about the Alliance. Especially since you've just been banned. And I will only do that on Tessa."

Nick texted the news to Pam, who started working with the Hamilton district attorney on a multi-jurisdiction prosecution plan. The network security concerns of the Kagents prompted the Hamilton prosecutors to wait, but not wait long. Lisa would face a quick hearing and trial on Tessa and then return to Earth for a series of trials in large cities across the planet, starting with Hamilton. Since Hamilton was where Lisa had caused loss of life, it would get first choice on where she was imprisoned.

By the time Nick and Lisa were on a plane to Hamilton, Pam had made arrangements for an offworld flight to Mars for her, Nick, and Lisa aboard a ship called the *Longburn*.

When the plane landed, Nick and Lisa were joined by a heavy police escort that took them straight from the airport to the liftport. Pam was part of a contingent of Hamilton officials who oversaw the signing of custody arrangements. Finally, Pam, Nick, and Lisa were escorted aboard the *Longburn*.

A bald-headed pilot named Izzy Goodburn regarded the prisoner with raw, murderous hatred. "Bridge was a good friend of mine," he said to Lisa as the police escorted her to the cargo hold. A cell there would hold her for the trip.

Lisa ignored him. She ignored everything. Nick's drones would provide round the clock surveillance of her. He and Pam left the cargo hold and joined Izzy on the bridge.

"We can't space her, Iz," Pam said, as she and the pilot hugged. Izzy kissed her full on the lips, to Nick's shock.

"So you two know each other?" Nick asked.

"Old flame," Izzy said, and shook Nick's hand. "It's good to meet you. Strap in and we'll make fire."

Yay, Nick thought as he strapped in for his first trip to another planet. Lisa was caged in back but seemed to have the upper hand, Pam had an old boyfriend flying them offworld, and Nick may never see Sally again.

CHAPTER TWENTY-TWO

CIEBRIAN BIETO HAD MEETINGS IN Cape Town, so his scheduling assistant arranged for Craig to meet Mr. Bieto there. Media reports said Bieto was intensely private and highly intelligent; Borbola's profiling had backed that up. Bieto was a study in calm, highly-focused energy. He had launched two corporate empires while building a brood of 12 children with his wife Ruby.

Borbola also mentioned that no less than five different people in Bieto's corporate holdings had profiled Craig before Bieto agreed to meet. Haruka had even texted Craig, during one of their marathon texting sessions, that Bieto had contacted her to vouch for Craig as well. Which she did, because she was completely infatuated with Craig, and the feeling was mutual.

The meeting was at Bieto's penthouse suite at the Sompa Fuor Hotel, an Earth-focused luxury hotel chain. Was it just coincidence that Craig had always wanted to see inside a Sompa Fuor? He once dreamed of honeymooning in Rio's Sompa Fuor with Basu. But when he had proposed to her, Basu had grudgingly admitted in her shy, halting tone that she had been boning someone else all along. Craig flew to Cape Town not knowing if he was twisting Bieto, or if it was the other way around, or if they would be allies.

Cape Town was tucked between wildly different-shaped mountains and the ocean. Despite the natural beauty and the pleasant climate, Craig got the vibe right at the hectic airport that this was a buzzer city. For centuries it had been the economic heart of southern Africa.

The airport shuttle whisked him onto Settlers Way Highway and into the business district. Skyscrapers lined Strand Street, but even the tallest barely reached the height of Lion's Head mountain in the distance.

The Sompa Fuor was tucked between the glass, concrete, and polymer towers that ran up and down Strand. But the Sompa Fuor stood out; its exterior consisted of dark, wood shingles and irregularly-placed stained glass windows. It looked like a cathedral constructed by a race of tree people.

The lobby took Craig's breath away. The walls on the left and right were lined with maroon silk drapes. Waterfalls cascaded down the far wall, filling the lobby with joyous crashing. Two ornate, curved staircases led to the second floor and a bank of bronze elevators. The staircases' balustrades portrayed a montage of hand-carved wooden animals and wilderness at different altitudes. Halfway up, palm trees turned to waves of grain to evergreen forests and finally, arctic icebergs.

The elevator deposited Craig in the lobby of the penthouse suite, complete with a fountain and benches. Bieto's scheduling assistant was sitting on a bench tapping away on his netpad. He waved Craig over and opened the suite door for him.

Craig didn't expect a fragrant breeze to greet him as he stepped inside.

The penthouse suite stretched about forty yards from the door. There were at least three sitting areas, an indoor pool, a kitchen, and what seemed like several bedrooms and suites off the great room.

The walls and roof were all windows that looked out over the ocean and the City Bowl, as the locals called the city tucked in between the mountain peaks.

Despite the high floor of the hotel, the breeze was warm. Cape Town had broiling summers, but the penthouse level was too high up to feel that warm. This was artificially heated. Dozens of plants and trees waved in the breeze. Borbola had reported that what prompted Ciebrian to join the Alliance was Cape Town's fight to preserve its biological diversity against terrestrial and offworld corporate developers.

Ciebrian Bieto was a thin man of medium height with the darkest skin Craig had ever seen. When he stood up from the brightly-striped sofa he was reclining in, he looked like a model who had stepped out of a clothes printer catalog: cream blazer, comfortable pants, business shirt with the buttons undone to look casual.

He smiled when he saw Craig and rushed over to pump his hand. The man had a smile that lit up the room. "It's so good to meet you. Come and sit down."

They sat in opposing chairs that were the same riot of color as the couch.

Ciebrian's smile stretched from ear to ear. "To business, then, because I don't have a lot of time, I'm afraid. The Alliance has been skirting the main problem. If the buzzers and the offworlders threaten our way of life, we should destroy them." He wagged a finger. "Not violently, of course, but cripple them financially, humiliate them. Like that bounty hunter who went after the Dragoons."

Craig's toes tensed. Ciebrian was referring to Borbola.

"The Dragoons are dying a slow death now. In two years, they'll be lucky if someone buys them before they go out of business. All because he smashed them right in the face." Ciebrian shook his fist. "He let everyone know that he damaged that entire company."

Was Ciebrian telling him subtly that he was aware of Borbola profiling him? That hint and meeting at the Sompa Fuor made Craig wonder if this Bieto had planned this to maximize Craig's receptiveness. Bieto was twisting him. Interesting.

"So, Lobbying should become an overt operation?" Craig asked.

Ciebrian spread his hands wide. "Exactly. If we can't implode a city subversively, then we should take it down any way possible."

"I can tell you from personal experience; that really doesn't work," Craig cautioned.

"Maybe so. But our usual methods haven't stopped the spread of the offworld lifestyle. We need to rethink them. Don't lose track of our basic mission: Our way of life is under attack and we are losing. We need every effective tool at our disposal to stop it."

Ciebrian was a firebrand, no doubt. But on the Board, he was alone on the fringe. He had the way of a prophet about him, though. People would recoil at Ciebrian's bold declarations and then gradually come around after further experience began to prove him right. But how far did Ciebrian want to go?

"If Lobbying were put back together, it could lead the way," Craig said, pretending to think aloud. "It could push for tariffs on offworld goods, demonize buzzer culture, advocate for more stable local policies."

Ciebrian shook his head. "Think grander. Find the pressure points of offworld societies and bash them. The Alliance's supporters have deep pockets and a far reach. Deploy economic weapons to strangle buzzer businesses and hurt offworlders, too. Use cultural weapons to reshape how people view offworlders and the buzzer lifestyle. Political weapons can ostracize them. Target whatever guards and supports the offworld societies, and disable those things. This is a fight for survival. We need to attack the buzzers on all fronts, whether down here or offworld."

"And you think that we should do this out in the open? That's quite a cultural change."

Ciebrian waved his hands. "Yes, do it publicly. We want to be noticed. We want the press watching as we smack the offworld societies right in the mouth."

Craig tapped furiously on his netpad. "You're talking about total societal war. Tearing down their society before they tear down ours. Convincing people to opt out is not enough."

"Exactly!" Ciebrian sat forward on his chair, wagging a finger madly. "That's what we need to do."

Craig smiled, despite himself. He hadn't figured Ciebrian would be a font of new ideas. But when you were a wealthy, innovative entrepreneur like Ciebrian, maybe you had the headspace to see things in new and different ways.

"You're not talking about a tactic like irradiating the center of a city, right? I tried that, once, and it failed."

Ciebrian laughed. "Nothing like that. We can choke supply lines using market forces. We can poison attitudes about offworlders with fear. Strike at the offworlders' homes and devalue the attraction of their buzzer culture."

"I have some quibbles with that," Craig said, "but am mostly in agreement."

"The problem," Ciebrian said, "is that the rest of the group does not share my views. Our views, right? We have a fundamental disagreement. How do you propose to address that?"

Craig waggled his netpad. "As a consultant, I'm trying to get all of you Board members to see beyond 'either/or' to seeing 'and.' That's where the truly innovative solutions lie. I have to find a way to boost the bottom line of businesses and carry this fight to the offworlders."

Ciebrian slapped his thighs and stood up. "Sounds perfect. You have my support and I believe we have an understanding."

Craig stood, nodded, and shook his hand.

Ciebrian added, "Contact me for any help you need. And please, stay in this suite until your flight home." He walked towards the door. "I have several meetings in town and then am leaving for Kuala Lumpur."

Craig looked around, amazed. "Are you serious?"

"The next three days are already paid for. It will make up for those hard years you had in the Indian backcountry." Ciebrian winked and walked into the suite's lobby. "Enjoy it, because you have a lot of work to do."

CHAPTER TWENTY-THREE

"NICK LINCOLN," CAPTAIN IZZY GOODBURN called over the *Longburn*'s intercom, "get your ass to the bridge. That's an order."

Nick pulled his weightless body along the corridor of the *Longburn* to the small space that Izzy insisted on calling a bridge. It was more like a cockpit with a couple of extra seats.

Pam was buckled into one of those seats and beamed at him. She had a cupcake in her hand with a sparkly candle burning on top. Nick thought fires on a spaceship were a bad thing, but he was the space noob here.

Izzy turned around in his pilot seat and motioned to the main viewer. "You only see your second planet once," he said. He flipped a switch to show the view from the stern scopes. Suddenly, the planet Tessa was hanging there, growing larger at a frightening rate.

And out of nowhere, Pam and Izzy broke into a soaring rendition of Happy Birthday. When they finished, Pam held out the cupcake.

Nick blew out the candle, which propelled him into the console on the upper bulkhead. He strapped himself down into another seat. "It's not my birthday," he pointed out.

Izzy grinned. "Old space travel tradition. When the first crew made it out to Mars, it was the mission commander's birthday. And they were just so happy to have made it. So, any time it's someone's first time seeing their second world, it's like their birthday on that world. Rite of passage before the decel."

Nick stared at the live image of Tessa. Going to the Moon had not been like this; he had seen the Moon every day of his life. And he finally understood his mother's worries about offworld lures. For the first time in his life, he didn't care if he ever returned to Earth. There was another planet below him, almost within reach.

Until that point, he had thought of Mars as a lifeless, reddish-orange rock with giant horizontal canyons that could be seen from space, nature's rust-covered rock pile. He had imagined tiny desert settlements made out of landing vehicle parts where people drank recycled urine. Hunter-gatherer backwardness mixed with modern technology.

Now he realized how truly ignorant he had been.

Clouds floated across an orange surface that had a smattering of green-and-blue splotches. Cities dotted the surface, connected to one another with silvery rail lines. Developments stretched from the day-lit horizon to the light-speckled night side. Millions of people going about their lives in cutting-edge cities.

Izzy activated a klaxon and a recorded voice issued instructions about securing for deceleration.

"Your cargo secured?" Izzy asked.

"This isn't Lisa's first trip," Pam said sourly.

But Nick checked the drones watching Lisa and nodded.

"Here we go," Izzy said and punched a virtual button on his screen.

The ship jerked backwards. Nick felt gravity flip again, pressing him into his seat as the engines fought against the inertia hurtling them towards Tessa.

Nick's eyes remained fixed to the stern viewer, watching the planet grow larger, but at a slower and slower pace.

Spacecraft and orbital platforms popped into focus as they drew closer. Ships rose, fell, zoomed into the distance, or came out of nowhere to zip by the *Longburn* on their way to orbital habitats off to the right. To Nick's left, a flock of passenger shuttles zoomed toward a cylindrical habitat hovering near the little rocky moon of Phobos.

Nick had never seen so many ships, habitats, and satellites before. They coated the planet in a thick swarm from pole to pole. A line of boxy freighters approached the docking nozzle of a rotating, cylindrical habitat. It was at least ten times the size of the biggest Earth hab and it hosted a lush, tropical climate.

"That's Fairhaven," Izzy explained. "That's where Bridge grew up."

Bridge's funeral had happened months ago, but Nick had not been ready to leave Earth and so, had missed it. Someday, he needed to visit the hab and pay his respects to the old jerk who had sacrificed himself for Nick, for Hamilton, for everyone.

Nick saw a thin line of freighters extending from the hab down to the planet's surface. "Is that an elevator?" he asked, dumbfounded.

"Yeah, those things are antiques," Izzy replied on his netpad. "The Werner Meade engines make direct flight cheaper and faster, and the elevators have been losing business for twenty years. Besides, this is more fun."

Nick looked over at Pam, who regarded him with a satisfied smile. He leaned over in his seat and hugged her.

"Now do you get it?" Pam asked. She meant that this was a place better suited to him. People dreamt big out here and then made it happen. Her home turf. She patted his hand. "Wait till we reach the surface."

The *Longburn* dropped through the atmosphere and the Great Ravine stretched along the northern horizon. As the ship dipped lower, the Ravine disappeared, replaced by a thin, gossamer silver thread running below them. The silver thread bisected bluish territory surrounding a small dome. A settlement. The silver thread was a railway. The map on Nick's viewer called it the SoConR, short for Southern Continental Railway.

The ship banked north to follow a spur from the SoConR. Orange-red desert stretched around the railway without a settlement in sight. Sunlight illuminated patches of the surface as the cloud cover began breaking up above them.

Finally, a small settlement flashed by, just a craggy orange building and a solar array next to some machinery. Then another cluster of buildings with vehicles moving about them. A small tented town was next, with outlying settlements spread around it.

"Are those plants?" Nick pointed to the blue-green stretches of landscape.

"Special scrubs, enclosed tree farms, lichen gardens, probably," Pam said. "Slow-motion terraforming. See these machines here?" She pointed at a metallic setup with a smokestack pumping white steam. "Oxygen and nitrogen farms."

The density of settlements and small towns grew, until Nick was watching large beige tents go by, connected by rail lines, and covered in plumes of dissipating gasses.

When the *Longburn* cleared the white oxygen clouds, Nick could see the giant, cream-colored tent of Monroe Morning, the planetary capital. The tent was a series of giant semi-transparent fabric sections that looked more like glass panes than fabric from this far up. A half-dozen skyscrapers poked through the tent like pillars holding it up. Surrounding the tent were plumes of oxygen and other exhausts, like an angelic take on a Victorian-era city skyline.

They landed at an open-air liftport outside the city tent. Umbilicals extended from the terminal and latched to the ship with thud and a hiss. Nick's stomach was grateful that gravity had returned, even if it was less than half of Earth's.

A cheerful customs officer came aboard to process them. Nick, Pam, and Izzy handed over their identification. The officer accepted Pam and Nick's Kagent credentials without batting an eye, but frowned at the three weapons Nick had brought with him. "This ain't no shooting gallery, pardner," she said in a broken, Ancient West accent. "No need for pew-pew-pew." She blew on an imaginary gun barrel and holstered her imaginary weapon.

Nick felt foolish and blushed. There had never been any question in his mind about the need to bring Bruiser, Slugger, and Thunker with him though. Not with Lisa aboard. "We have a prisoner in the back," he explained.

The customs officer nodded. "No worries, sheriff. We got some marshals waiting for you outside to help y'all out. But first I need to check your desperado's ID. Show me to the, uh, jail."

Walking down the *Longburn*'s central corridor felt strange in gravity after so many days without. Nick opened the cargo hold door. Lisa sat on the floor of the cell, her arms folded. The customs officer cleared her for entry and left the ship.

"Your mother is waiting for us on the arrival deck," Pam said to Lisa as they left the ship. "You can see her now before we turn you over."

"Thank you no."

Nick's first steps on Martian soil turned into stumbling down the transparent umbilical gangway. His stride was taking him further than he meant to. Pam walked ahead of him in smooth, practiced steps in the lower gravity. So did Lisa.

The terminal was made from old, dark-brown brick covered by a greenish-yellow moss. It had the dank, humid, homey feel of an old subterranean pub. Skylights admitted shafts of weak daylight tinged in sepia and orange.

A very tall, solemn man in a gray cloak was waiting for them with four other Kagents behind him. Linkfu Grunda had been one of the Kagents who came to Hamilton to help him and Bridge. He greeted Nick and Pam with a curt nod and looked at Lisa. "It's been a long time."

Lisa looked at him and the other Kagents with wide, frightened, angry eyes. "Yeah."

The quartet of Tessan Kagents all had hard looks on their middle-aged faces. Nick realized that they were friends of Bridge. Any fear he had of Lisa escaping once she was out of his sight disappeared. He probably had been the weak link in ferrying her this far.

"Let's go," Linkfu said, getting a firm grip on her arm. The

Kagents launched a visible perimeter of drones and marched Lisa away toward a security station.

Pam exhaled. "I'll be glad to not have her around for a while. Come on."

Meredith Radisson was waiting for them on the arrival deck. She was a stocky redhead, a decade older than Bridge, wearing a white Tessan cloak. Her vivacious blue eyes and warm smile seemed to reach across the distance and hug them both before they could reach her.

"Nick! Pam!" She hugged him tight and then did the same to Pam.

"It's so good to see both of you here, finally," Meredith said, a hand on each of their shoulders. "Pam, you must have some magical power to drag this boy away from Earth."

Pam smiled. "Lots of magic, I assure you."

Nick felt a pang looking at Meredith. He had never told her exactly what happened between him, Bridge, and Lisa. He felt compelled to blurt everything, but he didn't want to upset her. He decided to keep his mouth shut and let Pam and Meredith talk. His brain was stuck on the fact that he was walking on Mars, next to Meredith. It was every bit as otherworldly and awesome as he could have expected.

"I was going to have you stay with me," Meredith said as she showed them to a waiting taxi, "but that was before you caught, uh, her. The Council wants you to stay at the Nairobi Hotel during the hearing."

"I wish this could be a more joyous visit," Nick said.

Meredith shook him by the shoulder. "But it is. I've been wanting to talk to you for so long in person."

The taxi descended further underground and passed through utilitarian intersections with cross streets that opened up to dingy, shabby, subterranean neighborhoods.

"It's nicer further in," Pam noted. "Real estate values are lower the further away from the government center."

"Doesn't look safe," Nick said.

"All habitable spaces are certified at minimal levels of radiation."

"No, I meant crime," Nick said.

Meredith and Pam looked at each other in confusion.

"Oh, do you mean stranger crime?" Meredith asked. "It's negligible. Police drones survey all public space. Even in the poorer sections."

"So, this is where we would be staying if we were on our own," he joked. "If the Council hadn't paid for our hotel."

"Nonsense, I would have had you stay with me," Meredith said.

"Your parents live in an outlying subterranean settlement, right?" Nick asked Pam.

She nodded. "Never had a window in my bedroom. You'll see. It's not so bad."

"Oh, you're visiting your folks?" Meredith asked, with a flash in her blue eyes. "That's wonderful. Are you nervous, Nick?"

He laughed. "I wasn't until just now."

The taxi whooshed under an environmental barrier wall that marked where the tent started. The taxi emerged on a brief stretch of open road and they could see the transparent tent above them. The traffic streets were sunken, giving pedestrians the most daylight and freedom of movement. It meant that the city could have a wacky pedestrian layout that didn't interfere with traffic or mass transit. The taxi's map display showed that the pedestrian streets were really paths. Some curved, some bent at odd angles, and some were not big enough for a golf cart to fit down.

The buildings that had formed these paths were even crazier. Trapezoidal, hexagonal, triangular, massively cantilevered structures hung over the grassy paths. Tessan architecture looked like Antoni Gaudi and Frank Gehry had redesigned the Hanging Gardens of Babylon, while drunk. Buildings soared, bulged, and curved in flowing, organic forms, many of which Nick guessed would have collapsed in Earth gravity.

"What do you think?" Pam asked him.

Nick shook his head. "These look like a building inspector's feverish nightmare. They look like they'll topple over with a slight breeze, much less a quake. But it's the gravity and the materials that make these safe and sound, right? Please tell me it is."

The two women chuckled.

He had to admit it was a visual feast. Besides glass and steel, there were building exteriors of wood paneling, purple vines, tile mosaics, and changing light displays. Massive pylon-like towers rose to support the tent, dotted with windows that Nick realized meant they were apartment towers.

The taxi followed a circular route. The city's streets resembled a circular maze. The only way to the government center was through certain points in the surrounding ring roads.

Nick kept catching glimpses of the government center's spire, which looked like a frozen water fountain spewing up to the tent. He only saw glimpses of it between other buildings as they passed under neighborhoods of mid-rises. Neighborhoods gave way to office buildings, theaters, and restaurants.

The taxi stopped at Nick and Pam's hotel, a Kenyan-inspired four-star resort named The Nairobi. It was at the corner of the massive green space that surrounded the government center.

When Nick emerged from the taxi, standing outside on Mars, he found the air was cold, dry, and smelled like grass pollen. Nick, Pam, and Meredith climbed the stairs to the pedestrian level as the taxi zipped away. To their left was the Nairobi, a classy rectangular hotel that looked like it had been dropped into this strange city from the high street of the Kenyan city.

Across from the hotel was an immense park, with the government center's spire looming in the distance. The spire's base was out of view over the short horizon. Most of the park was an unending field of short, bright-green grass, but there were playing fields and picnic areas in heavy use, and forested groves where birds sang.

When Nick looked up, he could sort of see through the tent hundreds of meters above. The orange-white sky he had seen when the *Longburn* landed was tinted more blue by the tent panels. Still, it was the same old sun shining on his face.

"Let's drop our bags in the hotel and go for a walk," Pam suggested. "We need to get our Martian legs under us," she said to Nick.

They checked in at the hotel kiosk and a real, live human took their bags up to their room. Nick had expected a robot for some reason; some hotel chains on Earth used rolling robotic bellboys to keep costs low.

They loped across the pedestrian street and into the park. Pam and Meredith ignored the springy-looking crushed gravel path and walked right on the manicured lawn.

"Are we allowed to do that?" Nick asked.

"It's rebounder grass. It needs a good stomping to slow its growth," Meredith explained. "The paths are only for people who need a smoother surface."

They struck out across the lawn, heading for the government center spire. It looked like a crystal cathedral without any buttresses. The weak sunlight bounced, refracted, and reflected off millions of glass panes, painting rainbow-hued reflections on the grass.

The spire was surrounded at its base by half-a-dozen smaller spires to look like a water fountain frozen in time. Each sub-spire was a mid-rise office tower.

"Who's ready to eat?" Meredith asked.

"I'm hungry," Nick said.

Pam nodded. "Is that one place still open? With the koi pond?"

Meredith checked on her netpad and nodded. She led them out of the park and down a twisting path between buildings so close they actually did touch.

There were no street signs, traffic signals or building addresses. In a society built on the bedrock of constant net access, street names, addresses, and all that other information didn't need to be displayed. Most businesses had signs that were small and low-key.

Meredith took them to a cul-de-sac that ended at an open-air cafe with its own koi pond. They sat at a table near the pond and Meredith ordered half-a-dozen small dishes from the built-in menu.

The prospect of dinner with Meredith filled Nick with hope and dread. Eventually, the conversation had to touch on several unpleasant subjects: Bridge's death, Lisa's betrayal, his own failing business, or the investigation into Lisa's stolen Kagent netpad.

"This dinner won't be maudlin," Meredith announced after they ordered. "We're going to have fun and forget our troubles for an evening." She smiled at them both with her teeth bared.

Nick held up his hands defensively. "Okay, okay."

Meredith told several raucous stories about Bridge. He had pulled pranks on Meredith on their wedding day. He had apprehended a murderous nun in the middle of a production of Macbeth in the park wearing only his socks and carrying his netpad and his phallic stun-stick.

Before Nick knew it, dinner was eaten, his sides hurt from laughing, the streetlights had turned on, and a full stomach and travel-induced exhaustion crushed him.

He and Pam returned to the Nairobi. Pam preempted an oncoming migraine with a gel that knocked her out cold. So much for first-time sex on a different planet with lower gravity. But Nick was wiped out, too, and fell asleep before he could worry about what tomorrow would bring.

CHAPTER TWENTY-FOUR

RAIG'S STAY IN THE SOMPA Fuor came to an abrupt end. Penny sent him an urgent message in the middle of a three-course room service extravaganza on the suite's balcony as night settled in. She insisted that he come to New York immediately. She didn't say why and he knew better than to ask.

Ciebrian somehow knew and insisted that his suborbital jet could get Craig to New York in an hour. Twenty minutes later, he was aboard the missile-shaped plane, on a steep ascent into the night sky.

An hour later, Craig stepped off the plane into a sunny, windy day at Giuliani-Sinatra Airport. Craig already missed Cape Town and was irritated that instead of a peaceful night, he had another seven hours before sunset.

When he reached Penny's offices, good old Frank ushered him straight into Penny's office without a word. Craig said cheerfully, "What seems to be the trouble, ma'am?"

"Let's not be too familiar," Penny said tartly. "The Burgess people have made us an offer on a joint development project. Vacation and relaxation properties in or near Consortium members' boundaries, including new Stabilized Communities. It's a good offer. But a condition of the deal is the Alliance has to cease Lobbying campaigns."

"They want to kill Lobbying," Craig said.

Penny nodded. "Unsurprisingly, Mandy offered no opinion on

the proposal and the whole thing has fallen into our lap. You can imagine how ecstatic certain board members were."

Craig nodded. Some Burgess person either had known or lucked into the ultimate wedge issue for the Alliance. Profits versus the cause. It made him wonder if they had someone on the inside helping them.

"This is not part of any scheme of mine," Craig said. "I would try to pull the opposite trick."

Ms. Andrews cocked an eyebrow. "Not even to draw out Lobbying's enemies?"

He smiled. "I already know who they are. And I couldn't manipulate the entire Burgess Consortium to make an offer like this. I'd think bigger if I had that kind of pull with them." He leaned back in the couch cushion. It was some kind of stiff tweedy fabric that didn't give easily. Kind of like Penny.

"Dave Poole wants to take the deal," she said. "So do Haruka and a number of other board members."

Haruka, damn. Craig felt disappointed but unsurprised. "How would the Burgess people know we haven't lobbied their members? They would only know about the overt, cover campaign, not the actual lobbying."

"They insist on an open look at our organization and our finances if the deal progresses. They offered the same for us to make sure they were not hiding anything. It's standard business practice for partners, but the Alliance doesn't do partners, usually."

Kill Lobbying and wreck the decades-long secrecy of the Alliance? The Burgess Consortium was making a smart play. Craig shook his head. "Dangle a lot of money in exchange for us selling our soul and stripping naked for them."

Penny smiled appreciatively. "Precisely. You may be more Machiavellian than even Ciebrian. They want to end the conflict between our two organizations and to find a mutually beneficial way for us both to accomplish our goals."

Craig pulled up some information on the Stabilizer darknet and compared it to what he could access on the public nets with his netpad. "The Burgess Consortium is growing at such a fast rate that we'll just become its parks department in a few years."

"The offer goes right to the heart of the Board's disagreement," Penny said. "And it pressures us to resolve it. If we voted today, the Board would approve the deal. The Alliance needs the money. Ideas?"

It was like a real-life manifestation of a nightmare. He folded his arms. "My first impulse is to tell them to stick this deal high in their arse, but that's the Cajun in me. The mature move here would be to counter their proposal. Thirty years ago, the Alliance had a slate of changes they demanded from the buzzer cities. Limited hours for commercial activity. Closing financial exchanges once every 24 hours. Limited work weeks, vacation minimums, tariffs on offworld imports, noise pollution regulations, lower speed limits on roads. That kind of thing."

Penny asked, "Would the Consortium ever agree to that? It's a poison pill."

"Probably," Craig grinned. "But for a real estate development deal, they are reaching pretty far down our throat. This would test to see how serious they are."

Penny wasn't sold. "The rest of the Board would never counter with that."

Craig could have guessed. Some very slick buzzer was trying to twist the Alliance into giving up on its own cause. He needed time to figure this out.

"Stall," he said. "Tell them we need more time to develop a counterproposal, and that will give the Board some breathing room. I'm pretty sure we're getting played here, but I don't know how, exactly. The timing is terrible."

Craig consulted his network analysis of the Board. The personal, business, and ideological relationships of each member to all of the others twisted around as he spun it.

"What's your vote count on the deal?" Craig asked.

"Five to three in favor, the same line-up pro and against Lobbying."

Craig sat forward and cupped his hands between his knees. "I can't lobby them directly. I need to twist the weaker yes votes. Who's the weakest?"

"Your friend Salvador."

Craig brought up his notes on the Board relationships and beamed it to a viewer that Penny had underneath an oil painting of an old-fashioned city by the ocean.

"This is a social network schematic of the Board," Craig said. "Nothing special here; here are personal relationships, ideology and ethics, vote similarities. We use an analysis like this to twist local politicians and business leaders."

"Grand, but how do you change their minds?" Penny asked.

Craig thought for a second. "I'm not sure, yet. We need to change how they view the offer. Sal, he's concerned about conditions in the Communities. Could the deal divert funding from them to support the real estate development?"

"I hadn't thought about that," Penny said slowly.

Craig nodded. "Haruka, she's here to do good works, and she thinks Lobbying is dangerous and counterproductive." Craig thought about her thin black hair running through his fingers, the opulence, the privileged life. "So, I tell her we can eliminate Lobbying. Sacrifice it."

Penny turned pale, but Craig smiled. "Bless you, you're such a fighter. I've been thinking about this. Haruka may be open to a legitimate lobbying operation, without crashing cities. She's already suspicious that Poole is in it only for the business." He tapped his fingers against his chin. "If she felt that the Burgess offer was only about money, that could change her mind."

"How can you achieve all of this?" she asked, a hint of disbelief in her voice.

A thought occurred to him. He smiled at her. "Lady, I'm that good. You're the key. You express cautious support for the deal and surprise everyone. Then slowly back away as the negative details come out. It will build momentum against taking the deal."

Penny shook her head. "That's idiotic. We could just take the vote there and then we lose immediately, Craig."

Craig waved away her concern. "If you're taking a cautious approach, you can ask for more information. Make it a slow, methodical examination. Keep it focused on the business terms for Cooper and Dave. The negative information will come from somewhere else. The Alliance budget, or Community support."

Ciebrian, yes, the tycoon could tear the deal apart. He could pick apart any rosy financial estimates from Dave Poole or Cooper. Sal would be intent on higher income so the Alliance could better support the Communities.

Penny was confused. "What will that do? Other than make me look like a blottery old lady?"

"Hardly. We twist the Board's enthusiasm. Frame the discussion around all the good points first, which will seem natural. Your support will be a surprising endorsement of all the deal's benefits. They'll think, *Maybe this deal really is good if even Penny supports it.* But as its ugly warts come out, the initial enthusiasm will peak and drop. Slowly, the deal appears unfavorable to the Alliance."

Penny shook her head. "You want to play us like puppets."

Craig grinned wide. "It's what you hired me to do."

"Yes. I see. Very well. Make it happen quickly."

"Great to see you again, Ms. Andrews," Craig said, standing and making a small bow.

She nodded at him and he let himself out, saying goodbye to Frank. He had a lot of work to do.

CHAPTER TWENTY-FIVE

THE TESSAN KAGENT PRIVACY COUNCIL held its hearing on the top floor of a side spire in the government center. A swarm of drones scanned Nick and Pam's faces and then signaled to someone inside to open the double concrete doors. Beyond the doors, a Kagent with a long stun baton blocked their path and said, "All personal drones must be deactivated, and all weapons powered off."

When they both proved they had complied, the Kagent permitted them up the ramp that led up to the back of the hearing room. The top of the spire was a circular room with glass walls rising dozens of meters above the floor. To the left, there was a panoramic view of the park and the city beyond, with sunlight glinting off craft coming and going from the city's three liftports. To the right, the main spire dominated the view.

A ring of drones hovered ten meters high to record the proceedings from every angle. The last time Nick had seen that many drones was when Borbola's swarms were wiping Dragoons off of Hamilton's streets. Nick and Pam sat next to Meredith and the other Kagents in the audience gallery.

The five members of the Kagent Privacy Council sat on a dais of polished black-orange Martian marble. Nick had studied their publicly-available bios. The chair was Samir Smithson, an old friend of the Radissons. He had a reputation for being fair and even-handed, but today, he smoothed his black hair against his head several times and didn't smile.

Darren Vanvalkenburg was a privacy advocate who had feuded with Meredith for decades. He was a thin, gaunt man with piercing eyes who looked eager to get started.

Purva Kelk was a short woman with an easy smile who came out to greet Meredith and the other Kagents. She had a stellar reputation for screening projection models for biases and prejudices.

Hugh Manzano was an apprehension expert who was known for quiet takedowns. Nick recognized his large frame from the Kagents who had escorted Lisa away from the liftport security office.

Leslie Corso was a short woman with long straight gray hair. She was primarily concerned with the reputation and trust of Kagents. She had made public statements about how upset she was over the whole scandal possibly casting the Kagents in a bad light. Also, based on the stiff-necked posture that Meredith took when someone mentioned Leslie's name, the two apparently didn't get along well.

After some introductory formalities, Samir called the meeting to order and asked Nick to sit at the witness table and swear a truth oath.

"Nicholas Lincoln, we have read your statement about Lisa Radisson's ownership of a Kagent netpad," said Samir, "and your statement about your capture of her. May we proceed to questions?"

Nick nodded.

Darren went first. "I want to know how two Kagents ended up pointing guns at each other," he asked.

Nick replied, "Bridge and I disagreed on whether Lisa was still a threat without the Kagent netpad. I thought she needed to be apprehended anyway. Bridge did not, because he had outed her offworld background to the Alliance. But I didn't know that at the time."

"If you had known that, would you have let Lisa leave?" Purva asked.

Nick shook his head. "No. She was responsible for several crimes in Hamilton. Letting her go would have been illegal."

"But you didn't shoot her when she opened fire," pressed Darren.

"I couldn't. I didn't want to hurt her family, anymore." Nick was glad he had his back to Meredith right now.

Hugh Manzano dipped his bearded head closer to the microphone. "Uh, Nick, can you explain how she avoided Kagent surveillance?"

Nick nodded. "She hid in plain sight with facial disguises, padding, and even changed her walking gait. I couldn't single her out from other women until I noticed a birthmark on the back of her arm, right above her elbow. She probably didn't know it was there. I identified her at numerous Stabilizer events over the past decade and a half because of the birthmark. But ultimately, I only found her because she contacted me."

Samir, waited for other questions and then said, "If you had died and Lisa obtained both netpads, what would Bridge have done?"

"Bridge wouldn't have let her leave with either netpad," Nick said. "He pointed a gun at her, after all."

"But he was her stepfather," replied Darren. "I don't mean to disrespect his memory or upset his family, but wasn't it possible that he gave her the Kagent netpad?"

Nick shook his head vehemently. "Lisa is so estranged from her parents that they would not have helped her in obtaining a netpad. I'm certain of that."

Samir nodded. "Thank you, Nick for your time and service. I know this hasn't been easy for you. Let's take a short break before we hear from Lisa herself."

Nick returned to his seat next to Meredith as the council filed out. She put her arm around his shoulder and squeezed. "It's okay. You did the best you could in an impossible situation. And you did the right thing."

"I'm sorry you had to hear all of that," Nick said to her, looking at the floor.

"Look at me, Nick: I don't blame you at all."

Nick looked into her eyes. "What would you have done if you were me?"

"I would have shot them both," she declared without hesitation. "Several times each, possibly. You did better than I would have."

The council returned and Samir said, "Bring her in."

Lisa Radisson entered the hearing room escorted by a Kagent with a swarm of drones over her head. Her hands were manacled in front of her. She was wearing a light-green prison uniform. Behind her was a short woman in a business suit who looked irritated.

Lisa scanned the room for faces, noticed her mother, but didn't offer a flicker of recognition. She was guided to the witness table and sat down.

Meredith gasped and gripped Nick's arm hard enough to hurt. She hadn't seen her daughter in over 12 years, so he gritted his teeth and didn't complain.

Samir lead Lisa through the truth oath and other legal housekeeping. He said, "We want to know how you gained access to the Kagent nets, how you used that access, and other information about the Stabilizer Alliance. You have been charged with several dozen crimes by various authorities. You can do yourself a lot of good by being cooperative here today. Will you answer our questions truthfully?"

Lisa said, "Yes." Her tone was respectful but defiant.

"I'm advising you that the drones in this room will evaluate your biochem telltales for signs of lying and evasion. If they detect untruthfulness, we will call you out on it." When she nodded, Samir asked, "How did you obtain a Kagent netpad?"

"It's not my netpad."

"You're lying," Leslie announced, pointing at a display of Lisa's telltales on her netpad. "Don't waste our time."

Lisa cocked her head to the side and said nothing.

Purva asked gently, "Lisa, where did you go after you left home?"

Lisa replied, "I went to Earth. I attended Bucknell University for one year and then joined the Stabilizer Alliance through people I met at Bucknell."

Purva activated the viewer behind the dais. A map of Earth

appeared with cities highlighted with dates. "We have spotted you in these Stabilizer operations over the years. Tell us what you did for the Stabilizer Alliance."

Lisa replied, "I refuse to answer that question."

Purva nodded and continued. "Before teaching at Bucknell, Daniel Sloan was involved in some crashpoints, but most of his Stabilizer efforts were failures, the last one being the one in Shanghai right before he went to Bucknell. But after you two met, he and you went on a crashpoint-winning streak that lasted over a decade. We think it was because you had a Kagent netpad. Is that true?"

"Yes," Lisa said.

Darren said, "The netpad showed you how you could cause each crashpoint. The Stabilizers' successes could not have been accomplished otherwise. Is that true?"

Lisa's shoulders slumped. "I believe so. That's why I wanted to kill Nick Lincoln and take his netpad, to update the projections I was using."

Nick squirmed in his seat. He just wanted them to ask the question that was in the forefront of everyone's minds. But maybe they were warming her up, making her feel comfortable explaining smaller matters first.

Leslie asked, "Were you responsible for the attacks on Hamilton's airborne platforms, the mobs, and the spacecraft crash?"

Lisa's biochems spiked. "I don't know," she gritted out, her voice caught on snags.

Hugh pointed at Nick. "Why did you hide in Wertzville, where Nick Lincoln found you?"

Lisa replied, "I was not a threat to his family. I thought he would never look there because his family disowned him."

So far, Lisa's biochem telltales indicated she may be upset, but she was telling the truth. Samir looked up from his netpad. "Tell us what's happening inside the Stabilizer Alliance now."

She shook her head. "My contacts in headquarters cut me off completely after Hamilton. I don't know anything."

Her biochem telltales stayed true. Nick's faint hope that she had been in charge of the whole Alliance, or at least knew who was, evaporated.

Samir said, "Then tell us about how the Stabilizer Alliance operated when you were a part of it."

"I won't," Lisa replied, "unless you drop all charges against me."

Samir shook his head. "All of the charges won't be dropped, and you know it."

"Lisa, I'm impressed that you could pinpoint the crashpoints so exactly," Purva said. "How did you use the Sphere to predict crashpoints?"

Lisa shifted in her seat. "I simulated each city as an abstract thing, since the Sphere had limited information about Earth. I had bounty hunters map a city's social networks and profile the key players in government and business. We used our public relations firms to twist the local media to amplify our message."

"Brainwashing, you mean," Leslie said. "Wasn't it?"

Lisa squared her shoulders. "Each city is a fragile bubble, but some parts are too thick to break. With the Sphere, I could find the fragile parts and pop the bubble."

Purva's face paled. "But how did you access the Kagent models without accessing the Kagent nets?"

"I had someone set it up that way. I just needed the models, not the offworld data," Lisa's hand restraints clanked on the witness table. "The person who knew how to do that was a friend in the Preservationists and he's dead now."

Lisa's lawyer, Sherrie Edick, put her hand on Lisa's arm and whispered in her ear. Lisa nodded and said, "I'm not answering any questions about the Preservationists."

Nick looked from Lisa to her legal counsel. In a flash, he realized that she was probably an attorney for the Preservationists, not for Lisa. Leslie, Darren, and Hugh were fuming now that the Preservationists had come up. Pam tightened her hand into a fist.

"How do you know that he's dead?" Hugh asked, his face returning to its normal color. "The Preservationists don't hold funerals. They tend to die in depressurized tunnels or in firefights with the police or Kagents."

Lisa simply said, "He died before I left Tessa. Not because of me."

"Why don't you give us his name so we can check?" Hugh asked.

"Ms. Radisson already said she wouldn't answer questions about Preservationists," her lawyer said.

Hugh looked murderous. "Offhand, Lisa, how many people would you estimate that you have killed, directly or indirectly?"

"I refuse to answer that question."

"Were these deaths sanctioned or ordered by the Stabbies?" Leslie asked, letting the nickname drip with venom.

"The Alliance does not use or condone violent tactics," Lisa stated.

A silent pause ran for a full five seconds as Hugh tried to contain himself. "Do you know that you murdered Bridge?"

Lisa stiffened. "I did not kill him."

Leslie leaned forward. "You shot him underneath the baggage claim in Hamilton. That is where he died."

Lisa looked over her shoulder back at Nick. "Lincoln shot Bridge, not me. I'm sure he didn't mean to."

Leslie shook her head. "The forensics don't match any of his weapons. Bridge didn't fire any weapon he had. You took yours with you. And you fired it several times in that room."

Lisa sat back and then her shoulders started to shake. Her breath caught in her throat. "Oh, my God. Oh, my God. I didn't know." Eventually, Lisa brought her ragged, violent breathing back to normal.

Meredith gripped Nick's forearm more tightly. She keened so quietly that Nick, sitting shoulder-to-shoulder with her, didn't know if he had heard it or imagined it.

"You shot him down in cold blood," Hugh said in angry disbelief.

"It was an accident," Lisa snarled. "I would do anything to take it back." Her voice broke at the end and she covered her face.

Darren looked down the line of his fellow interrogators, and they all gave him a tight-lipped nod. She was softened up now, emotional, perhaps more willing to confess or explain the truth. "I am very sorry to hear that, but we must continue," he said. "Without the Kagent nets, why do you think your crashpoint projections were any good?"

Lisa's shoulders relaxed, but her voice quaked and her biochem telltales were still spiking. "They were probably pretty bad, but in the land of the stupid, a half-wit can be king. Until Hamilton, when I saw there were Kagents there. The city's unorthodox strategy was hard to counter. I feared that you all were far ahead of me. I needed to upgrade."

Nick's assumption that her projections were on par with his was what had led her to trap him and nearly make the assumption self-fulfilling. That left a sour feeling in his stomach.

Samir folded his hands, irritated. "Lisa, where did you get the netpad from?"

Nick held his breath. This was the question every Kagent had. This was where Nick hoped Lisa would detail exactly how she had defeated Kagent security, hacked the access, and made off with a copy of the Sphere.

Lisa put her hands in her lap and said calmly, "My mother gave it to me."

CHAPTER TWENTY-SIX

LISA'S BIOCHEM READINGS SHOWED SHE was telling the truth. Everyone looked at Meredith.

"Bullshit," Meredith said, loud enough for the Council to hear. She appeared too calm to be lying, but Nick didn't have his smartshades on to see for sure.

"And she handed it over to you knowingly and willingly," Samir said. "Violating the fundamental rule of Kagent privacy security? Putting her entire career at risk?"

"Yes." Still telling the truth.

"Why would she do that?"

Lisa shrugged. "I don't know. She let me have the netpad."

Nick chewed his lip. Could she be tricking the biochem readings?

"Don't you think you've done enough damage to your family?" Hugh growled. "You left. For ten years, they didn't know if you were alive or dead. And then, when Bridge finally found you, you killed him."

"Do you have a question, Mr. Manzano?" Sherrie Edick asked.

"Yes, I do. Lisa, are you hoping to hurt your mother by saying this?"

Lisa nodded. "Of course. But it's still true." Everyone watched the biochems.

"What happened to Bridge was an accident," Purva said smoothly, "but what you're doing right now is not. It won't help you to lie."

No, Nick thought, *but it would hurt the Kagents. It could help the Stabilizers.*

Samir steepled his fingers together. "Tell us exactly how she gave it to you."

Good, thought Nick, he wanted to see if she could trick the biochem telltales for an extended period of time. It was the only way to prove that Lisa was just twisting the knife by lying.

Lisa's biochem telltales did change, showing her face flushing. It was anger and possibly lying. Nick looked up and could see Lisa's arms shaking.

"My 13th birthday party was cancelled so she and Dad could prep for Franchise Day," Lisa said, her voice cracking. "She always resented that she gave birth so close to such an important holiday. Took her out of action for yet another important stretch of the career. Anyway, she felt guilty about it and she wanted me to follow in her footsteps as well, so she took me into the office."

Lisa cleared her throat. "There were all kinds of equipment in the office. The next generation of secure netpads. I had seen her use the Sphere hundreds of times, so I knew how to get around in it. My mother gave me a netpad with the Sphere on it."

Damned if her telltales were all running true. Meredith saw the same thing and emitted a tiny gasp.

The gaze of every Council member stayed on Lisa and then snapped to Meredith. A soft crescendo of noise built as the spectators sitting around Nick and Meredith became antsy and chatty.

"Meredith, could you come to the witness table and explain this?" Samir asked. Meredith nearly leapt out of her seat and sat on the other side of Lisa's attorney, as far from Lisa as she could get. But that couldn't change the fact that this was a mother-daughter battle royale.

Samir swore in Meredith and then said, "Your response?"

Meredith cleared her throat and took one look down the table at Lisa. It was a look of cold anger, possibly hatred. "I have never given her or any other non-Kagent access to the Kagent nets or a Kagent netpad."

Darren leaned forward. "Do you know how Lisa came to possess this netpad?"

"I gave her a Kagent training netpad when she was younger. We had hoped she would be interested in becoming a Kagent one day, but she turned out to be more like my mother than my grandmother. But I never gave her a real Kagent netpad, even on her 13th birthday."

Meredith's telltales also showed true.

"Is it possible," Leslie asked, "that you accidentally left a netpad at home or in the office that she could have taken?"

Meredith shifted uncomfortably in her chair. "It's possible. I didn't watch my netpad when I was sleeping. But she could not have accessed it, as you know. Nor would she have been able to steal it without my notice. Any netpad not checked in after 30 days is destroyed remotely."

Darren nodded. "Can you explain how she obtained the netpad?"

"I can't," Meredith said. "There were beta-test netpads that had limited access to the Sphere when a new generation of netpad was in the testing phase. It could be one of those models. But the biometric access locks would never let her or any unauthorized person in. It's not a matter of cracking a passcode on the netpad. She would have had to fool the Simons guarding access to the net."

"You do realize that the burden of proof here lies with you, not her," Darren said in a low tone.

"I'm fully aware of that," Meredith stated.

Nick closed his eyes. If Meredith couldn't prove that she wasn't responsible for giving Lisa the netpad, and access to the Sphere, she would be considered responsible. The Kagent rules were tough, but since the privacy of every single person on Tessa was in the hands of each individual Kagent, a Kagent had to be responsible for any breach.

Unless Meredith could find and prove some other explanation, she would be expelled. Radisson Associates would probably fold as a business. And it would likely damage the careers of the other Kagents she worked with, including Nick, her protege.

With one ridiculous-but-hard-to-refute accusation, Lisa had just struck a huge blow against all Kagents. And helped the Stabilizers.

Leslie looked horrified. "I move, with much sadness, to suspend Meredith until this is settled."

Hugh shook his head. "No. It's bad enough she has to defend herself against her husband's killer. We need to give her some time to prepare that defense."

Leslie shook her head. "Hugh, I understand. But this will be an unprecedented scandal for the Kagent industry. Meredith is a highly respected senior Kagent and her family has a long history in the industry. But even for her, we can't let her leave here today, with these accusations hanging over her head, without taking action. We have to protect the industry." She turned to Meredith. "You understand, don't you?"

Meredith nodded. "Perfectly. I agree with Leslie."

"However," Purva said. "We should also consider that Lisa's accusation furthers the Alliance's interests and ties us up in recriminations. This could be a tactical move by the Alliance to undermine us."

Yes, thought Nick. *Go Purva.*

Samir nodded. "It is a good point. We shouldn't let our principles and rules become weapons to be used against us. This breach is bigger than simply Meredith's reputation and privileges as a Kagent."

Hugh added, "Lets issue a Warrant for interested Kagents to investigate this. That way, we can get to the bottom of Lisa's accusations quickly, patch any security holes we find, and do justice by Meredith."

Darren held up a hand. "I oppose handing out a Warrant with a broad investigatory scope to any Kagent who wants it. What if a well-meaning Kagent wants to protect the industry badly enough to fake proof that Lisa has lied and somehow beat the biochem test? We have to choose carefully."

Purva added, "There have been no Kagent traitors because the Simons guarding our nets would detect them. I think the same would happen to anyone trying to frame Lisa to clear Meredith's name. We need as many Kagents as can be spared to work on this."

Darren grimaced, but didn't respond.

Samir motioned for a vote. "In favor of granting a Warrant to interested Kagents to investigate how Lisa obtained this netpad and how it was able to gain unauthorized access to the Kagent nets."

Leslie, Samir, Purva, and Hugh raised their hands and the motion passed.

"Meredith, you may investigate this, as well, and do everything else you can for your defense," Samir said. "But in the meantime, I need you to hand over your netpad and the Simons will suspend your net access."

Meredith stood, her head high, and approached the dais to hand over her netpad.

Samir motioned to someone by the hearing room's door. "Take the prisoner back to Holding."

"Samir," Meredith said, folding her arms and glaring at Lisa, "I want to talk to my daughter first."

Samir nodded and adjourned the hearing. Meredith followed Lisa, her lawyer, a swarm of drones, and their Kagent escort out of the hearing room.

Nick looked at Pam, Pearl, and Linkfu. Lisa had just beheaded the effort of Kagents on Earth. She was a human grenade. "Now what?"

CHAPTER TWENTY-SEVEN

CRAIG WAITED WITH A CROWD to cross Fifth Avenue. Everyone was on their netpads or chittering in their harsh Yankee staccato about their self-absorbed lives. They just had to make use of the minute wait any way they could.

He thought acting that way was so stupid, really, because New York Jersey was quite nice, even in winter. Craig gazed at the tall buildings around him and the reflection of clouds sliding by in their windows.

He didn't know where the term 'buzzer' started, but it easily could have been here. These people created a frenetic background buzz with their talking and hurrying. It grated on his nerves.

Finally, the red blur of sidelights on passing cars turned yellow as they stopped at the intersection. The cars' sidelights flipped to a white pedestrian walk sign. The impatient multitudes on opposing sidewalks surged towards one another.

Craig's netpad buzzed in the middle of the street. He ignored it until he was across the street. He didn't want to do anything these people did. He ducked in a gel shop, eager to get out of the cold wind barreling down Fifth, and answered.

"We need to talk," Borbola said. "In person."

Craig replied, "I'm in New York Jersey."

"I know. Meet me in office 726 at this address on West 39th street."

The line went dead and Craig looked at the map Borbola had sent. It wasn't too far. He rejoined the churning mass of buzzers outside and tried to forget the cold. He found the address, an office building, but nothing was listed for the seventh floor. The hallway that the elevator deposited him in was littered with empty paint buckets and scraps of wall compound. Wiring dangled from an open ceiling panel over an aluminum ladder.

Office 726 was still under construction. The metal detector doorframe was installed, but wasn't active and had no nameplate. The receptionist man-trap was in place, but he walked straight through it to a waiting room without a stick of furniture.

Borbola called out through the auto reception desk, his voice magnified by a cheap speaker. "I'm in the office with the light on."

Craig found the bounty hunter standing against the back wall of a windowless interior office. He closed the door behind him. "How did you know where I was?"

Borbola replied, "I have eyes everywhere. And since you refuse to use online chat rooms, I had to find you. Have a seat." He motioned to a ladder in the corner.

"I'll stand, too, if you don't mind," Craig said.

He wanted to be on eye level with the pacing bounty hunter. He wanted to see Borbola's body language and his facial expressions. Also, Craig didn't talk business over a viewer or from an inferior physical position.

"A Kagent has captured Lisa Radisson," Borbola said.

"The offworld mole," Craig said. Daniel's protege-gone-rogue after the Hamilton disaster. The Alliance had exiled her. That she had been in the Alliance for so many years, but hid her offworlder background the whole time, had shaken the Alliance to its knees. Now, every volunteer was profiled by bounty hunters to make sure that they had not lied about their background.

Borbola shook his head. "She wasn't a spy for the offworlders. She was a refugee," he said. "She hates Kagents and has just accused her own mother of violating the Kagent privacy code. If anyone should be worried about her, it's the Kagents."

"Her mother is a Kagent?" Craig said. "What if she talks about the Alliance? She knows about our previous type of lobbying operations."

"And those are really gone for good?" Borbola asked.

Craig nodded, confused about what the bounty hunter was hinting at.

Borbola shook his head. "She won't talk. She is a true believer, like you. Would you have talked if they caught you after Shanghai?"

Craig shook his head. "I would have killed myself."

Borbola paced back and forth, struggling with something.

"I can handle whatever it is you're thinking," Craig said with a smile.

Borbola didn't return the smile. "The Kagents believe your Alliance could become a mortal threat to offworld society. Terrorists bent on destruction. That's why they are interfering so much down here."

Craig scowled. "If they think the Alliance is a pack of dangerous terrorists, why did the Burgess Consortium offer to partner with the Alliance on real estate development?"

Borbola looked surprised. "They did? The Kagents may be trying to neuter the Alliance."

Were the Kagents lobbying the Alliance? That would be ironic. Maybe these Kagents realized they couldn't predict the future and were using the more reliable lobbying techniques to twist others. That actually made them more of a threat in Craig's opinion.

"How far have they gotten inside the Alliance?" Craig asked.

Borbola held up his hands. "My sources say not far. The darknets are buttoned up tight and they don't have any way to get info. Even capturing Lisa didn't help."

Craig folded his arms. There were limits to how much he wanted Borbola to know about Alliance operations. And the mention of offworlders nosing around the Alliance jogged his memory. "There was an offworlder on the Burgess negotiating team. At least, she seemed like an offworlder to me."

"Can you ID her?" Borbola said.

Craig nodded. "Yeah. I chatted with her." He messed around with his netpad. He never used a Simon, so he manually had to dig for any video or stills of the Burgess negotiation team when they were in Celebration.

He found a still shot from a public cam on the Celebration boardwalk on a bright sunny day.

"Here." He showed the bounty hunter the picture. "That's her."

Borbola's eyes went wide. "Pam Sullivan is a Kagent. An offworlder, but wearing Earth clothes to fit in. She's a negotiation expert. She works with the Kagent who is hunting the Alliance. When was this taken?"

Craig swallowed. "Less than a month ago."

Borbola nodded. "You need to tell your people to sweep any sensitive locations for every kind of bug. Microscopic drones, like the ones I used in Hamilton against the Dragoons."

Craig's mouth hung open. "Are you fucking kidding me?" Kagents planting dust-like listening devices all over headquarters was a lot worse than tricking the Alliance into a bad deal. The Alliance was careful to avoid bounty hunter surveillance, even to the point of blocking satellites from spying overhead.

Borbola waved his arm around the office. "That's why we are meeting here. No surveillance. Are you starting to understand how serious this is?"

"Yes," Craig replied. He sent a message to Penny about the threat to headquarters. The Kagents sounded like Lobbyists.

Borbola paced around the windowless room. "These guys can predict the future and they're hell-bent on interfering with affairs on Earth. They must know that the Burgess deal will damage the Alliance and that there is a good chance the Alliance will accept."

Craig smiled, not looking up from his netpad. "Now, that's just paranoid."

Borbola stopped pacing. "I've seen it. How do you think they beat the Alliance in Hamilton last year?"

"That was a total fuck-up on our part, not because of a crystal ball," Craig retorted.

Borbola said, "They have had a decent track record for over a century. Their forecasts are grounded in math and science."

Craig shook his head. "Go study chaos theory and quantum mechanics for a while, then psychology. Predicting the physical world is nearly impossible, but predicting how an entire solar system of messy people will behave? Or even one city? Ridiculous."

Borbola shook his head. "They want to jam the buzzer culture, as you call it, down your throats. There's only so much I can do to help here without more cooperation on your part. You have to take this seriously."

"Oh, I am. They are offworld bounty hunters with superior tech," Craig said. "But how come they didn't predict that you and I would meet right here today? Come on. At best, their predictions are abstract, like what marketing firms and business analysts produce."

Borbola shook his head. "Whether you believe they can predict the future or not, they believe the Alliance will become incredibly dangerous. And they are acting on it."

Craig had heard about the bounty hunter's penchant for playing two sides against each other. He rarely took up a cause, as he had against the Dragoons. There was an entire cottage industry on the public nets in speculating about what motivated the man. Craig put his hands on his hips. "You going to drum up business by setting off a Kagent-Stabilizer war? Are you working for them, too?"

Borbola held up his hands and said, "No way. The Kagent down here, Nick Lincoln, I know this guy. I know what he's capable of."

"Lincoln? Was he one of the Kagents at Hamilton two years ago?"

"Yes. Partners with Pam Sullivan. He's from one of your Communities. He has inside knowledge of the Alliance to start with and he's the one spying on you."

Craig looked up Lincoln on the Alliance's darknets. "We just exiled him a little while ago. He has been visiting Communities all across the continent, lately."

Borbola nodded. "He's just the first wave, the goddamn spotter for the offworlders. You need my help, Craig."

Craig was so relieved to hear it that he just nodded wildly. "Wait. What? We already have you on retainer."

Borbola looked at Craig for a silent moment and then said, "I want to join the Alliance."

Craig's hands fell to his sides. "You're not exactly known as the most trustworthy person in the world, Eldred. No offense."

Borbola chewed his lip. "None taken. You shouldn't trust me. Don't let me in to your systems or darknets. Keep me away from anything you think is too sensitive."

Craig wasn't believing this. "Why now? What changed?"

Borbola sighed. "I can't believe I'm saying this, but the Kagents are a serious threat. They will not stop because they think the Alliance is a mortal threat to offworld society. Some of them, people I know well, have tossed aside their own moral code to do this. They need to be stopped for the Alliance to survive. For Earth to have a chance to determine its own fate. They've become just as bad as the Dragoons."

Craig understood. "And you think the real estate deal makes the Alliance complicit in spreading offworld culture. We can't co-exist."

Borbola nodded. "By the time the Alliance realizes its mistake, it'll be marginalized and ineffective."

"I'll be lucky if I can sabotage this deal," Craig said. He wiped his forehead. "How do we stop them?"

Borbola grinned. "I know how. I used to be a Kagent."

Craig took a step back. "What the hell?"

"Have you ever been offworld? You wouldn't understand, then. You may not believe they can predict the future, but I've seen them do it. I trained with them. They are your greatest threat. Unless you have other people dropping spy dust on your headquarters."

Craig walked over and shook his hand. "You've got a long way to go to earn the Alliance's trust. Letting you in isn't even my call, I'm just a consultant. Are you willing to agree to the Alliance lifestyle philosophy?"

Borbola's eyes blazed with intensity. "At its heart, the Stabilizer mantra is for people to be left alone to live life the way they want to. Without interference, directly or indirectly, from offworlders. I've been committed to that ideal for a long time. I just don't care about community playgrounds and limited work week regulations."

"Well, dang, that sounds close enough to me. I'll have to set you up with my friend Sal to get in formally. But let me be the first to say, 'Welcome to the Stabilizer Alliance.'"

CHAPTER TWENTY-EIGHT

"COME ON, NICK. WE CAN'T be late," Pam said from the bathroom. Nick was out of bed, finally, but not making much progress in getting dressed. The quicker she moved, the more he slowed down. It just felt wrong to leave a day after Meredith was suspended, even if she had gone into seclusion.

Pam planted a firm kiss on his lips. His eyes fluttered as he came out of his stupor. "Understand that we're not missing that train, no matter what," she said.

Nick nodded and dressed. "I think I'm still getting acclimated to the conditions down here," he said.

"That's crap," Pam replied. She hurried him out of the hotel room and to the south-side train station. They made it onto the cross-continental bound for Concordia with only seconds to spare.

It would take three hours to reach the Concordia outer suburbs. Nick fidgeted as the raw Martian desert rushed by. Pam slapped him on the shoulder at one point to make him stop moving.

"You need to do something," she said. "Meredith doesn't want you trying to save her or stewing about it. Do what you are supposed to do."

He grimaced. "That sounds all perfect and everything, but I feel like ripping these seats apart."

"How's the Celebration spying going that I almost sacrificed my life for?" Pam asked, elbowing him. "You have a couple of hours."

He accessed the same Celebration intel. "I need to focus on

what I can do," Nick repeated to himself over and over. He donned his smartshades and inserted the earpiece. "Cross, what's the latest on our Celebration intelligence?"

Ever since Pam deployed those drones in Celebration, Cross had been building a database of people identified as working at headquarters, any conversations they had about Alliance business and whom they interacted with. Spying on people in public didn't violate any privacy laws; it was the same as walking down the street with your ears and eyes open.

Initially, the drone-intel was excellent. The drones Pam had dropped inside the headquarters building recorded conversations, saw internal documents on viewers, and generally soaked up all the information they could about the people who worked there.

Cross constructed an organization chart for several offices in the Alliance's personnel department. She also uncovered an office romance, a back-stabbing boss, and several friendships between Community Liaison and Accounting. There was a group picnic between the two components planned for the spring. Nick felt like all this insider info was the break he had needed.

But then the drones started to die. The Alliance did routine sweeps for listening devices and within three days, all of the drones inside headquarters were jammed or offline.

He hadn't despaired at that point, because he still had drones scattered all over Celebration and figured they would fill the gaps. Cross kept three-dozen drones in the open-air white tablecloth restaurant by the lakefront. The business lunch conversations alone would be more informative than cracking into a document database.

No Privacy Warrant needed, no leaning on Eldred Borbola and his unsavory tactics.

But Nick was disappointed again and again with the summaries that Cross provided of these conversations. The Alliance conducted a lot of boring business and had more than its fair share of meaningless office gossip.

He frowned and watched the orange desert zip by. "Cross, how many drones are still operating?"

"Twenty-three percent."

"Hope springs eternal. Let's see where we are," Nick said, trying to keep desperation out of his voice. This was probably it, though. If he couldn't compile a better understanding of the Alliance from these drones, he probably never would. This was the point of no return, his last chance to crack open the Alliance without needing a Warrant or Borbola.

Cross displayed the social network map of the Alliance she pieced together from the drones and highlighted the new connections and nodes. Romantic connections were pink, friendly were blue, business were black, and unknown were gray. Most of the connections were a simple black line indicating a business relationship. Very few nodes had more than two connections.

"Okay, we have a new romantic relationship between Rhoda and Gerry in Finance," Nick said. "And Terence in Accounts transferred to Finance. Not that we know what he does there. We don't have any audio of him."

Pam said, "I've used body language analysis models to estimate the relationships between people when based on a short video clip of them together. And knowing how they related to one another is almost as useful as knowing what their goals and negotiating styles are. Play some footage of Terence."

A group of Stabilizers walked to the lakefront for lunch, and Pam's model identified the boss, the senior and junior employees, and how much they liked one another. Terence was one of the senior employees.

"And reading his lips reveals that he talks about soccer. Only soccer. Always soccer. Maybe he transferred because his office got tired of hearing about soccer," Pam said.

Nick said, "Just great. How's the org chart looking for the entire Alliance now, Cross?" Five more nodes fell into place. "There's not much new here, is there?" he said.

Pam identified the pretty boys in fancy suits coming and going who were lawyers on retainer to the Alliance or to Pooled Developments. She had rubbed elbows with them during the Burgess Consortium negotiations. They weren't employed by the Alliance. It helped limit the number of people who may be Alliance employees.

Nick rubbed the bridge of his nose. "Any sign of some kind of clandestine operations bureau? Intel? Protests? Crashpoints Bureau?"

"None," Cross said.

"Well, that tells us something, too. Either it's offsite, much better hidden than we thought, or not directly attached to the Alliance. Or they shut it down already, which would be so great, that has to be wishful thinking."

Nick looked at the multi-colored web of interlocking spokes and nodes of the Alliance HQ social network. He had already stared at this growing web for hours, trying to fit various typical organizational structures on it. He spun it around and turned it inside out. There just wasn't enough data to know much about how the Alliance operated or who the key executives were.

"You're not wasting time playing with the network schematic again, are you?" Cross reproached him.

Nick gave the schematic a little twist. "Maybe there are former employees who we could turn into informants."

"You're grasping now," Cross said.

Nick sighed. "Okay, okay. Anything new about Pooled Developments, Pam?" She had given Nick a full debrief about the real estate developer and what she could glean about their ties to the Alliance. "Is it just business between them and the Alliance?"

"David Poole hasn't been back to Celebration since I was there," Pam said. "His lawyers have returned twice."

The connection between Poole and the Stabilizer Alliance raised the hairs on the back on Nick's neck. There was something there, but he didn't know what. Nick leaned back in his train seat and looked at Pam. "Is it time to give up on this angle?"

"Yes," Cross answered.

Pam smiled sadly. "You need that Privacy Warrant."

Nick's shoulders slumped. "I know, I know."

His girlfriend's mouth formed a thin line. "But the projections aren't certain enough to convince the Council that it's an emergency. You don't have a smoking gun here about the Alliance's intentions. And they already turned you down before."

Nick drummed his fingers on the armrest. "They know how dangerous the Alliance has been."

Pam conceded that point, but replied, "Borbola has made them nervous about Kagents being accused of interfering with Earth. They're afraid of a backlash. And then, there's Meredith's situation."

Nick shrugged. "But how does that affect me?"

Pam shook her head sadly. "The Kagent Privacy Council is skittish about Warrants. It's a poorly-kept secret on the Kagent nets. A few years ago, a murderer on Venus nearly disappeared because the Privacy Council there hesitated for two days before granting one."

"Great. All that adds up to is another 'no.'"

"What will you do next?" Pam asked.

Nick blew out a breath and let his lips flap. "There's only one option left."

"No," Pam said.

Nick nodded. "Yes. Either Borbola discovered something I can use to spring a Warrant, or I've failed."

CHAPTER TWENTY-NINE

CRAIG FOUND HIMSELF WITH A rare weekend at his one-bedroom condo in downtown Celebration. He spent an entire day studying the Burgess offer and the Alliance's balance sheets and budgets. And then he pinged Sal if now was a good time to talk and Sal pinged back yes. Seconds later, Craig put the netpad to his ear and said, "Sal, how are you?"

"The water supply in Corpus Christi is contaminated again. We just don't have the firepower down there to stop these fuel companies from dumping their sludge upstream."

"You need me to help you out?" Craig said. If Sal declined, then he was just bellyaching and had it under control.

"Oh, no, bless you Craig. You have bigger projects to pursue. What can I help you with?"

Craig couldn't bring up the real estate deal directly. "I'm trying to make the numbers work for a more integrated strategy. This takes some shifting around of funding and I wanted to see what you think."

"Sure, sure. I've been saying for years that the Communities are under-supported," Sal replied. "And if we want to convert the heathen buzzers, we need to give them an attractive alternative."

"Speaking of heathen buzzers," Craig said with a smile, "any bounty hunters show up at your mission recently?"

"What? Oh, do you mean Eldred? Yes, yes, he did. Filled out all the forms. He hasn't chosen a Community yet, because he travels so much."

"Good, good. I knew you could take care of him," Craig said, "Sorry, back to your attractive alternative."

"Yes. We were talking about shutting down Lobbying," Sal said quietly. "We need that money. I didn't have the heart to tell you before."

"It's okay. You're right though, Lobbying is dang expensive. But shutting it would mean losing some valuable assets," Craig said.

"But Community subsidies have been flat for years. When I think of the kids hurt because we paid for idiotic crusades against richer cities, oh, my blood pressure rockets."

Lobbying was the second-biggest chunk of the Alliance budget. Buying media outlets, maintaining operatives in the field, staging *faux*-political movements, and gathering the intel to crash a city was enormously expensive. Lisa Radisson's Rocky Mountain missile barrage against Hamilton had cost about two years' worth of the average Community subsidy.

Craig chuckled. "Calm down, *padre*. That's why I think we could reorient Lobbying to support the Communities and do so at much lower cost."

"You're blowing smoke up my ass, now, hotshot," Sal retorted.

"Come, now, Brother Salvador," Craig said. "Lobbying could help support the Communities, which support the Alliance businesses, which continue to fund Lobbying. More attractive Communities increase our recruitment, which gives our businesses another boost."

"Now you're blowing sweeter smoke up my ass. Give me an example."

Craig replied, "When I ran into you down in 'Rouge, what were you railing against?"

"Parish was screwing with our water rights, try to make us swallow a doubling of the water fees or get some chemical plant's wastewater pipe shoved into our supply."

"And how did you fight them on this?"

Sal said, "I went to the damn meeting with about a dozen people and we let them know how unfair it was. We had people in the Community message the heck out of the Council."

It sounded so simplistic. It was like some civics classroom exercise. Could Sal be that naive after all these years? "And did that work?"

Sal huffed. "No."

"Here's how I would have done it with Lobbying," Craig said. "A scout team figures out how to maximize our influence, given the parish's personalities, agendas, and social networks. A media team runs a marketing campaign to make our case, in public through the media, and behind closed doors to your targets. The leverage team figures out the political economic leverage that our businesses can bring: jobs, product discounts, contributions to favored charities, whatever. Finally, the grass-roots team organizes the efforts on the ground: the letter-writing, calling, protesting, etc. You wouldn't lose."

"That sounds like old-fashioned politics," Sal said. "Not city-killing."

Craig laughed. "Exactly. No one else can run those kinds of sophisticated operations on the local level except corporate conglomerates. We'd be even with them for once, or have the advantage. Either way, it would still be a fraction of the cost of our current Lobbyist budget and a hell of a lot more ethical."

Sal didn't respond for a moment. "The thing is that we have already spent the Lobbyist budget elsewhere. Or we plan to. And this Burgess real estate development deal requires a lot of upfront capital."

After studying the Alliance's financials, Craig had developed a lot more sympathy for Dave Poole, who must have cringed watching his companies' donations to the Alliance pour down the drain with little to show for it.

But Salvador March counted souls he had bandaged, as he put it, not return on investment. He looked at the Alliance balance sheet and saw poverty and misery in Communities that could be alleviated with more funding. His New York Jersey ministry saw burned-out buzzers reject a better life because it came with a lower living standard.

"I thought you were hoping to get a piece of the Lobbyist budget for the Communities," Craig said. "But I've been looking at the numbers, and the subsidies won't go up under this real estate deal."

"I know," Sal lamented. "It's a longer-term payoff. The additional revenue will allow the subsidies to rise after the first 15 years."

"They got your support with the promise of an increase in 15 years?" Craig asked.

Sal said, "Cooper assures me that we have little downside risk because the Burgess people would put up half of the investment. Even Penny supports the deal. But the money will have to come from either Lobbying or the Community subsidies."

"It's a good point," Craig conceded. "This would give us a toehold in every Burgess Consortium city and zone. If we had some higher-end examples of the Stabilized life, right there in every city, that could improve recruiting. And maybe those developments could cross-subsidize the older Communities, so the existing Communities don't have to lose purchasing power for the next two decades."

The gears turned in Sal's head. "I hadn't thought about this, but these newer developments could overshadow our existing Communities," he said. "They may expect the Alliance to be a resort manager and homeowner association, and not care about its social justice mission." Disappointment weighed heavily on every word.

Craig sent Sal his own budget proposal. "What if we did this, instead?" The proposal diverted three-quarters of this year's Lobbying budget to boost Community subsidies. "The Alliance couldn't afford the Burgess deal though."

"An immediate increase in the subsidies? Ha, ha, you know me too well, old friend," Sal said.

"Duh. Of course I do. This moves the Communities closer to self-sufficiency; it'll boost recruitment. Plus, it puts tighter reins on Lobbying, focuses them on directly supporting the Communities."

Sal said, "Where's the downside, Craig? Don't tell me there isn't one."

"Selling the other Board members on it. Lobbying is their shock troops, their army of spies and saboteurs."

"You'll have to give them another army, or they'll never approve this move." Sal replied. "So, where's this other army?"

"The businesses that support the Alliance. Their financial muscle. Instead of just being our biggest donors, they become our biggest weapons against the offworlders and the buzzers."

"And you think the business folk will agree?" Sal asked. "Ciebrian, Coop, Dave, Haruka? Cooper is the only true believer in the cause among them. You think he and Ciebrian will agree to become the Alliance's muscle?"

"If they gain market share in the process. There's another subtle benefit here, Sal. With Lobbyists helping Communities in the political realm, and our businesses backing them with raw economic power, we may actually slow the spread of buzzer culture."

Sal replied, "This sounds like a wholesale change In what the Alliance does."

"No, the mission doesn't change, just the strategy and tactics," Craig said looking out at the lake. "We're just integrating the tactics better so they adhere to our nonviolent philosophy and have a higher probability of success." He licked his lips. "What do you think?"

"I'll raise these concerns. It doesn't mean I'll oppose the Burgess offer though. I mean Penny Andrews has been warm to it, Coop and Dave are behind it. But we need to discuss these concerns. You have a long way to go before the Board opts for your alternative instead of money on the table. You need to understand that."

Craig chuckled. "You're a start. Will you help me?"

Sal grinned. "Oh, now you want me to jump in this hole with you? Like when you cherry-bombed the toilets in middle school?" Craig was about to retort, but Sal continued, "You're giving the Communities a gift on a platter here. I'll do whatever you need me to. But we can't just oppose the deal without mentioning the alternative of yours. Are you ready for that?"

"Yes, Father."

"Good to hear, my son. I'll also see if what you've told me matches up with whatever you're selling the others. Just to make sure this isn't an old Lassiter snow job."

"So cynical for a Catholic priest," Craig lamented. "You're spending too much time in New York Jersey."

"Ha, ha. I'll keep that in mind when I'm eating with the sinners at Ray's Pizza," Sal laughed. "Speaking of, when was the last time you went to confession?"

It was Craig's turn to laugh.

CHAPTER THIRTY

Pam's parents lived in Cecilia, a rural settlement beyond the suburbs of Concordia, Tessa's largest city. Pam said it bothered the hell out of her as a young teen, because she was so close to all of the excitement of Concordia, but had no way of going there. Her parents preferred the quieter, more-isolated life out in the rocks. It was a factor in why Pam had emancipated as young as she did.

She and Nick arrived in Concordia in mid-morning. Nick was intrigued to see skyscrapers poking through the eight tent roofs that covered the bulk of the city, but Pam rushed him along to catch the midday ferry that ran out to her parents' place. It was part-dune buggy, part-hollowed-out boulder. The boulderized surface provided radiation shielding and the buggy's ten tires negotiated the debris-strewn rock fields between Concordia's northwestern edge and her parents' village.

Pam didn't recognize the driver or any of the other people who filled the 20 seat cabin. Her parents had told her that the homestead's population had grown a lot since her last visit. The oxygen and greenhouse gas farming had been doing well and a rail spur out from the nearest suburb was due to open soon.

When she and Nick disembarked from the ferry, walked through the umbilical and emerged in the village square, it seemed to Pam that the space had doubled since her last time there. The grocery store had moved to a bigger space by the open-air fruit market, replaced by a hardware store and a clothing manufacturer. Two new walkways had been carved out to the south and the north. All the changes made Pam feel just the slightest bit old.

"Well, ain't this the happening burg," Nick remarked. "The Kagent nets say it's on track to be a small city in 20 years, if the population growth projections are right."

"Mom and Dad are very proud of this, by the way," Pam said.

Nick grinned. "You mean Hunter and Angie."

How come he didn't seem nervous in the least to be meeting her parents? Didn't he realize he would be scrutinized? Or was it that he didn't care? Pam had become just a tiny bit concerned.

Her parents found them seconds later. Hugs were exchanged all around and then her mother stepped back to look them over. "Oh, what a cute couple. Put your arm around her, Nick, so I can get a picture."

Pam's smile became just a hair more brittle.

"Actually, don't bother with the arm," Dad said. Was he acting protective about her?

The four of them chit-chatted about the trip the whole klick-and-a-half back to the house. And then her mother explained the chemical farming that most of the town residents did.

The idea of chemical farmers who lived beneath their fields, which were automated machines tended by tele-operated drones, clearly struck Nick as strange. But Pam considered this key to his Tessan education, and key to understanding her better. There were still times when the culture gap between them lurked like a big, itchy pimple.

Mom managed to ask only 14 embarrassing questions before they reached the house, including how long Nick and Pam had been living together. Dad scowled uncomfortably during that entire exchange.

They went inside and settled in those ugly floral print chairs Mom insisted on using in her front room. Pam thought it was a tacky decorating choice when the entire house was crammed floor to ceiling with actual plants.

"So, Nick, how is the Kagent business treating you?" Dad asked.

Nick grinned. "Roughly. I'm still feeling my way."

Dad nodded with that nod he did when he was trying to look tolerant of an answer he didn't like. He harbored a dislike for Earthers, as he called them. Pam had told him that Nick was the most un-Earther Earther she had met, but she didn't know if he believed her.

"Having trouble getting into the stream of things?" Dad said. "It must be tough for you, with the childhood you had, you didn't get a chance to make streaming a lifelong habit."

"True," Nick replied. "Climbing the learning curve on the business end is harder though."

Dad grunted. "We've been there before. The tricky thing is knowing when to hire more help, so you don't work over forty hours a week."

Nick laughed. "Forty a week sounds like a vacation."

Dad didn't smile. "I haven't worked over forty hours a week since before Pam was born. You've got to learn to manage your time to manage your business."

"Pam, can you help me out in here?" Mom called from the kitchen. Pam didn't want to leave the two most important men in her life just yet. Especially because it sounded like things could go downhill very fast. But when her mother called again, Pam went.

"So," Mom said as she chopped vegetables. They were local vegetables, engineered for Tessan conditions. The image took Pam back to her childhood. "How are things between you and Nick?"

Pam hesitated, almost spitting out a stock answer. "It's a little tense with his business in trouble. And I had to drag him offworld."

"That's nice, but I meant the sex," Mom said. "The real barometer of a relationship."

Pam couldn't help but blush and blurt, "Ah, a little less frequent than usual." She spun that a lot more positively than she should have. Nick had withdrawn after losing the Burgess Consortium contract. Like he wasn't worthy of her. She felt so bad for him that she let it slide.

Mom asked her to prep the water, tea, and the fresh-squeezed fruit juice her father preferred. "Don't let him slip away. I like him. He looks up to you; not a lot of men are wired to do that."

Pam arranged things on the tray to carry out to them. "I don't have any plans to."

"You two are sleeping in the same room here tonight."

"Lets not upset Dad."

"Don't worry about him. He is just checking Nick out. In case he's a keeper. He knows better than to act on his protective urges."

"Even still, I think Nick and I should go back on the last ferry tonight."

Mom killed that notion with one dark look. It had been over two years since Pam had been home. They could stay here until the Kagent Privacy Council called Nick back. Hell, they both could work out of here for weeks if they needed to.

"I'm sorry." She hugged her mother from behind. "I miss you guys so much, but I don't want to impose."

Her mother kissed her on the forehead and then carried the vegetable tray out to the front room. "Drinks and snacks, men."

Everyone situated themselves with something to drink and whatever the men had been discussing stopped.

"So," Mom said, getting comfy next to Dad, "are you two going to make this permanent at some point? If you have children, will they be raised on Earth or somewhere else? Excuse me, Hunter, but I have questions."

Nick actually warmed to the challenge. "No plans, yet. But the longer I'm down here, the more open I am to living here. If the Earth Kagent thing falls apart."

Pam raised an eyebrow. "What about your family?"

Nick shrugged. "Dez is still pissed about Sally. She won't return my calls. I've never felt more at home than I have on this planet."

Pam understood: he had met Meredith and other Kagents. He

had discovered that they were his people, his mental tribe, and he was juiced on that. And he was trying to forget the pain of possibly losing his family forever.

Nick and her parents got along about as well as she expected. Neither of her parents had spent much time around Earthers. While her father was suspicious, her mother was curious. Dad gave Nick a pat on the back, his way of saying that he approved.

"That wasn't so bad," Nick whispered when he and Pam went to bed.

"No, they like you." Pam stretched her arm out and gathered Nick into a hug. "My mother was concerned about our sex life."

Nick rubbed her arm. "Me, too. When we get back to the Nairobi, we can work on that."

"Why wait?"

He chuckled. "In your parents' house? With them in the next room?"

She rubbed his thigh. "Walls of rock are soundproof."

A dull tone sounded from the dresser where his netpad lay. It signaled an incoming priority message. Pam and Nick watched each other's reaction in the darkness. Nick walked over to it.

"It's dark in here. Did I wake you two?" Cross said over the small speaker.

"Never mind," Nick said and thumbed his way around for a few seconds. Pam watched his face, lit by the glow of the netpad. An irritated frown gave way to a grim frown. He shut off the netpad slowly.

"The Kagent Privacy Council has suspended Meredith indefinitely. Pearl will take over running the firm. They have also denied my petition for a Warrant on the Stabilizers." He came back to bed.

Pam rubbed his back. "I'm sorry."

Nick buried his face in the pillow and gave a short, frustrated yell. "Think your parents heard that? I feel like I helped Lisa cause

183

this to happen. And for nothing. We would have been better off if I never saw her back home."

"I know," she said.

"I should have shot her two years ago." He faced her. "Think of how much better things would be. For Bridge, Meredith, my family."

"That's not helpful thinking, Nick. Focus on what your next step should be."

He sighed. "I have no choice but to rely on Borbola. But without Meredith helping me, I don't think I can figure out a way to twist the Alliance." He sighed heavily and tossed himself to face the other direction. "Which means we'll be right back where we were two years ago, without Meredith or Bridge, and possibly with a tougher Alliance than we faced then."

"We need to get back to Earth as fast as we can," Pam added. "We can leave tomorrow."

"Or we could just stay here and let Earth go fuck itself."

"You don't really believe that," Pam said, testing him.

Nick grunted and turned over to face the wall. "What do I have left on Earth?"

Pam didn't have an answer. She put a hand on his back to comfort him.

"Okay, I'm just pissed. The Stabilizers are twisting us, it feels like. I can't walk away from that. We have to go back."

The news about Meredith wiped away any desire Pam had like warm bread crumbs swept away by a cold, wet towel. First the poor woman loses her daughter, her husband, and now her life's work and business.

Pam rolled on her back and stared at the familiar textured ceiling above her. She didn't fall asleep for hours.

CHAPTER THIRTY-ONE

HEINZ SHOWED CRAIG INTO A conference room in the basement of Coop's faux fire station. It was a subterranean rec room with a classy old billiards table sitting under a blue pendant lamp in the corner.

Cooper came in a minute later with Arianna in tow. He shook hands with Craig, but sat at the far end of the table. It was a distancing move, confirming what Craig had suspected. This wouldn't be a cozy chat with good old Uncle Coop.

Craig put the billiards ball down on the green felt table and adopted his most sober look as he sat down. "I'll be straight with you. I know that Ms. Andrews, you, and many of the others are in favor of the Burgess Consortium deal. But my analysis shows it isn't good for the Alliance. It ties up the budget for the foreseeable future and would nearly eliminate all other activities, including Lobbying."

"You don't miss much," Cooper said through a nasty smile. "I admire anyone who knows their business and tells truth to power. This deal is designed to put the Alliance on a stronger financial footing. Maybe even make the Communities self-financing."

Craig shook his head. "That's unlikely. The profits depend on meeting rosy enrollment projections. If enrollment undershoots, the Alliance will hemorrhage money. Which will decimate the Communities and Lobbying."

Cooper raised an eyebrow. "Well-done, Craig."

Craig leaned forward. "What are you really up to? You didn't establish the Alliance to make money. Every time we crash a city, the economic damage hurts GoldLand's businesses, too. Vacation resorts are luxury goods. You must make most of your profits from buzzers. So, you were willing to take a net loss on the Alliance, because you believed in the cause. But now it looks like you are trying to shut it down."

Cooper steepled his hands on the conference table. They were as unblemished as a child's hands. "I wanted to be Walt Disney, Robin Hood, and Werner Meade. You know who all three are? Good. I sell the wealthy a taste of the Stabilized life, funnel their money to help the Stabilized, while trying to revolutionize how we live our lives. GoldLand is an elaborate, efficient wealth redistribution scheme. But the Alliance has fallen short on two out of three of those goals."

Craig nodded. Despite disagreeing with him, he really liked Cooper. The guy knew how to maximize his return on investment.

"I want the Alliance to take on the wealth redistribution itself," Cooper said. "The Alliance can't be Werner Meade and Robin Hood at the same time. But Lobbying's failure was pivotal. It's time to change course. I supported Lobbying longer than you've even know about it, but it's time to let it die. It's work can be done on a grander scale, by Poole, me, and Ciebrian."

Craig felt his stomach drop away. He didn't see any way to reconcile that view with those of Penny, Ciebrian or his own. "So, you're giving up on the Alliance?"

Cooper waved a hand around. "No. The Alliance is best as a humanitarian organization, building the Communities. That's its strength, its value-add. We should lean on that."

Craig was dumbstruck. He looked at Arianna and Heinz, but they didn't seem surprised in the least. "That won't do anything to stop the spread of the offworld lifestyle," he said.

"The Alliance hasn't been successful in that, anyway, has it?" Cooper asked. "Have you ever been offworld?"

Craig shook his head. "I grew up poor in Baton Rouge; never had the chance."

"You should go and see what we're up against, you really should. They have better technology, better infrastructure, higher education levels, and tons more wealth. And the kicker is, *they don't work more hours than us*. It's the damnedest thing. We see the buzzers down here putting in sixty, eighty hour weeks, all stressed out, but that's not the way it is offworld. The only way we can keep up with offworlders is to run ourselves into the ground. And whenever we try to upset their sweet deal, they have these Kagents defending them."

Craig stewed, tired of the fawning over these offworld nerd-ninjas. The Stabilizers had been running circles around them for years. Until the Hamilton campaign. "Kagents are just bounty hunters with cloaks."

Cooper waved off his rebuttal with a wry, condescending smile. "I sent our Seoul movie studio on a trip offworld to research a Kagent-versus-Dragoon game based on the Hamilton battle. Arianna, tell Craig what the Seoul movie scouts found. Tell him."

Arianna stepped forward and cleared her throat. "Kagents provide investigative and analytical services to nearly every sector of offworld society. They analyze trends and forecast economic conditions, demographic changes, social and political changes, and even fashion trends."

Craig cocked an eyebrow at the old man, unimpressed. "There are plenty of pundits and prognosticators. They all have lousy track records."

"Not the Kagents," Arianna replied. "They actually publish their forecasting accuracy. And they do well and do so consistently."

Cooper added, "The Kagents are a dire threat to the Alliance. We need to create a paradigm shift in lifestyle, like Werner Meade did in education. The Alliance can be a living example of that lifestyle. Making this deal with the Burgess Consortium is a big step in that direction."

"I don't think the Board and the rank-and-file will want to change the Alliance fundamentally like that," Craig said.

Cooper's smile vanished. "The best we can do is to turn the Alliance into a Community management organization. Take the fight elsewhere."

Craig shook his head, confused. "How does that stop the buzzer culture from spreading?"

The smile returned briefly. "It doesn't. That's why we brought you on. Tell me how to make it work."

Craig thought quickly. There actually was a way, but he doubted Cooper would go for it. He spread his hands. "Take a two-pronged approach. The Communities need help financially and politically. Lobbying refocuses to actually lobby for Communities in their neighboring zones. The more Stabilized the surrounding region, the more competitive we'll be economically. No subterfuge, no stealth terrorism. Now, that's a much smaller, lower-cost operation. Let the Kagents chase around actual Lobbyists, thinking they're dangerous.

"Second, just like you said, use the economic, business, and financial muscle behind GoldLand and Pooled for the same goals. But take the fight to the offworld societies." Craig cut the air with his hand. "Ciebrian calls it total societal war. Non-violent destruction of the offworld economic and political infrastructure. Ignore the buzzers and the Burgess Consortium, go hit the offworld culture at its source. That would stop the spread."

"What does that entail?" Heinz asked.

Craig said, "Buying offworld companies, choking supply lines, raising prices, slowing trade."

Cooper listened closely while his assistant and attorney exchanged notes. "Turn GoldLand into a weapon for the cause? I like the concept, I do, but our wealth is minuscule compared to offworld. We don't have that kind of capital on hand."

Arianna added, "Operating offworld, on their turf, puts us at a huge competitive disadvantage."

Craig replied, "I'm not talking about a frontal attack that will draw attention. Just aggressive business moves. Meanwhile, we run an old school Lobbying operation against the offworlders. And the Kagents."

The old man winced. "What about retaliation? What happens when the Kagents see this coming? They would come after GoldLand. We can't expose the Alliance's financial backers to risks like that."

Craig didn't have an answer for that. "I'll admit this idea is a work in progress. But the businesses are not connected to the Alliance. Our organization is hidden from bounty hunters, Kagents, and the public. We can pivot, change course, and they won't know if it's us or something natural."

"Your plan needs work," Cooper said. "And we don't have the time to hash it out. We have to act on this Burgess deal now, or it disappears. We can make the Alliance more financially secure with the Consortium and then explore your ideas later."

Craig bit his tongue. It was a patronizing dismissal, a sweet lollipop of a brush off. He knew the real estate deal was a dire threat to the existing Communities. If it failed, they would be screwed financially. If it succeeded, the Alliance would have two tiers of Stabilized people. His rusty, hard-luck childhood told him in no uncertain terms that at best, the richer, newer Stabilizers wouldn't give a shit about the existing, poorer ones. Cooper was abandoning them just like he was abandoning Lobbying and what the Alliance stood for.

"What if they are mutually exclusive?" Craig asked.

Anger flashed over Cooper's face. "I think Ciebrian has been whispering in your ear. He just wants to hit his offworld competitors. He's about the business, the bottom line, and always has been."

But so are you, Craig thought. Hitting the offworlders would reverberate down to the wealthy buzzers whom Cooper's companies sold over-priced amusements to. Considering that they were sitting inside an old fashioned rescue station in a life-sized monument to nostalgia, it shouldn't surprise him that Cooper resisted new thinking.

Arianna murmured something about Cooper's next engagement. Cooper stood with a little difficulty and kept his hand on the back of the chair. "I'd appreciate it if you ran ideas by me before discussing them with the other Board members. I can give you the history and context for why some things will work and others won't. It would save you time and help you find workable solutions."

Craig was wondering if another Board member would try to supervise him. Coop was the first, probably because he felt he was losing his grip on Craig. Craig stood up, to stay on eye level with the corporate giant. "I can't do that. I'm happy to bounce ideas off of you, but I need to operate freely."

Coop drew himself up to his full height. "You're too smart to be getting played by Ciebrian or Penny. I know you're in the tank for their point of view."

Craig returned the dead eye. "I'm not anyone's tool. I'm doing what I can to find a way for the Alliance to succeed. Not fail in a profitable way."

Good old Uncle Coop's eyes became as deadly as a shark's. "Remember, I may lose a vote here or there, but never on the important issues. I am the goddamn Stabilizer Alliance."

CHAPTER THIRTY-TWO

EVERY TIME NICK WALKED IN Councilor Abby Burgess' office, he got a big, warm hug. She had been his biggest backer on the Burgess Consortium board and she, he, and Pam had become close friends. Pam even babysat her two kids when Abby left town on Consortium business.

This time was no different, even though a cold rain had coated his jacket and hair. Behind her, the rain hit her windows in angry waves and became a full-on, clattering downpour.

"It's so good to see you," Abby said. "I'm sorry for calling you here on such short notice, right after you got back. How was Mars?"

Nick exhaled a big breath. "It's amazing. Met Pam's parents and that went well, even though we left early. But Lisa Radisson's accusations are like a heart attack. Kagents are still picking up the pieces, trying to cope. I'm without a mentor at the moment. I can't find a way to twist the Stabilizers."

"I'm sorry," Abby said. "The timing is unfortunate. Take off your jacket and have a seat."

He tossed the jacket on the other guest chair and sat down in front of her desk. Maybe the world felt so heavy on his shoulders because the gravity was higher here on the blue marble.

Abby sat on the edge of her desk and looked him straight in the eye. "Nick, honey, I have bad news."

Nick's eyes flitted to the picture of Juan on the wall. He remembered hearing the bad news that Juan, Abby's ex-husband

and his best client, had been gunned down. That had been bad news. Her tone suggested it was nothing that bad. Pam hadn't been mangled in a freak thresher accident on the agricultural trade tour she was hosting for Taiwanese food distributors today.

"The Stabilizer Alliance has declined the Consortium's offer," she said. She let that sink in for a second before continuing. "They stated in quite-clear terms that they are not interested in pursuing any agreement with us."

Nick tasted defeat in his mouth, and it was bitter like stomach acid. The Consortium had dangled the money, engaged the Alliance, and lost, all because of his idea. The Consortium leaders would probably never trust him again; he could just imagine what Minister Seraprondi thought of him now. On top of all that, it left the world sinking towards disaster again.

His threat index projections wouldn't be two-tailed, anymore. The Alliance would regroup, rededicate itself to destroying everything, and it would be a fight for survival. Nick's thoughts wandered around this new, horrible fact, trying to find a way to accept it.

He looked up at Abby. "I don't know what to say. I'm sorry. I could never figure out who makes those decisions in the Alliance, so we weren't able to tailor it like I hoped."

Abby held up a hand. "You did a great thing here. The Alliance had to stop and think about the offer. General Lasson thinks you may have bought the Consortium enough time to extend our advantages over them. And it may pay dividends later. It may convince them that they can work with us on other issues."

Nick grinned. "If you're trying to comfort me, it's not working. You sound like a politician."

"A better politician than me would say that this was a constructive exercise. We made progress. We're in a better position than before. Thanks to you."

Nick shrugged. "Okay, that speech made me feel a little better."

Abby tilted her head to the side. "What do we do next?"

"I thought I would have an inside look at their organization by this point. I grew up on their darknets, you know?" Nick threw his hands in the air. "But I don't know anything more about their leadership than I did before."

Abby swung the foot that dangled off the side of the desk. "You must have had a contingency plan."

"I wish I did. The projected path the Stabbies are on right now is pretty dismal. Damn, I was really hoping we could have prevented this."

The disappointment was like a gaping stomach wound on his soul. He felt his insides falling out through that hole. He hadn't felt this way since that moment years ago when he had realized how bad his bounty hunting job really was.

"I'd like to tell the others that you have something in the works," Abby said.

Nick snorted. "Come on, a bunch of them didn't think this was a good idea in the first place. And why would I tell them for free?"

Abby smirked. "Only a bounty hunter wants to talk about getting paid when the world is on the line."

Nick rubbed a hand across his chin, unable to return the smirk. "Kagents have expenses, too."

Abby folded her hands, like he had seen her do when her two boys acted up. "You are angry. It will take you a little while to come to grips with this."

Nick nodded. "Did they hire someone, yet, for the job you wanted me to do?"

"Yes. A local guy named Rave James."

"I know Rave. He's good." In fact, Nick would have recruited him as a Kagent, if he ever succeeded enough to afford a coworker. Nick thought about paths not taken. If he had taken that job with the Consortium, he was pretty sure their offer to the Stabbies would have failed then, too.

"But he's not you," Abby pointed out. "How do you think we should handle the Alliance at this point?"

"Find their terrorist group and take them down. They are just too much of an unknown to plan for."

Abby took the hint and became more serious. "Do you have a projection of whether that approach would succeed?"

Nick shook his head. "I've been failing to do that all along. I stopped trying to predict my own success. I thought the Consortium offer would work. Maybe I just wanted to believe it would."

Abby hopped down off the desk and laid a hand on his shoulder. "Don't worry about it now. You've got to digest this. I have no doubt you'll come up with something that works."

Nick appreciated her support, but there was little comfort for him in her words. Not just because she was a politician but because he believed her. It just meant more pressure on him to not fail. He stood up. He needed to go for a walk. He didn't care that it was raining hard outside. He needed to pound pavement and let his brain run in circles for a while.

"Nick," Abby said in a commanding tone.

He turned around, and realized he had drifted towards the door.

"I'm going to tell Pam to keep a close eye on you tonight," she said.

He shook his head, embarrassed.

"You did a good thing trying to get the Consortium and the Stabilizers to play nice. You're carrying on the legacy of an old friend of mine." She tilted her head toward Juan's portrait. "He failed, he won, he stumbled, but he never gave up. We're all better off because of it."

Nick looked at the portrait and then back at her. People accused politicians of twisting the public with nice words. The funny thing was that it worked. Nick felt her words rummaging around in his brainpan, firing off endorphins and squashing the billowing blackness of a dark mood that was trying to take control. Juan struggled too, but he kept going.

A small smile played across his lips. He walked back to where she was standing, bent down, and kissed Abby on the cheek. "Thank you, I needed that," he said. She squeezed his arm in return, as if to say that she didn't mean it as a politician or a client, but as a friend.

She watched him grab his jacket and leave the office without another word. His eyes watered up as he reached the marble hallway. He owed a lot of people who had helped him get to this point. Juan, Bridge, Meredith, Pam, and Abby had all stepped up to help him achieve more. He couldn't let them down, give up and flee. He hurried outside to pound pavement and think about how he could go after the Alliance.

CHAPTER THIRTY-THREE

PENNY'S SUMMONS UNSETTLED CRAIG. HIS own count of Board votes suggested that the Burgess deal would probably lose, but there could be more wrinkles. Sal could have changed his mind again. Cooper could be working over his colleagues.

His plane landed in a deluged Brooklyn. If the temperature had dropped a few degrees more, it would have been a blizzard. The denizens were wet, cold, and angry at the weather-induced flight delays. Apparently it had been raining for five days straight.

He taxied into Manhattan, which took forever, and entered a different world up in Penny's suite in the Empire State Building II. The rain fell silently against the large windows and the low clouds made the storm appear distant and hazy. Frank handed him tea and Penny was waiting for him, sitting behind her desk. She looked like she hadn't been hit by a raindrop in years.

"You did it," Penny said with a small smile. "We rejected the Burgess offer. You have done yeoman's work here, Craig, yeoman's work."

Craig clapped his hands together in victory and whooped. "I wasn't sure, but I had a good feeling." He sat back and relaxed muscles he didn't realize had been clenched. "Have you ever had Ray's Pizza?" he asked.

Penny pursed her lips. "I don't eat Italian."

Craig grinned. "Come on, let's go get a slice. To celebrate."

"I'll pass, Craig, but thank you. We should focus on next steps."

Penny dipped her head in appreciation. "We had to make a deal to win Cooper's vote. We have to fire you, I'm afraid."

Craig's mouth opened a little, but nothing came out.

Penny shook her head. "The others wouldn't vote against his position. He is the last remaining founding member on the Board. We wouldn't oppose him on fundamental matters." She paused. "He is quite angry at you for undermining the Burgess deal. This was his condition."

Craig rubbed his face with both hands. "If that's what it took to kill this deal, though, then it's worth it." He wasn't just saying that—he believed it. "What's the Alliance going to do now?"

Penny raised an eyebrow. "It does seem like we are back to square one. Which is untenable. But Dave and Ciebrian have started talking. They think there may be a way forward that uses Lobbying and some of your ideas."

Saving Lobbying had been the whole point at the beginning. But he hadn't expected to stumble across a path to victory over the offworlders.

"Well," he said, slapping both thighs and standing. There wasn't anything more to say. "I'm sorry I caused you any trouble, Ms. Andrews."

She rose, too, and shook his hand. "You really did do a fine job. I owe both you and Daniel. You can keep the expense account for the next 90 days, to get yourself back on your feet again. But the Board-level access on the Alliance net was cut off a few minutes ago." She walked him to the office door. "I hate to leave you in the lurch like this. Do you have any idea what you'll do next?"

He had spent most of his early life trying to get out of Baton Rouge and his middle age not returning there. He wasn't spending his old age anywhere near it. "No, I'll figure it out, though, if no one is trying to arrest me for a few days."

"It almost goes without saying that I would be happy to make some calls on your behalf if you would like."

He nodded and walked out of the office. He said goodbye to

Frank, who didn't respond. Not having his next gig lined up didn't bother him nearly as much as the demise of his grand plan. What the hell, maybe Penny had considered him expendable from day one. Maybe the anti-Burgess part of the Board had twisted him.

He reached street level and the doorman hailed a taxi for him. He dashed under the doorman's umbrella through the tinny downpour, his breath coming out in steamy plumes. New York Jersey was sure as hell not an option for starting over again. He told the taxi to take him to the nearest airport.

Craig stretched out on the back seat so he didn't have to look at the city flashing by. He called Daniel. "I got fired," he said and explained what happened.

Daniel gasped. "I'm sorry. The Board is so divided that you would have made a mortal enemy somewhere down the line. It was an impossible job. Even for you. Damn it, I feel like I set you up to fail."

"No way," Craig replied. "You gave me my life back and a chance to save the one thing I really care about."

Daniel sighed. "Small comfort, right? The Alliance is still lost."

"You don't know the half of it. The thing that really singes my ass hair is that I figured out how the Alliance can beat the offworlders." He explained the grand plan, Ciebrian's total societal war combined with Sal's desire for more Community support.

Daniel whistled. "Ingenious. But you didn't expect them to welcome such bold thinking with open arms, did you?"

Craig shook his head. "I thought I had a chance because time was short and they were so desperate. But all I think I did was shock them enough that they prefer the funk they've been in, instead."

Daniel chuckled. "Yeah, you'd have to run a hardcore op on them."

"What's hardcore, anymore?" Craig asked, thinking of radioactive isotopes spreading over Shanghai. That was hardcore.

"You were playing an inside game," Daniel said. "Trying to win them over by aligning interests, smooth-talking: retail stuff. Hardcore is wholesale, outside events that change the game and do the twisting for you. In the aftermath of Lisa's betrayal, I learned the scope of what she was doing. A lot of it was flat-out terrible, but she did manage to use outside factors to do much of the work."

"Okay, smart guy, I've got a 90-day expense account and a borrowed condo in Celebration. Not much to go change the world. What do you have?"

"Don't get pissy," Daniel said.

"I'm not... okay, I'm pissy." Damn it, he should have known this firing would get at him. Getting outmaneuvered by that old man, who had been running his own ops against his fellow Board members for decades, probably. Stupid limbic system, idiotic subconscious, and asinine lizard impulses clouding his thinking. "Whatever are you talking about, dear Daniel?"

"That's better. I mean a scare, a threat, a scandal. It takes some serious resources or some serious balls. You're talking about Cooper Mangold-level people here. They don't scare easily."

"My expense account should cover that," Craig joked. But Daniel was right: He needed to twist some Board members from behind the scenes and without leaving fingerprints. An outside event, something that scared the shit out of them. Like dropping a fucking orbital habitat on Orlando.

"You'll figure it out, pal. But I have to get back to my class," Daniel said. "Good luck. If you need anything, call anyone else."

"Screw you, ya turd," Craig said jovially and hung up.

The cab pulled up to a Ray's Pizza as the rain drummed the roof like the fists of a hundred angry prairie dogs. No doorman with an umbrella to escort Craig this time.

He dashed inside and thumped his fist on the counter, grinning like a jackal. "Give me whatever's hot," he said to the guy shoveling pizzas out of the oven.

He took a steaming slice and a cup of water to a seat by the window. He poured a thick coat of crushed red pepper on top of the onion and cheese. He shoved the slice in his mouth and proceeded to burn the ever-loving shit out of his tongue. Deliciously painful.

He always thought clearer when he ate spicy food.

Craig chewed and thought and burned, and then chewed and thought and burned some more. He drained his cup of water.

The guy slinging pies put another cup on the counter. "You sure that's hot enough for ya, Chief?"

"It's perfect," Craig said as he downed the water, swished it around in his mouth. He slammed the cup on the counter and motioned for a refill.

"Here you go, smart guy. Take the whole pitcher," the pizza guy said, his distaste for Craig oozing out of every hair-covered pore on his face. "It's on the house."

"Thank you, sir. Go Yankees." Craig nodded to the blue pennants hanging above the counter.

"Yeah, which ones? Basketball, hockey, or baseball?"

Craig returned to his seat. Loved the pizza; hated the city. "All of them."

The pizza guy harrumphed and went back to his work.

Craig fired up another slice and tortured the nerves in his throat and mouth. Finally, the pain cleared away his pissed-off thoughts. He was ready to call Haruka. She answered instantly.

"You knew," he said.

There was a pause. "I almost told Penny to let me tell you what happened, but... but that would have revealed too much about us."

"I'm not mad," Craig said. "I would have told you to vote for it. This was a temp job and it could have gotten between us."

She sighed. "If it makes you feel any better, I voted against this compromise. I wanted that deal with the Consortium."

"You stubborn, stubborn woman," Craig mused. She could have sunk the compromise. What would Cooper have done then? Or did Cooper have her all figured out?

"I want to bring you home with me," she said.

That was out of the blue. "Really? You must really like me."

"Ha, ha. I need to update my father about what's happened on the Board. He knows how to deal with Cooper. The two of them started the Alliance together."

CHAPTER THIRTY-FOUR

"IS THIS SECURE?" NICK ASKED, peering around the virtual dining pavilion. His avatar, wearing a tuxedo, sat at a table with a white-linen tablecloth. Borbola's grinning face covered the head of an avatar in a tuxedo who sat across from him.

The other diners, all dressed in old-fashioned formal wear, sat nearly elbow-to-elbow with him, definitely within earshot. Oddly, he couldn't hear exactly what they were saying, but he could hear an orchestra playing on the far end of the grand four-story dining pavilion and a murmur of conversation and silverware clinking on china.

"Haven't you heard of the Satin Patio?" Borbola's face frowned. "It's the most secure chatroom on any net."

The dining room was lined with pillars that framed a view of the Amalfi Coast on one side and luscious Italian gardens on the other. The sun was setting in a sky filled with brilliant purples, pinks, and oranges.

Borbola insisted on meeting online like this because they were unable to meet in person. If Nick didn't know better, he would have thought the bounty hunter was shooting for a romantic date with this setting.

"What are you doing in Denver?" Borbola asked.

Nick replied, "The Stabilizer operations wing is based out of Celebration. I've traced key protestors in their latest campaigns back to specific Communities. A lot of them came from this area and they are one of the more militant branches. I'm hoping that their terrorist wing is located here." He didn't mention that he was grasping at a few last desperate ploys.

"Oh, I thought for a second that Pam tossed your sorry ass out," Borbola said and laughed.

"Not yet," Nick replied, only chuckling.

Was this camaraderie between the two of them now? How damn odd.

"I only kid because I have no respect for you whatsoever," Borbola said.

"The feeling is mutual. So, why meet here?" Nick asked. "Trying to wine and dine me?"

Borbola grinned. "This chat room has been in business for over eighty years. It was based on the set of some dramatic scene in the film, *Peace of a Prince.* People get engaged here. Ask me some other time how I took it over. Right now, I have to know how you decided that Celebration isn't their secret terrorist base?"

A waiter came to fill their virtual water glasses and Nick paused.

"You really don't have to worry about being eavesdropped on in here," Borbola said. His avatar cupped his hands together. "We are in a protected instance of this chat room. The other avatars in here only see randomly-generated body language from us and the conversation is actually someone else's conversation turned into a murmured audio slush."

Nick looked around. "Someone may still be able to parse it. Read lips or something."

Borbola shook his head. "No. I own the chatroom." He laughed at Nick's surprised expression. "Used to be the most reputable, secure private chatroom in the world. Then I hacked it, its value plummeted, and I bought it cheap. I only let them see what I want them to see."

"You *hacked* it?" Nick said skeptically.

"Let's say I obtained system access from the site's security lead after some enhanced intimidation."

Nick indicated the silk drapes blowing in the breeze. "Classic Borbola. But this is nice. A sign of your decorating tastes?"

"No way. This eye candy is part of the brand. This is what makes the money. So what have you learned?"

"Okay." Nick felt his lack of business sense rear its ugly head. "The Stabilizers aren't as careful about what they say on the streets of Celebration. They have accountants, Community sales, and public relations people in Celebration, but no spies, soldiers, or executives." He paused. He was ready to plead for any new scrap of information. Without a Warrant, without the Burgess deal to force the Alliance to open itself to more scrutiny, he was tapped out. "What do you have?"

Borbola frowned. "Well, I guess that's a lot for you. Me, I got names of Alliance executives, I think."

Hope coursed through Nick's body. "What? Who? Speak!"

Borbola said, "The Stabilizers are still navel-gazing and they have brought in a consultant to assess the situation. He's one of their old warhorses from the terrorist side of the shop."

"Stop pausing for effect. The name of this old warhorse?"

"Craig Lassiter. Middle-aged guy from somewhere in the South, if his accent is legitimate. I profiled him and surprise, there's not much there. He must be a Stabilizer born and raised, like you. Here's a physical description."

Borbola's avatar leaned across the table and placed a slip of paper in front of Nick's avatar. When Nick picked it up, the paper turned into a data file. Nick opened it. There was a brief description and a blurry picture of the man. Craig Lassiter looked like an all-American guy's guy. Nick put the file aside for now and Cross began running down what she could on Lassiter.

"Unfortunately, your fears are well-founded," Borbola continued, making his avatar do a casual hand gesture. "The Stabilizers were looking at everything from peaceful engagement to all-out conflict with the rest of the solar system. But this Lassiter guy, or his allies, convinced the Alliance to reject the Burgess Consortium offer. He is leading the charge for all-out war."

Nick shook his head. His enemy had a name now. An enormous improvement compared to five minutes ago. "All-out war? Do you mean like the Tessan Preservationists, blowing up settlements, or the Flashing 12s down here way back when? Or are you talking figurative, like a public relations campaign or a crashpoint push?"

Borbola activated his avatar's shrug emotion. "Honestly, I don't know. Lassiter was the jerk who tried to fry Shanghai two decades ago with some nuclear bomb. The campaign there was failing and he thought spreading radiation in the city center would make it uninhabitable. It would literally kill the city, while technically not hurting anyone. But the Chinese stopped him before he could press the button. It's in that file I gave you."

Cross displayed a twenty-year old internal Alliance document condemning Craig Lassiter and exiling him from the organization. Nick blinked. "And they brought this wacko back to consult?"

Borbola laughed a little. "Yeah, it's crazy. Sensible people on the inside are worried that he's back. Do you think this will spring a Warrant?"

Nick rubbed the back of his head. "I hope so. It sounds like the Alliance is ready to toss out its nonviolent ideals. Cross, what can you find on the Stabbies in Shanghai 20 years back?"

Cross posted a summary of news articles in the Shanghai press from that time. A twenty-year old news report about the Alliance disavowing an operative who worked for them in Shanghai. Suspected use of radiological weapons, a manhunt in China, it matched what Borbola found. "Something almost happened like that," Nick reported to Borbola, "but nothing mentions Lassiter by name. It just says 'the foreign suspect' escaped."

Borbola looked crestfallen. "That document has to be enough. We're so close I can feel it."

Nick smiled. "My Simon just found a photo of Lassiter, in Shanghai, with Daniel Sloan around that time." He showed Borbola the image on his netpad. "But not with his arms wrapped around a dirty bomb."

"He did disappear right after and didn't surface until now, right?" Borbola asked with desperation in his voice. "And Sloan continued on right along. That should mean something to your Kagents."

Nick shrugged. "I hope so."

"Seriously, Nick, I'm not playing around. I don't know what all-out war means in this context. But supposedly, it involves a lot of damage to offworld communities and cities down here. Of course," Borbola smiled, "it's only the damage down here that concerns me."

"What kind of damage?"

Borbola replied, "My source says they haven't figured that out, yet. Could be physical, economic, cultural, or something else. Hell, maybe spiritual. No one down here wants to see any more crashes, especially me. Every crash of a city down here undermines our independence from the offworlders."

Nick scratched his head in real life, causing his face to wobble on his avatar's body in the Satin Patio. "How did you find this out?"

Borbola grinned. "My source says the Alliance's executive council has been split on strategy. The militants want to hit us hard, but the doves want a nicer approach, like you've pushed for. But Lassiter is working them over, bringing them around to the militant side, apparently."

That tracked with Nick's projections. He felt vindicated but, at the same time, terrified. Knowing there was a see-sawing debate they could influence was one thing. Knowing that there was an accomplished operative on the inside working against them already, and winning, wasn't.

"Why is your source telling you this? What is his angle?" Borbola's source was probably someone who opposed Lassiter's war-like approach.

Borbola activated the throw-hands-in-the-air gesture. "You're asking if they're playing me?" He laughed. "They could be pushing their own agenda, fighting some office politics battle. Or someone could be playing them. But my source is alarmed at how things have developed. The Burgess offer being rejected shocked them."

"Your contact could be the key," Nick ventured. Getting a mole on the inside could secure a Warrant and give them the leverage to twist the Alliance. Maybe the Consortium didn't need the real estate deal to infiltrate the Alliance after all.

Borbola grimaced. "I don't know if this person wants out, themselves. They are hoping that I can do something and let them avoid trouble. I don't think they'll go for much more involvement. You don't want to know how much enhanced intimidation it took to pry free the Lassiter exile file."

In real life, Nick rubbed his hands together in excitement. They felt hot and clammy despite the cold weather outside his hotel. "If they won't talk, see if you can have them find us someone who will work for us. Start their own cell inside the organization."

Borbola rolled his eyes. "Nick, I'm lucky I got this far. I was hoping you could just run with this. This whole thing is making me nervous. You know my concerns. I don't want these guys doing anything that brings your offworld friends down here."

Nick puffed out his cheeks in frustration. Even if Craig Lassiter himself walked up to him right now and gave up everything, Nick doubted that would be enough. He threw up his hands. "I'll take what I can get. This probably isn't enough to spring a Warrant. You mentioned more names."

"Yeah, but I bet you need a Warrant to get any use out of them. My source had a list of attendees at an Alliance fundraising event in Malta from before the Hamilton operation. So no Craig Lassiter. I don't know if these people are Alliance execs, donors, or just good-looking dates." Borbola handed over another virtual slip of paper.

Cross posted the names on the viewer. Nick recognized a few surnames, from the ranks of the rich and famous. Without knowing more, there was no way to obtain a Warrant to profile them. No profile, no learning their agendas and behaviors, or finding ways to twist them to do the right thing.

Borbola looked particularly sheepish and said, "The upper management ranks of the Alliance rarely meet together in person and most of the people who work for them rarely ever see them, my source says. They could be on this list or not. It's possible that the Alliance just has a professional fundraiser handle everything and these are just rich people looking for a good party."

Nick nodded. "So this may be worthless."

Borbola shook his head. "Or priceless. My source thought this would be just as useful, but didn't explain why."

Nick raised an eyebrow. "He doesn't have a Kagent netpad, does he?"

"Ha, not that I know of. But just because the Alliance doesn't look as dangerous as the Dragoons or the Flashing 12s, it doesn't mean they can't be as destructive," Borbola said. "All so these assholes can make a last-ditch effort to protect their siestas and profit margins."

"Profit margins?" Nick repeated.

Borbola looked taken aback. "Yeah. Some of the donors on that list run conglomerates that have been fighting offworld competition for years. I'm just speculating based on where they sit," he added quickly. "If we can talk twist them, I'm ready to help."

Nick hadn't considered why people would want to donate to the Alliance. Growing up in a Community, he'd thought people supported the idea of a limited work week because they liked kids. Offworld competition explained why the deep-pockets crowd may want to oppose the offworlders besides lifestyle ideology.

"I don't think anyone wants to make use of your persuasion skills," Nick joked. He looked at the list. Cross annotated the list with the reasons why each individual was either famous, wealthy, or both.

Borbola knitted his brows together. "Is there some way you could deduce who the Alliance sugar daddies are from your other intel?"

Nick looked down at the virtual place setting in front of him. High quality virtual china, it looked like. "I've tried. My Simon tried.

Pam tried. There just isn't enough out there. The Alliance doesn't release an annual report or a list of donors."

Borbola shook his head. "No, I meant figuring out who's running the Alliance out there in the world. Who acts sympathetic to them or could finance them?"

Nick had never thought of just guessing based on what was available on the public nets. It smacked of desperation. He, Borbola, and third-graders with a book report due, scraping together whatever they could. "I can't do it without a Warrant. If I can't get one for the Alliance itself, I'll never get one for people who attend their fundraisers. And these people are probably all privacy-blocked to hell." He thought for a second. "Why don't you track them down? Off the BHN. Old school."

Borbola looked uncomfortable. "Time is running out to start that now. It took me years of tailing Dragoons until I could ID the execs, much less tie them to a chair for a friendly chat."

Nick put a hand on his hip. "Just make some guesses, say less than a hundred, and profile them yourself. Then tell me if you find anything promising."

Borbola made a useless gesture with his hand. "Could you even use that information? Or will it violate your precious Kagent ethics?"

"Uh...." Nick hadn't considered that, either. Now he realized why Borbola was being quiet about his sources; he was protecting Nick from violating any Kagent privacy rules. For all Nick knew, Borbola could have read a copy of a Stabilizer company newsletter.

"Okay, Eldred, I'll add this data to mine. See if it spurs anything."

Borbola shrugged helplessly. "I'll keep pumping my source."

That struck Nick as a complete lie. Borbola knew more than he let on, and Nick doubted it was only for Nick's own good.

Borbola looked around at the other diners and grinned. "I'd tell you to stay and enjoy this, but you're too damn maudlin to do that. I'd rather fill this instance with a paying customer. Ciao."

Nick blinked and found himself staring at a blank viewer in his hotel room in the Rockies. He dropped his face into his hands and rubbed vigorously. Well, at least he had a name. He set to work confirming that Borbola was indeed right about Craig Lassiter's public nets records being mostly nonexistent.

[What the hell is he hiding?] he asked Cross.

[You think he's hiding something?]

"Absolutely," Nick said. [May be because of Kagent ethics. Or maybe not. Notice that in that chatroom, I couldn't see any of his bio telltales to see if he was lying.]

[What can you do about it?]

Even if Nick had a Warrant on Borbola, the bounty hunter was famously untraceable. That fact bothered Nick like an ant crawling under his skull.

[Nothing. I can't do anything about it at all,] he said. All he could do was learn as much as he could about Craig Lassiter.

CHAPTER THIRTY-FIVE

HARUKA AND HER EXECUTIVE JET were in San Francisco, so Craig had to slum it in a commercial sub-orbital flight to meet her. Shortly after they took off for Manila, she enrolled him in the Ten Mile High Club. They would be staying in separate buildings at the family compound, she explained as she got dressed, and this was their only chance. The Gallardos were old-school Catholics, she reminded him.

They landed in the Manila airport and a car was waiting for them in the sunny heat and humidity. The older gentleman 'driver' named Ed gave Haruka a big hug; apparently, they had known each other for most of their lives.

The car drove the three of them from the airport into streets flooded with jeepneys, bicycles, and three-wheeled scooters. The car turned onto the South Luzon Expressway and headed toward Dasmarinas, the upscale neighborhood where the Gallardo 'city' house was located.

Ed and Haruka talked in what Craig guessed was Tagalong. At one point, she slipped her arm through Craig's and patted it while explaining something that included the word 'Shanghai.'

Ed smiled and asked in impeccable English what Craig did for a living. Craig smiled, murmured something about being a consultant between jobs. Ed nodded and Haruka distracted him by asking a question about her father, Craig guessed, because they both grew somber and talked in low terms.

The car pulled into a gated compound with elaborate cream-colored archways that looked vaguely Moroccan. The driveway was made of concentric circles of brick set into concrete.

The house buzzed with activity and in under a minute, Craig was mobbed by a dozen relatives, most of them children and teenagers, who turned out to be Haruka's nieces and nephews. Her arrival home had prompted a reunion of sorts at her parents' compound.

Haruka pulled Craig toward the kitchen one step at a time as he feverishly shook hands and tried to remember names. The kitchen looked like it had been carved out of huge blocks of brown stone, with a tile floor outlined by brown marble.

"Craig Lassiter," said Haruka's mother, a tall, severe-looking woman in her seventies with orange hair. She walked over in high heels to give him a big, bling-encrusted hug.

Haruka's sisters greeted him with less warmth and more curiosity. One looked just like her mother, another like Haruka. They were busy cooking something that smelled sweet and pungent.

After some polite conversation, Haruka escorted Craig out to the veranda, which overlooked a sun-baked lawn of bright-green grass. Two more brothers were out here, one of whom was about Craig's age and completely gray. An old man in a motorized chair sat between the brothers and his face lit up when he saw Haruka. She bent down to hug him and kiss his forehead.

She turned to Craig. "This is my father, Manuel Gallardo."

Craig took the old man's featherlight hand in both of his. "It is an honor, sir, to meet one of the Alliance's founders."

Manuel shook it. "It's a pleasure to meet such an interesting man as yourself. From Shanghai to India to Celebration. Have a seat. Joshua is CEO and Kenji is his most trusted advisor. Rookie-rook, tell us what is new."

Haruka didn't look at Craig's surprised expression at hearing her nickname. She sat down in a deck chair, serious as ever, and explained the compromise vote by the Board.

Manuel's eyes flitted to Craig when she mentioned how the compromise got him fired, but then they returned to her.

When Haruka finished, Joshua said, "That leaves the Alliance no better off." He exchanged a concerned look with his father and brother. "I have to face shareholders next month. We've been expecting that the Alliance would make a major move. Otherwise, our revenue will continue to erode."

"Offworld competitors have been chipping way at our market share in 13 separate industries," Haruka added.

"Cooper took advantage of the fact that you, Craig, wouldn't know enough about the deal-making dynamics among the board members," Manuel said. "He crafted that compromise to remove you from the picture."

"He's cutting off his own nose to spite his face," Kenji said, his hand slicing the air.

"I agree," Craig said. "Why would he do that?" he asked Manuel.

The old man blinked rapidly for a few seconds, like he was recalling information at a high rate of speed. "Cooper and I have grown used to fearing the offworlders and the buzzers. In the early days, confronting them directly seemed suicidal. Cooper was sly enough to find a way to get richer off them. But deep down, he defers to them."

Craig nodded. People, even the rich and powerful, were often shaped by their first major experiences as adults in a given avenue of life, whether it was in love, business, or play.

Cooper had been steeped in the kind of subversive direct action that the Stabilizers had been founded on. It was political guerrilla warfare, designed to harass a superior enemy. It was also predicated on a fear of that enemy's superiority.

Haruka said, "Craig has a plan that could defeat the offworlders, actually make progress against offworld culture spreading down here. But Cooper saw it as a threat."

She prompted him to describe the plan, which he did. Kenji was visibly excited about it and couldn't stop grinning like a maniac. Joshua nodded soberly, but also seemed positive.

Haruka looked at her father for a reaction. When he didn't speak, she said, "Father, what are your thoughts?"

Manuel Gallardo chuckled. "I'm keeping my thoughts to myself. This is for your generation to decide. I will support whatever course Joshua decides to take."

Joshua sat there like an emotionless statue. "Even if this more aggressive plan fails, it could buy us time, room to maneuver. The alternative is just to go out of business slowly."

Manuel regarded Craig with narrowed eyes. "Conventional political lobbying is much less effective."

Craig nodded. "You're right. But it makes the buzzer cities more Stabilized, and our Communities more competitive and more self-sufficient. It's a win all around."

Kenji grimaced. "It seems slow-moving."

Craig smiled and looked at each one of them. "The societal war against the offworlders is the aggressive part. The businesses have to cripple the offworlders economically. But I would need your help to do that. And Cooper's. See the dilemma?"

Joshua Gallardo shook his head slowly. "We can't take on our offworld competitors. In telecommunications, transport, fashion design, entertainment, a number of other industries. We're slowly losing on all of those fronts."

Craig kept smiling. "You won't be competing with them in any of those markets." He laid out Ciebrian's idea about how to hit the offworlders where they were economically vulnerable.

First, Kenji's eyes lit up, then his father's, and finally Joshua's.

"Cooper didn't like this plan, did he?" Manuel asked.

Kenji slapped his thigh. "Cooper needs to go."

Haruka said, "He's the godfather of the Alliance."

Manuel shook his head. "It's not a lifetime appointment. A unanimous Board vote can remove him." He shifted in his seat and it was the first sign of discomfort that he had exhibited. Was it because he was part of a group that would turn on his decades-long comrade? No, it was physical pain; he winced as he took a deep breath.

Everyone looked at everyone else.

Manuel shook his head, impatient. "I taught you children how to deal with a foe stronger than you. Turn their strength against them."

Kenji, Haruka, and Craig furrowed their brows, thinking.

After thirty seconds, Joshua said, "Father, why don't you tell us what you are driving at?" His impatience was thinly veiled.

Manuel waved his hand. "I don't have an answer for you. I don't know how that may work."

"We need leverage from the outside of the Alliance," Haruka said. "An outside event. We'll never budge things internally."

Yes, Daniel had told Craig that, and he might have mentioned that to Haruka. "Yes," Craig shook his head, "The internal strategy clearly didn't work."

Manuel scrutinized Craig. "What are your long-term plans?"

Craig held up his hands. "I'm playing it by ear."

Manuel took a labored breath. "If we take Cooper off the Board, we need you to make a commitment to the Alliance."

Craig looked at Haruka and she nodded slightly. This was that loyalty, family thing she had told him about. The Gallardos trusted each other because they were so tightly interwoven by family, by wealth, by expectations, and by commitment.

Craig replied, "It's not like I have a lot of other choices. The Alliance has been my surrogate family all of my life. Yes, I'll be part of it."

"Craig, my father is asking you to run the Alliance," Joshua said. "You have a good vision. You have field experience and leadership skills."

Haruka couldn't be a Board member, his boss, if he was running the show. Were they making him choose between the Alliance and Haruka? The tropical humidity was punching through his Cajun defenses and sweat trickled down his back. He put a hand on

Haruka's knee. "Haruka and I want to stay together but I don't want to jeopardize her position on the Board."

"Don't worry about me," Haruka said.

Craig looked deep into her eyes trying to understand what she was hinting, but she looked away with a little smile wriggling across her lips.

Joshua said. "We'll take care of that."

"Good," Craig replied. "But someone has to convince Cooper that he should retire."

They batted around a number of ideas, some outlandish, some scary. Cooper Mangold couldn't be bought off, or be found with a prostitute, and no one wanted to poison or assassinate him.

Rejecting those violent possibilities reminded Craig of Borbola. The bounty hunter was an asset he shouldn't overlook. He could be invaluable, his propensity to create carnage aside. After all, the bastard had taken on the Dragoon corporate franchise and whipped the piss out of it. Could he do the same to GoldLand Entertainment? Or to Mangold personally? He had a hard time believing that even a bounty hunter like Borbola could penetrate the protective layers of security that Cooper had wrapped himself in.

Borbola's worth wasn't his combat abilities, Craig realized. It was his access to information. When Craig's attention returned to the conversation, Kenji was animatedly discussing an elaborate plot to ostracize Cooper.

Manuel raised his hand to quiet his younger son. "Cooper's son is the designated heir apparent. But Bobby Mangold doesn't share all of his father's beliefs."

Haruka shook her head. "There's little chance he would conspire against his father."

"We don't need to conspire with him. We just need to twist him, indirectly," Craig said. "Cooper is slowing down and Bobby has to be watching for signs he needs to step in. If we play on his concerns and hopes, he'll act on his own."

If only they could discredit Cooper like Lisa Radisson had

discredited her own mother and the Kagents. She had made one accusation, possibly baseless, that had messed up the Kagents. If there was a way for Borbola to twist Cooper, it would leave the Gallardos, other board members, and himself free from suspicion.

Craig snapped his fingers and grinned. A plan coalesced in his head. It would be so iron, as the kids said these days.

By the time Haruka's sister Mimi alerted them that dinner would be served, the sun was low in the sky, Kenji and Craig were grinning like jackals, Manuel and Haruka were pleased, and Joshua was making phone calls to take down Cooper Mangold.

CHAPTER THIRTY-SIX

CROSS SOUNDED THE APARTMENT'S ALARM. Nick was at his workstation and instantly reached for Bruiser. He and Pam exchanged a cautious glance. Their apartment was a converted greenhouse on the roof of the building; people didn't wander by. Plus it was pretty cold outside today.

Nick and Pam both had made enemies in the Stabilizer Alliance, the Dragoons, and among the disreputable bounty hunter ranks. They had posted a round-the-clock drone early warning system around the apartment building.

Cross posted an image of the visitor. It was a woman in a full-length biker bodysuit, covered in ID badges and building passes. A courier. She walked towards the greenhouse door with a package. She wore a civilian form of smartshades and was in a hurry. The drones' scan for weapons was negative.

The courier rang the apartment's doorbell. "I have a package for Nick Lincoln. I need a signature," she said in a business-like tone that dripped with impatience and boredom.

"Anything dangerous in the package?" Nick asked Cross.

[Not that our sensors can spot.]

"Cross, can you scan the sender barcode?" Pam asked.

"Samir, Kagent Privacy Council," Cross replied over the nearest speaker.

Nick's fear turned to confusion and finally to hope. Pam actually broke into a smile. Nick let the courier into the glass mantrap that served as their front hallway.

"Tight security here," the courier observed. "I need ID and signature from Nicholas Lincoln. Company rules." Nick handed over his ID, thumbed his print for a signature, and she handed over the manila package and left.

Nick hefted the package. It still was warm from where ever the courier had come from to deliver it. He ripped it open, his face wracked with an irrepressible expression of glee.

Inside was a portfolio of black-marbled leather with the words 'Privacy Warrant' stamped in gold. It reminded Nick of his father's bookshelves full of printed books: It smelled of ink, paper, and leather. He wanted to close his eyes and hold it to his nose and drink in the smell.

Such a portfolio might be nothing special on Earth, but it was worth its weight in electronics since it had been shipped all the way from Tessa. Nick held it in his hands like it was a sacred ancient document.

Nick said, "Pam, babe, love, it's here! They did it!"

She had ducked into the bedroom and emerged just now, pulling a shirt over her head. "A Warrant? That's great."

Nick sat down at his workstation and opened the portfolio. Inside was black ink on soft beige paper pages that explained that Nicholas Lincoln was the sole bearer of this Warrant to investigate the Stabilizer Alliance and anyone who worked for it. It defined 'investigate' to include profiling individuals connected to the Stabilizers on any and all nets he could find information.

At the bottom of the page were handwritten signatures of every member of the Kagent Privacy Council. There was a second paper page behind the Warrant. It listed all the ways in which Nick could screw this up and have himself tossed out of the Kagent profession forever. The list was long but clear. It was nothing he hadn't seen before.

"I've never seen one," Pam said, looking over his shoulder. She felt the paper and ran her fingers over the black ink. "You realize how large a deal this is, right?"

"How big a deal, you mean," he said. He hefted the portfolio again. The Stabilizer Alliance had just lost any hope of privacy that the law could give them. Nick would be able to track every move of Alliance personnel that registered on the BHN and his own embryonic Kagent net. It was a sign of confidence in him, his plan, his abilities, and the urgent need to expose the Stabilizer threat. "Yes, I know."

"So, what's your plan, hotshot?" Pam asked with a grin.

Nick smiled at her and stood up. "First, my trusty Simon will profile every known Stabilizer on the BHN while I make dinner. Second, while distracted by making dinner, my subconscious will stew on this subject. Third, after dinner, I will have the information I need to execute a dazzling plan with confidence and aplomb."

She grinned and kissed him on the head. "What I can do to help?"

Nick walked into the kitchen, keeping the Warrant close by. "Cut vegetables. And keep the emotional support coming. I'm going to need it."

Pam shook her head. "I meant, what can I do to help with the Stabilizers?"

"Ah," Nick washed his hands in the sink. "Prep various organizational models so I figure out who the leadership is." He retrieved a pot to make an old family recipe: a simple peasant soup of pasta, veggies, and odds and ends. Family legend had it that the recipe had come over the border with his Hispanic ancestors centuries ago. "Hopefully, Lassiter will lead me to some of the Alliance leaders. Once I know one piece, I think—I hope—I can crack the others. I have a feeling that if I do get in, my access may be limited, so if you can project what the rest looks like, I can maximize my time on their darknet or however I get in. It's still kind of a rough plan."

Pam watched him stack ingredients on the counter. "Are you making that stupid soup again?"

Nick pulled his hand away like the pot was too hot to touch. "Oh, my God, I am!"

"You need to expand your portfolio in the kitchen. I have certain standards," she teased. His upbeat confidence was spreading across the apartment. Good.

Nick focused on cooking, and of course they didn't talk about work while they ate. Instead, Pam offered suggestions of other things he could try cooking, things that were not this soup. She volunteered to clean the dishes so he could get into using the Warrant. She tossed the brown enzyme wash tablet in the sink and it began fizzing and foaming, just like on their first night together. Nick smiled at the memory as he scooped up the Warrant and went to his corner.

"Cross, give me everything on Craig Lassiter," he said. He cracked his knuckles, which caused Pam to growl at him from the kitchen. She hated when he did that.

Cross posted Lassiter's profile on the viewer. Born in a Baton Rouge Community, military service in Louisiana for a few years. Then he'd disappeared; no trace on any amoeba nets, the BHN, or the Kagent nets. Which meant he went back into the Alliance, hiding on their darknets. Maybe in a Community.

[I spotted him recently in airports in Baton Rouge, New York Jersey, Cape Town, Shanghai, and Orlando. But he was by himself, even on the city streets, in each one.]

Nick leaned forward. "He went back to Shanghai recently? Show me what you got."

Cross posted half-a-dozen clips on the viewer. Lassiter walking by a security cam in the airport. Lassiter climbing in a private car at the airport terminal. A long-distance shot of Lassiter in a crowd of Asian people. Him exiting a cab at the airport several days later. And the last still was of him walking through the airport.

"Can we get any other cam coverage?"

[Shanghai limits its exposure to the BHN. Access to public cams requires a formal request, with a valid search warrant.]

Nick caressed the Warrant; not a problem now. There was nothing holding him back. "Make the request," he said. "And let them know that this was the Stabilizer who tried dirty-bombing them decades ago."

Nick scrolled back further back in his profile. The BHN picked up Lassiter from 25 years back, in Stabilizer protests, exiting Stabilizer safe houses and 50 still images of him with Daniel Sloan, looking like close friends.

Alarm bells went off in Nick's head; from Lassiter to Sloan to Lisa Radisson. Was Sloan running things behind the scenes? Were the three of them working together?

He reviewed the Sloan profile that Cross updated in seconds. Sloan had disappeared after Hamilton and stayed that way. Most likely cooling his heals in a Community. There was no sign of contact between the two Stabilizers since Shanghai. Lassiter next popped up on his recent flight into Celebration. Out of India. Interesting.

"Any Indian footage of Lassiter, Cross?"

[Just Lassiter hurrying through the Lucknow airport. Not surprising; much of India isn't hooked into the BHN. There is a cultural taboo against remote surveillance.]

"Cue up what we have on Lassiter in Celebration recently," Nick said. "Profile everyone he talks with. Scan the audio or lip sync it."

[There were a lot of near misses, but I have a partial match of Lassiter talking in a golf cart with David Poole, the real estate developer.] The image was fuzzy and there wasn't enough to reconstruct what they said.

"Poole is on the list too, right? Label him a warpather and go profile the shit out of him," Nick said with a grin.

[His profile will be ready with the others in just a minute.]

"Great," Nick replied. "Can we track Lassiter's financials or communications? They can't all be routed through the Stabilizer darknets."

[No, but all Stabilizer communications are encrypted.]

"Just break the encryption, then," Nick said with fake impatience.

Break the encryption. Right. Cross didn't even dignify that with a response. "Okay, can we identify his friends? We know about Daniel Sloan. Scan the rest for any sign that Lassiter has seen them."

[If he sticks to the Communities, we'll never spot him,] Cross pointed out. [Unless he takes public transport between them again.]

Why would Lassiter risk returning to Shanghai, in public? It could because of the Stabbies. Or anything else, too. Nick looked at Lassiter's most recent appearances on security cameras linked to the BHN. "He's been jetting around a lot lately. Taking risks. Looks like he flew to the west coast recently and then disappeared. Shit. He must be up to something."

[He disappeared from view shortly after leaving the terminal too,] Cross added. [There's nothing more on Lassiter.]

Nick shook his head. "There has to be more we can tease out. Wait, you're telling me there isn't much chance, aren't you?"

[I didn't want to be rude.]

"Let's keep going." Nick spent another hour re-examining each piece of data on Lassiter before concluding that Cross was right. Darkness had fallen and the drone guards had to be swapped out for a freshly-charged set.

"I'm going to tell myself that I didn't just waste a bunch of time," Nick said. "Alliance donor suspect list on screen, please. Let's go through the anti-offworld people, first, with affiliations and business ties."

[Manuel Gallardo, Suzanne Rosanna, Ciebrian Bieto, Viktor Mamchev, Muhammed Nellis, Mary Eastland, and David Poole: all rich and powerful businesspeople.] Cross posted profiles of each person and the businesses the person owned.

Nick paged through the Manuel Gallardo profile. "This is really thin."

[All of them are completely untouchable on the BHN. They have first-class privacy blocks on all of their data. The only reason we know where any of them live or whom they are married to is because there is a feature article about them in a business or society article.]

"But we have a Warrant." Nick punched the air with his fist.

[They buy offworld-level privacy protection, possibly including alerts if someone attempts to probe them. If you want to get at their data, you need an Earth-bound warrant, about sixteen lawyers, and ninety days of legal squabbling, if the last time this happened is any indication.]

Nick sighed. "What's on the public nets about them then? Gossip columns. Great." According to the gossip columns Cross posted, these people bought art, had messed-up kids, and seemed to only go to charity events.

"Who might have a business reason to oppose offworld business?"

Manuel Gallardo and Ciebrian Bieto topped the list. Ironically, both were hermits; Gallardo due to illness and Bieto because he was a weird recluse.

"Okay, who has businesses tied to offworld interests?" Nick's heart was racing. These were the people who would have supported the Burgess Consortium deal, if they were in the Alliance. They could be key allies for the Kagents to reach out to, he hoped. His optimism was melting away as he encountered one bust after another.

[All I have is David Poole's birth record. The public nets have reported on him, but much of it is unverified by a second source.]

"Born, raised, and lives in Texas. Houston." Nick said. "Not far from where Lassiter grew up in Baton Rouge. These two could be tight. That suggests that he's on Lassiter's side, but the Burgess offer would make his company a lot of money. Maybe he's not tied to the Alliance, could be just a friend of Lassiter."

Poole had a no-nonsense man's man reputation and never smiled for a picture. He had worked his way up from carrying a hammer to running a multinational construction company that broke ground on three continents each month.

"Sort his company developments by price tag and whether they were in a Community or not," Nick said. "Pooled may have built most new Communities from the last quarter-century, but look, his company has to make its money on developing in cities like Hamilton, too. Hmmm."

Cross displayed a chart showing that over 60% of Pooled developments in the last ten years were in Burgess Consortium members. Only 20% of the developments were in Communities.

Location, location, location, Nick's dad always said. Development money followed that same rule. "So, why would he want to hurt his main customers, and his own business? He doesn't seem like a sacrificial ideologue, does he? If he weren't golfing with Lassiter, I'd think he'd back the Burgess offer."

Nick returned to the fuzzy video of Poole driving Lassiter to the Celebration golf course. Were they buddies, enemies, or business associates? Poole was the only connection between the fundraiser list and Lassiter. "Can we analyze their body language? I really want to know their relationship."

[I'll compare older videos of these two to conduct a body language analysis.] Cross posted clips and stills of Lassiter and Poole both together and apart. The clips of Poole showed him walking down the street with a pack of well-dressed men and walking alone.

"Those guys Poole is walking with there are the Pooled negotiators," Pam chimed in. "We met with them on the real estate deal."

Nick turned toward her. "Good to know. I thought you were reading a trade agreement."

Her gave him a sultry smile. "I am."

Nick smiled, but turned back to the viewer. "What's the body language analysis say, Cross?"

All human cultures had similar expressions for emotions. The body language analysis used facial expressions, physical touching, proximity measures, and classic dominance, subservience, awkwardness, and familiarity poses to estimate the relationship between two people interacting. The same software that allowed Cross to recognize the emotions of the humans she interacted with also allowed a Simon to estimate the relationship and emotions of two people interacting with one another.

[Poole sees Lassiter as a subordinate, and Lassiter treats him like a superior. But when they part, Lassiter is the respected subordinate. Lassiter smiles a lot, and actually mimics Poole's mannerisms and body language.]

"So Lassiter knows how to play people?" Nick looked over his shoulder at Pam. "He's a pretty handsome guy. Did he flirt with you?"

"Of course he did," Pam said, acting offended that Nick had to ask. "He was suave and sexy. But too old for me." She giggled and dipped her head back into her reading. Nick turned back to the viewer and mused about Craig Lassiter wanting to bed Pam.

Nick's mental wheels spun. Poole was a real estate business guy, in Alliance headquarters, talking with Lassiter. Doing business on the golf course. And they went from strangers to friends after a couple holes of golf. Was Poole in charge of the entire Alliance? "Do we have anyone Lassiter met in Celebration with who acted like his superior?"

[None that we have evidence of.]

Nick looked at the clock and stepped back from the viewer. He looked at the bleak darkness outside. The weather was wet, cold, and raw.

"I need a break." Nick got a cold glass of water and walked around the apartment until condensation ran down his hand.

It was a shame the Warrant had showed up after he had spent most of the day on his Earth-focused Kagent net. He looked at his viewer from across the apartment. He still had so much to do, but his brain was sagging. Time was running out though.

"Nick, you look tired. It's late."

[Listen to her] flashed across his viewer.

He turned to Pam and nodded, "I'm done for today."

CHAPTER THIRTY-SEVEN

HOUSTON WAS UNDER SIEGE AGAIN.

Every person Craig encountered throughout the Orlando airport felt compelled to remind him of this fact. He wondered if they truly expected him to cancel his flight because they happened to mention that fact. He wouldn't admit it to anyone, but the troubles there sent a thrill up his spine.

Besides, no commercial airliner had been shot down over Texas for at least three years. You had to take your risks, Craig had told Haruka while he waited to board. The flight was pleasant. The plane didn't even have to make a combat landing, and as the engines cycled down, Craig didn't hear any distant sounds of shelling. The terminal looked almost normal, except for the large numbers of Houston Republic Armed Forces eyeing all the passengers as they deplaned.

Craig waited an hour to clear the frisk line. Then he had to bite his tongue to not crack wise when the beefy young security guard gently groped his balls and rifled through his bag. One loon tapes a tiny grenade to his scrotum five years ago and everyone scores a free testicular exam.

Poole had sent a Rolling Fortress convoy to pick him up. These weren't civilian Rolling Fortress; they were painted a concrete gray and layered in extra armor. When Craig climbed in, a young guard inside handed him a helmet and helped strap him into seat restraints before strapping herself back in.

"Your boss picked a hell of a place to hole up in," Craig said to the guard while he adjusted his chin strap. "Who's attacking this time?"

The guard replied, "White Mules. They splintered off from the Values Coalition a few months back. Odds are they'll get beaten back within a week, but they almost took Baytown." She shook her head. "This place is straight-up crazy sometimes."

The convoy sped off south towards downtown, along highways without signs. Stern-looking HRAF soldiers brandishing giant assault rifles waved them through checkpoint after checkpoint.

The city itself seemed unperturbed by the violence at its borders and went about its business. Craig doffed the helmet. Climbing out of the Fortress, he craned his head to look up at the tallest building in Houston. The guard followed him in and keyed in a special elevator code. They rose forty floors above the street. When he stepped off the elevator, he heard the artillery thunder in the distance. The guard escorted him into a secure conference room. The lights were dim and the sounds outside died off when the door was closed.

Dave Poole sat at the conference table, poking numbers out of the air to build a spreadsheet. The last time Craig had seen Dave, the industrialist was happy, smiling, with a golf club in his hand and the sun on his face.

Now, dim orange light from the spreadsheet created deep shadows on his dour face and he had a gigantic gun holstered on his hip.

"Thanks for coming out here to meet me," he said, walking over to shake Craig's hand. He closed up the spreadsheet and synched his netpad to an old viewer on the wall.

"Do you normally hang out in war zones?" Craig asked, jabbing a thumb back at the door.

"Eh, those guys don't amount to much," Dave said. "It's the Austinites that keep me up at night. Either way, this is home and I don't run." He tapped at a console in the table and Ciebrian appeared on the viewer.

"Hello, men, it's good to see you both again," the South African said with a nod. "Craig, I'm so sorry we had to let you go. You say the word and I'll set you up with a job anywhere around the world."

"Thanks. I appreciate that," Craig said.

"Yeah, we've all been through those ups and downs before." Poole looked around the room and shook his head. "Hell, a month ago, I was looking at a big fat expansion. Now I'm hiding from threats." He filled an empty glass with water and took a long drink.

"A number of board members were profiled," Ciebrian explained. "Dave, me, Penny, Father March. I have alerts posted whenever someone tries to access private data on any of us. Even Father March, who can't afford his own privacy block."

"Doesn't that happen often?" Craig asked. "You are all business celebrities. I read press profiles of you all when I got the job."

"On the public nets, sure. But this was the bounty hunter databases." Dave shook his head. "That's disturbing. Whenever something like this happens, it could be someone out to harass you, ruin your personal life, or even kill you. A serious security threat."

Apparently, it scared him more than sitting 40 floors up while artillery shells zoomed by, fired by half-trained twenty-something dudes with poor math skills.

"Do we know who did the profiling?" Craig looked from Dave to Ciebrian. "My sources say that the Kagents have been trying to profile the Alliance, to figure out how to stop us. But I don't know who was behind these attempts."

Ciebrian shook his head.

"I'm afraid I do," Dave Poole said with a frown. "A Kagent working for offworld partners of a GoldLand subsidiary."

Craig frowned. "I don't know what to say." Besides thank you Eldred Borbola for setting up Cooper like this.

"Cooper? Actually that makes some sense to me," Ciebrian said. "He really thought the Burgess offer was the Alliance's last hope to contain the offworlders. He's getting desperate, Dave, I've been telling you that."

Craig shook his head. "Kagents are like bounty hunters on performance gels. They have tiny drones that spy everywhere. Celebration was infested with them recently and it took a solid week to clean them out. God only knows what they may have heard or saw."

Dave turned a shade of green. "Goddamn it."

Ciebrian said, "A number of our financial contributors were profiled, many that aren't on the Board, like Manuel Gallardo. But they all have some connection to the Alliance. The Kagents are probably targeting the Alliance's potential financial supporters."

"The Kagents want to destroy the Alliance so offworlders can buy out Earth unopposed," Craig added. "One of the Burgess negotiators was a Kagent. I ran into her in Celebration. They even violated their own ethics to come after us." He explained Lisa Radisson accusations.

There was a pause as Ciebrian and Dave digested that.

Ciebrian wagged a finger. "Cooper is a founding member. He loses the vote on the deal, he probably fears that he's losing his grip on the Alliance. He may be trying to make a move against us all."

Dave sighed. "It don't look good, that's for damn sure. But are you saying that he's working with these Kagents? Against us, against the Alliance?" He shook his head. "We should just talk to him before we do anything rash."

Ciebrian looked at Craig and back at Dave. "I would be shocked if he did anything besides deny it. Let me talk to Bobby and see what he knows."

"You know, Dave, you voted in favor of the deal, too," Craig pointed out. "Why would Cooper have the Kagents profile you, too?"

Dave frowned again. "I don't know. We've also lost a couple of projects with GoldLand recently. I didn't think much of it at the time, but now it's troublesome."

Ciebrian shrugged. "It could be another sign that he wants to move against us. At the time, firing Craig seemed like a small price to pay, no offense, to get Cooper's vote against the Burgess deal. Now it seems like the first step to taking control of the Alliance."

Dave frowned. "That's paranoid."

"'Paranoia' is just another word for due diligence," Ciebrian replied.

"You're saying the Kagents are coming after us?" Dave said. "We have an old saying around here: Once is a coincidence; twice is enemy intent."

"Then it's enemy intent," Ciebrian said. "That real estate deal was their first attempt to cripple the Alliance's capabilities. I know you didn't think so, Dave, but it was. This profiling is the second attack on us. This means war. Not too much different than what's happening up there in Houston right now."

Craig nodded. "The Kagents have wanted a way into the Alliance's organizational structure; they spied on Celebration. They are a fundamental threat to the Alliance and the cause."

Dave Poole rubbed his chin. "Ciebrian, you may be wrong, but to be safe we have to assume you're right." He spread his hands. "The Alliance is supposed to protect our identities. It just occurred to me that if we're exposed, we should leave the Board, to protect the other members and the Alliance."

"That would leave Cooper completely in charge," Ciebrian grumbled. "I'd have to rethink my support for the Alliance."

Craig tensed. He didn't know about that particular rule. Were they about to break off from the Alliance and take their considerable financial resources with them? He'd had no idea the Board members squabbled this much. He said, "If they drove you out, the offworlders would ultimately win. Let's not forget the Alliance's basic mission. If Cooper is working with the Kagents, he's abandoned it."

Ciebrian sighed and threw his hands up. "Cooper may be well-meaning, but it's time for him to leave the Board."

Dave sighed. "I've known Coop a long time, almost forty years. He's been a mentor to me, Ciebrian, a father figure. I'm having a hard time believing that he would sell out all of us to the Kagents."

"I know," the South African said. "I went to school with his son Bobby. In fact, I should talk to him before I come to any conclusions, either."

Dave smiled. "I would appreciate it if you did that, old pal."

Ciebrian nodded and signed off.

"Sorry for dragging you out here," Dave said to Craig. "Technically, none of this is your concern." He reached for an armored jacket. "I'll run you back to Bush myself so you can catch a flight back to Florida. I'm going to tour the front lines, anyway. Run up around the 610."

"Ho-ho, you have to let me ride along for that," Craig said.

Dave's eyebrows shot up. "You really want to see a live, old-fashioned Texan battlefield?"

"Hell, growing up in Louisiana, that's what we played all day."

Dave narrowed his eyes. "You ever see any actual action, Lassiter? This ain't like watching a tornado in the distance."

Craig saluted. "256th Infantry Brigade, Louisiana Regional Army, Sergeant Lassiter reporting. Helped put down the Shrimper Rebellion of '78."

Dave looked him up and down, and shook his head. "You're a crazy squirrel like the rest of us, Lassiter. I'm only going out there because I can't stand being holed up in here. And the rockets are so pretty at night."

Craig grabbed the helmet and body armor that Dave handed him. "Sounds like fun."

CHAPTER THIRTY-EIGHT

IT HAD BEEN A GRAY cold morning with no sign of the sun. Nick kept yawning as he trudged through data requests and small projects. He should have been excited since these jobs actually paid, unlike his profiling of Craig Lassiter.

Pam blocked Nick from going to his workstation though. She held up a protein bar and his bike helmet. "You need some exercise before you do anything else."

"I was streaming."

"Streaming doesn't involve snoring," Pam pointed out with a wry grin.

Nick pouted. "Don't you have to be at a meeting in the office or something?"

She shoved the bike helmet into his chest. "Get your blood moving, Lincoln, oxygenate your brain. You'll work more effectively. Come on."

Nick smiled when she wasn't looking, knowing she was right. She knew when to kick him in the butt.

A cold drizzle fell across the city when they wheeled onto the bike lane. Cars streamed by continuously on their left. They biked around the Palisades, up to Nelsa Park, and then back home. Nick focused on not slipping on the wet ground and keeping up with Pam, who had become an avid biker.

The exercise only held the raw cold at bay until they returned to their apartment building. As they climbed upstairs to the apartment

Nick was wet, chilled, and exhausted. But not so much that he could still appreciate how Pam's wet clothes and hair clung to her hips and back. The scent of cold rain and the elated post-exercise rush all jacked his mood and shifted the contents of his pants.

He let his mind wander to the last time he felt her bare hips, listened to her talk in stark and direct terms and push the limits of what he was comfortable with in bed. He wanted more of those memories, but first he needed to needed to get work done.

He dragged a chair from the kitchen over to his workstation. His legs needed to take a break. "Cross, where were we?"

[You seem distracted, to put it nicely,] Cross texted on the viewer. She was reading his bio telltales. Throbbing erections were clear as day on infrared.

"Never mind that." Nick reviewed the Lassiter and Poole footage again. "So, Lassiter is meeting with people high up in the Alliance. Poole could be an executive, the CEO, or just a donor who hangs out at headquarters for fun. Lassiter acts like the talk went well for him, which is bad for us. Maybe Poole joined the warpath, or at least turned against the Burgess real estate offer."

[That's a lot of inference and deduction based on a video of two guys far away playing golf.]

"Yeah, but what else do we have? I'd kill for some audio of that meeting."

[You would have to deploy more drones in town to get around the privacy blocks the BHN puts over the people Lassiter is with. And that would mean sending someone back to Celebration.]

Nick's instincts tingled because there was some thought lurking about Lassiter disappearing into other people's privacy blocks. If he couldn't track Lassiter inside those privacy blocks, he could at least track him when the privacy block moved across security cam footage. Two years ago, he had tracked Lisa Radisson by tracking the instances where someone evaded Hamilton street surveillance in a certain way.

"Track all of Lassiter's known movements and flag every time he disappears into someone else's privacy block. Chances are, it's another Alliance higher up like Poole. Or a rich donor. Either way, we may learn who it is. Start with Celebration."

Cross posted a series of graphics, timelines, and thumbnail video clips. "I have several blocks in the Orlando area. Many are around GoldLand properties. But, like Hamilton and the Stabilizer Alliance itself, they don't sell their data to the BHN, so it may not be a personal privacy block."

Nick smiled. The self-defeating drawback about using a privacy block was that the user couldn't hide the block itself from surveillance. It was like running down a street wrapped in a black sheet. No one may be able to identify you, but everyone could see you.

"Maybe Lassiter wanted to ride roller coasters," Nick mused. "Is there any overhead satellite coverage of the GoldLand properties? Or do they block satellites like the Stabilizers do?"

"The entire Orlando region is missing detailed satellite coverage," Cross reported. "There are low-resolution still images, however. But not enough to see individual buildings or vehicles."

Nick grimaced and stretched out his left leg to work out a kink in the muscle. His calf muscles would be screaming tomorrow. "Okay, let's run through all the other instances where he disappeared into a privacy block."

"Shanghai, when he left the airport terminal." Cross posted the footage. Lassiter stepped outside and the BHN coverage blacked out.

Nick leaned forward in his seat. "How big is that privacy block? Can you show me a time lapse of how big the privacy block is and where it goes?"

Cross posted an overhead shot of Shanghai on the viewer. The privacy block was relatively small, about the size of a car or truck. It left the airport arrival pickup and traveled across the city. There were about a dozen other privacy blocks of similar size traveling around town at the same time.

"When did Lassiter next appear," Nick said.

The next time he surfaced was in a park an hour later, and only for two minutes at a restroom. After that, it was two days before he was spotted leaving a posh hotel. He disappeared again and reappeared at the airport a day later to fly back to Florida.

"Can I just see the street cams where his car was traveling?" Nick asked.

Cross displayed a blurred picture from the street cam. The vehicle Lassiter was riding in was dark in color, but other than that, there was no identifying characteristic.

"Okay, dead end. A first-class block is first-class." Nick stood and walked into the kitchen to get a drink of water. "Follow the privacy block until it moves from the car."

The car stopped and the privacy block shifted to a nearby park. Lassiter must have stuck with the privacy block, or stayed in the car, which turned out to be a rented black luxury vehicle.

Nick searched the rental car company's records for who had taken it on this day, but he hit another privacy block.

The fuzzed-out privacy block walked around the park, into a building and back out an hour later. It returned to the car, which took the privacy-blocked Lassiter and guests to a posh hotel in Lujiazui. The hotel had its own giant privacy block on the whole building.

The next security cam footage of Lassiter was him leaving the hotel entrance a few days later and returning to the airport. Whoever had generated that privacy block around Lassiter evidently stayed at the hotel or left some other time.

"We know the privacy block isn't for him. He also didn't go through that hotel entrance until he left for the airport. He either snuck out some other way, or he never left the hotel. And I can think of only one reason to not leave a hotel." Nick whispered with a salacious grin.

[Let's not forget that you have hormones rattling around your brain.]

"I can't argue that. He could have attended a conference, or a meeting, or a wedding, for all we know. There could be another privacy-protecting donor or one of the executives," Nick said. "It's unlikely someone completely unrelated to the Alliance flew him out to Shanghai and back. Which people on the donor list have businesses in Shanghai?"

[Manuel Gallardo, Viktor Mamchev, Ciebrian Bieto, and Mary Eastland.] Cross posted the office locations on a Shanghai city map. [Lassiter didn't go near any of their offices or locations.]

Nick twirled a stylus around his fingers. "Did he ever talk to anyone on this donor list in the open?"

[Father Salvador March and Lassiter met up outside their home Community in Southern Louisiana shortly after Lassiter returned from India. Father March runs various religious missions in New York Jersey, Louisiana, and the Carolinas. He travels between them quite frequently. And he did not have a privacy block then, but he does now.]

"He's on the donor list, but his name is crossed off." Nick looked at Father March's profile. A poor Catholic priest who helped the downtrodden: gel addicts, the mentally ill, and the poor. There was probably plenty of burned-out buzzers, as Nick's mother liked to say, in all of those cities and zones.

Lassiter and March. They had met in a municipal building and talked about some local issues, according to the lip-read transcript Cross compiled from a security cam. The two men went outside and walked away, their backs to the camera. And no audio. They turned a corner and disappeared off the limited security in that parish.

"You've got to be kidding," Nick said. But he looked at the good father's profile closely. Between living in Stabilizer Communities and frequenting areas that were poor in many ways, including surveillance devices, he was only trackable about a third of the time. And that was when he was in New York Jersey. If Nick could find March, he might reach Lassiter. But to do that, he would have to be there in person. Dumping drones wouldn't work if they ran out of power and Lassiter disappeared again.

"Does March ever meet with anyone else on the donor list?" Nick asked.

[Not that's visible. But with privacy blocks involved, it's impossible to know for certain.]

"Show me." Nick hoped there was some crossover with Lassiter, and that he could deduce who these hidden individuals were. He was thinking that whoever March talked to had to be a prime candidate for twisting, if those people were in the Alliance.

All of March's interactions with privacy blocks were in New York Jersey, either at his mission, his church, or just passing privacy-conscious people on the street.

Nick swallowed his disappointment. He turned from the viewer. Pam was studiously trying not to watch him as she read her netpad on the couch.

"I'm making progress," he said. It came out sounding defensive. "I may have a way to catch Lassiter. He has a friend he visits in New York Jersey and I may just have to stake it out."

Pam looked up at him with sultry eyes. "Good. Now come here and massage my lips."

He grinned and joined her on the couch. She gave him a quick kiss and then pushed him away.

"Not on the cock-block couch," she said and stood up. Nick followed her towards the bedroom.

CHAPTER THIRTY-NINE

NICK PULLED PAM INTO A close embrace as he kicked the door closed. They kissed tenderly then urgently. Nick's hands slid along her hips and sides.

She smelled of citrus and cinnamon. The pungent odors of the greenhouse faded away when she was this close. "Everything will be okay," she said.

"I believe you," he said and kissed her again.

She pulled his shirt open, the micro-velcro parting silently, and ran her hand across his skin until his nipples stiffened. He pulled her hips close so she could feel what else had stiffened.

She smiled and then dove for his mouth tongue-first. The air in Nick's lungs ebbed eventually, and his skin became prickly and hot. He pulled back to recover and she pushed off of him.

She back-pedaled towards the bed and tossed her t-shirt and panties across the room as she went. The contrast between her pale skin and black hair, brown eyes, maroon nipples, and the black triangle between her legs invigorated him like splashing through a cold stream on a hot day.

She pulled his clothes off when he approached, something she enjoyed doing. He cupped his hand around her side but she dodged away.

He chased after her and she giggled, but he had her cornered. She grabbed him, using her index finger to send little electric thrills through his balls. He cupped her small breasts and kneaded them roughly enough that she closed her eyes and purred.

She pulled him against her, pressing herself against the greenhouse's stained glass wall. She opened her right leg and he felt warmth envelope him.

They rocked against the wall. She gently-but-steadily pushed him deeper on each thrust. His thumbs flicked her nipples and he buried his face in her hair.

She crushed him as he came. The climax roller-coasted in three waves. Then she was kissing him again, on the ear, the cheek, his lips, his neck.

She pushed him back to the bed and straddled his stomach. Her hair was a curtain framing her deeply-aroused face. She drove herself against his waistline, dry-humping his torso.

The humping wasn't dry, though.

Nick's hands slid up her inner thighs until his thumbs met. Her eyes shut and she bent over him, her black hair tickling his forehead. His hands had no choice but to return to her breasts. He gripped them roughly, supporting her weight, and she blew a breath through gritted teeth. The salty, musky tang of sex began to arouse him again.

Pam kissed him on the forehead, nose, lips. She slid back, smiled ferociously, and licked above his left knee. Her tongue wandered left, right, and then up his thigh. She was in a kinkier place than he was comfortable with, but he had learned it was better not to stop her.

She lapped at his goose-bumped skin, her tongue circled around and ventured to his other thigh. She went slow enough to be just shy of torturous. Nick twisted the bed sheet in his hand.

Pam chuckled, but it was a husky, throaty chuckle and she nudged him with her tongue. She flicked her tongue around the base and then worked her way up to the tip.

Nick's old-fashioned Earth sensibilities, as Pam had mocked them, rushed back for a second. He couldn't help it; it just felt doing this was demeaning to the giver, regardless of who they were. But hell, she enjoyed it. She had told him a long while ago that where she came from, it was a perfectly acceptable expression of sexual power and who was he to deny her? She thought his hangup was silly and no reason she couldn't indulge herself. Once, she even told him to just lay back and think of the Sphere.

A hot, soft waterfall descended on him as she indulged.

He was on the rebound, no doubt. But not so early that it didn't feel damn good. He hardened quickly.

She let him go, running her tongue across her teeth like a tiger savoring the last bits of its meal.

She rolled over onto her side, tugging at him to come along. The blow job was just a setup, he realized.

His fingers traced their way down to where her legs met. She inhaled deeply as his fingers circled. She manhandled him and inserted him again.

He rode along with her thrusting, his finger circling mercilessly between their bodies. His arm was bent at an odd angle, but he didn't care. Things were starting to feel really good inside her. He was not letting go for anything.

She metered his thrusting with her hands, her sharp nails scratching his cheeks. She faltered as a spasm took hold and bit her lip. Then she opened her eyes and looked up at him, her eyes locked on.

"Cum with me," she panted. She cupped his face in her hand. "Look at me."

He opened his eyes, not realizing he had closed them. The moment became twice as intense. His fingers reversed direction. Her thigh muscles tensed and her stomach went rigid against his arm.

Still, she stared at him, her brown eyes wide and twinkling. Her hand fell to his shoulder and the intensity ratcheted upwards. Nick could feel pressure building.

She climaxed with her enlarged pupils searching his, her

body a giant vise, squeezing him. She spasmed and gasped and spasmed again.

With another thrust, he broke loose, his eyes still locked on hers. He kept coming and coming as they slowed down, until there was nothing left inside of him, but he didn't blink.

As he collapsed into her arms, it felt like they had pounded away all the stupid complications, distractions, disappointments, and concerns. There was something elemental that existed between them underneath all that superficial crap. Something unbreakable and intricately compatible.

He kissed her deeply, not caring where her mouth had been a few minutes ago. His horniness was washed away and replaced with contentment. He felt wildly, massively, passionately in love with her. He had never had such an intense, naked moment with anyone before.

She held him close and tight, the two still interconnected, and she caressed his back. They exchanged a round of 'I love you's' that seemed utterly incapable of expressing what they were both feeling.

He thought, if they could just tap into this love, they could withstand all the crap the rest of the world threw at them. He might even succeed in the impossible tasks he had assigned himself.

She said, "You have an odd look on your face."

"What?"

She thought about it. "Confidence." She wrapped her legs around his back. "I like it."

"Are you going to let me up?" he asked.

She frowned. "No. Stay here. Enjoy the moment."

He relented and snaked his hands under her back. Then he tucked his face into her soft hair, a homey sanctuary he didn't ever want to leave. Of all the moments in one's lifespan, it was best to spend as many as possible like this. He relaxed and hung on as long as she let him.

CHAPTER FORTY

CRAIG HAD TO GO BACK to New York Jersey if he wanted to catch up with Sal, who was working in his Brooklyn mission during a cold snap. Craig was concerned about the Kagents profiling his friend's life without any privacy blocks to stop them. Sal had family back in South Haven and he was the most exposed of all the Board members.

Brooklyn hadn't changed in over a hundred years. When the old 19th and 20th century buildings had begun to crumble, developers replaced them with the then-latest craze in construction: a narrow, glazed-white brick that had the strength of steel and was insulated like fiberglass. Like a lot of 22nd century fads, it was manufactured offworld in zero-g kilns and had the novelty of looking unlike anything else.

A few decades later, the bricks faded and turned a fleshy pink. Rather than accept a house or apartment building that looked like a pile of pink flesh, people painted them with any number of neutral grays, to bring back the early 22nd century look. Now, the buildings in need of a fresh coat of paint resembled squarish elephants with cracked gray skin and fleshy, open wounds.

Craig stepped off the bus to the saltwater smell of the ocean, a blue sky, crowded streets, and a cold, whistling wind. The gray houses stretched down the street in both directions, with only a handful of pink bricks peeking out underneath.

He found a Ray's Pizza near the mission and texted Sal to join him. He could eat pizza all day in this place. The smell of tomato, basil, and baked dough was like a gel high.

The Italian *padre* showed up half-an-hour later, not even wearing a coat. They hugged, ordered a pizza, and sat down. Sal cupped his hands together and blew in them to warm them. "What will you do now?" he asked. "Start over again? At your age?"

Craig shrugged. "I'll figure something out."

The pizza arrived and Sal grumbled about there being too much before they each took a slice. Craig, with his mouth full, told him to take the extras back to the mission.

"You're a dumbass, sacrificing the job to kill a perfectly good deal," Sal said after he swallowed a bite. He washed it down with cold water in a white paper cup.

"I didn't come up here to argue about that again," Craig said. "I'm checking to see if you're okay with people profiling you and all that crap." It was only half-true. He had come back to the city for another reason entirely, but needed an excuse.

"I'm fine," Sal said. "My life is an open book for any who want to look around. Other than certain obligations, you know." He balled up his napkin and tossed it on his plate. "Why am I eating this shit? It's horrible for my poor arteries."

Craig said around a mouthful, "Have some more red pepper; you're going to heaven, anyway."

Sal laughed. "You bastard." He drank more water. "So, what's with you and Haruka Gallardo? Don't deny it. Mandy DeCasas has been blabbing about it to everyone."

"Oh, you don't want to know." Craig saw that this wouldn't appease his friend, so he swallowed and wiped his hands. "It's debauched and sinful. We're a thing, possibly serious. Happy?"

Sal grinned in a way that was anything but priestly. "'Serious'? She's Catholic, you know. She's rich, too. Is that why you let Coop fire you?"

"I'm no gold digger," Craig said, offended.

Sal punched him in the arm, as he always had done when Craig blasphemed.

"Here comes virgin Salvador, brother of Christ," Craig said. He used his teeth to tear at the soft, juicy dough that always sat right in front of the crust.

"What about settling back home?"

Craig eyed him warily. "There's enough unemployed Lassiters down there. But now that you mention it, maybe I can use Haruka's family money to move my mother some place nicer, away from my brother and his wife."

Sal shook his head. "Craig, Craig. What kind of Stabilizer are you?"

"Eh, I'd rather settle in with her family. Go boating in the South China Sea with her nephews and nieces. So, how's the buzzer salvage business here in Sin City?"

"Come with me and see. Stop eating that shit; you've had enough." Sal took Craig's plate and tossed it in the nearest trash can.

"Hey!" Craig said with his mouth full.

"Haruka will thank me. Let's go."

Craig swore under his breath and followed his old friend outside. The wind had stopped and the temperature was rising.

"We've expanded our services," Sal said as they weaved around a sidewalk art sale. "We offer massage therapy, career counseling, and stress management."

"Palliative care, huh? Given up on recruitment, then?"

Sal shook his head. "We do whatever it takes to get people in the door."

They reached Nostrand Avenue, turned north, and stopped at a brownstone building that was a faded grey with pink cracks. A sign above the door read, 'Stability Mission.'

"Come on, let's go inside," Sal said. "You've seen the worst of New York Jersey; now see some redemption."

Craig grimaced. "You mean losers, gelheads, addicts. You know they make me unexplainably angry."

"Like you're much better at this point." Sal said as he hiked up the brownstone's steps.

Craig followed him inside. It was dark and dingy. There was a tiny chapel off the entrance.

"The Alliance doesn't pay for maintenance, anymore. I had to do a fundraiser to just replace the wood paneling in the chapel."

Craig pointed at water stains on the ceiling. "It still looks like shit. You proselytizing in the mission, *padre*? Baptizing converts in a tub upstairs?"

"We only provide non-denominational services and counseling," Sal said. He talked to a receptionist AI named Margy at the front desk.

"You have three bbbzzeeesshhhh waiting to see you," Margy said with a lisp of static.

Sal gave Craig a knowing look. "It's hard to convince people the stable lifestyle is better when this is their first brush with it. Only about one out of every twelve ships out for a Community. Most buzzers just want a shoulder to cry on. You want to sit in on an interview?"

Craig held up a hand. "No, thanks. I might slug someone. I should be off." He pulled Sal into a hug.

"Peace be with you, bro," Sal said. "Keep in touch."

Craig turned to the front door, which also was in bad need of a coat of paint. "I'll send you more pictures of naked Tahitians."

"My bishop didn't think that was funny!" Sal yelled, but Craig was already out the door.

245

CHAPTER FORTY-ONE

CRAIG HADN'T BEEN TO CONEY Island since he and Dan had led a protest march along the seawall twenty-odd years ago. It was one of the few spots he liked in the Big Apple.

There weren't any taxis within sight, so Craig walked south towards Avenue U, where he could see more traffic. The white puffy clouds beelined it across the blue sky and he needed the exercise.

Two blocks later, Craig had the feeling someone was watching him. A man walked by him, entranced by his netpad. A little girl in a stroller coming towards him looked at him with her hand in a tentative wave. Craig waved back and the girl broke into a smile. The mother was fussing with a blanket and didn't notice. The kid lunged to look back at him and he waved again.

As Craig turned back the way he came, someone appeared in front of him and said, "Can I ask you something?" Craig found a young guy with spiky black hair standing in front of him, wearing shades, three weapons and looking like a bounty hunter.

"I'm too busy right now," Craig said, stepping to the side to pass him.

"No, you're not. Craig."

Craig tensed and looked around for a street camera. There was one hanging over the corner up ahead. But would that matter? This so-called Kagent could shoot him, or zap him, long before Borbola swooped in.

Craig squinted at the guy, as if he were trying to recognize him.

But he had a good idea that this Nick Lincoln, the offworld bounty hunter who was after him. "If you know who I am, then message me later." He started walking past Lincoln, looking at the street camera, hoping someone was watching this. The cam looked really far away, though. "Stop, Craig! You're coming with me," the man said.

Craig turned around and looked at him. The pizza in his belly began doing the backstroke. But Lincoln wasn't even reaching for one of his weapons. He couldn't force Craig to do anything out here on the heavily-surveilled streets of New York Jersey.

Craig smiled. "Go screw."

"Wrong answer," Lincoln said.

Craig heard a buzzing noise and felt a sharp shock on top of his head. It made his scalp tingle. "Ow! what the hell?"

He looked up to see what bit him. There was a small cloud of gnats flying right above his head. Except, they weren't flying random patterns like real gnats would. These gnats were flying in perfect circles and figure eights. And they weren't gnats.

A taxi stopped at the curb and the door cracked open.

"Get in," Lincoln demanded. "I can knock you out and drag you in there, or you can spare yourself the headache."

There was no way Craig was getting in that cab. He looked around, but the street was pretty empty. The mother with the kid had turned the corner.

Craig spread his hands. "Not till you tell me what I'm charged with. Otherwise, the cops can come and sort this all out." It might buy him time.

Lincoln looked down at his netpad. "Okay, we'll call the cops. They'll be real sympathetic to the guy who tried to start a civil war here once."

Craig's smile fell away.

He was considering what to do when there was a buzz-like whistling noise and the taxi lurched backwards like a giant gnat had stung it.

There was a smoking hole in the taxi's rear engine compartment.

247

Craig's netpad rang with an incoming call chime. A special chime he had reserved for another bounty hunter. His netpad had an incoming message: *Run.*

"Shit," said Nick Lincoln in front of him.

Craig looked up and saw the gnats above him get attacked by other gnats. Some of them sparked and fell into his hair. He frantically brushed them out, hoping they wouldn't burn him, and started running.

He ran up an old-fashioned asphalt parking lot. The backside of the businesses offered no escape. There was a backyard ahead walled off by a pink-brick wall about as tall as he was.

He contemplated hiding in the parking lot by the dumpsters, but the gnats had him spooked. He needed to put some distance between them and him.

He climbed the fence, his feet slipping against the smooth, plasticky bricks. Finally, he was up and over, and dropped into the yard behind. Pain lanced up from his left ankle to shin, but he hobbled at top speed.

The backyard had a picnic table, grill, bicycle, and—Thank God – a driveway leading to the next street.

He hurried down the driveway. *Stupid,* he realized. He should have gone up to Avenue S and found a deli to hide in. Out here, he was visible and susceptible to whatever tiny offworld drones Lincoln had.

His netpad chimed again. It was Borbola calling. "Why are you running? I chased him off. Dumbass didn't expect a drone fight out here."

"You didn't get him?" Craig asked.

"No, but he's headed west. You're safe. I've got eyes on you. I'll meet you."

Craig found himself breathing hard. Climbing that damn fence hadn't been easy. He felt his ankle and rotated his foot. He really hoped he hadn't broken or sprained it.

"Why the hell did you let him get so close?" he asked. He could see Borbola at the end of the block and let the man come to him.

Borbola shrugged. "I couldn't scare him off by letting him see my drones. That was some tricky-ass work I just did back there."

The bounty hunter was close enough that Craig killed the call. "He could have killed me."

Borbola grinned. "Relax. Don't you know what it means to be bait?"

Craig didn't answer. Yes, he was bait and the Kagent had fallen for it. "Did you get everything you need?"

Borbola tapped the thigh pocket that his netpad was tucked inside of. "Police cam footage."

Mention of the police made him uneasy. "Good. I want to get out of here."

"First, let's get a taco," Borbola said.

"You're hungry *now*?"

The bounty hunter turned around. "Yeah. I know this taco place down at Coney Island. And you need to walk that off."

"What if it's broken?"

Borbola tapped his netpad and started walking. "It's not."

CHAPTER FORTY-TWO

"CROSS, WHO THE HELL WAS that back there?"

[I don't know. Clearly, those were offworld drones. It looked like they were handled by a trained user.]

"Were they handled sophisticated enough to be controlled by a Simon?" Nick asked. He knew that if you watched a drone swarm carefully, you could tell if they were following pre-programmed flight patterns or if someone was manipulating them on manual. A human could manually control a couple of sub-swarms, but not thousands individually.

[Either it was a Simon or a sophisticated program.]

"Borbola doesn't use a Simon, does he?" Nick asked.

[He didn't use an advanced one against the Dragoons at the Hamilton liftport. Why would you think it was him?]

Nick thought about it. "Check to see if any other Kagents are down here. You can search by Kagent netpad locators."

[There aren't any. Borbola is the only known non-Kagent to use offworld drones on Earth.]

"Shit. Who else could it be but Borbola?" Nick tried to wrap his brain around that. Borbola had fed him the information about Lassiter, from his 'source' inside Alliance. If Borbola had betrayed Nick, Lassiter could be the source. Why betray Lassiter to Nick, if Borbola had to protect him? Who was twisting whom, then?

Cross posted the security cam feeds around Nostrand Avenue coming through on the BHN. They were blinking out one by one down S Avenue at around walking speed. [NYJPD have not mentioned an outage. It has to be a BHN block.]

"Someone is blocking the feeds from reaching the BHN." Nick wanted to cry. "A bounty hunter. It has to be Borbola."

[Borbola? Why would he help Lassiter?]

Indeed, why? Borbola thought the Alliance was a threat. Was he using Nick to dig deeper into the Alliance, using the Alliance to mess with Nick, or playing them both against the other for some reason, or just for fun? He had no idea.

Did the reason matter, though? Nick mentally kicked himself for ever trusting Borbola. He had played Nick for some purpose and had a reason to protect Lassiter right now. If Bridge were alive, he probably would have talked Nick out of cooperating with the bounty hunter.

"Track the outages," Nick noted. "I want to make another attempt on Craig Lassiter. See what Borbola does, if it is him."

[There is a large and extensive field of drones surrounding each outage. The chances that you could apprehend Lassiter are very low.]

Cross posted a map of several square blocks of Brooklyn on Nick's smartshades. Infrared from the city's overhead assets clearly showed a speckling field of tiny heat signatures moving down Avenue S. The drone field was almost twice as large as what Nick had.

Nick zoomed in and the map went black. Another block on the BHN. Nick shook his head. He was hoping to surprise Lassiter during a quiet moment and take him to a secure spot for extensive questioning. He was sure he could have broken open the whole Alliance at that point. But not if Borbola and his drone air force were protecting Lassiter. *I need proof that the bounty hunter really is Borbola. I just can't believe it, otherwise. If a former Kagent has thrown in with the Stabilizers, it could be almost as bad as Lisa having a netpad.*

Nick zoomed out on the Brooklyn map. "The drone field is collapsing."

251

[They are getting in a taxi. Destination is Giuliani-Sinatra Airport, according to the taxi company.]

"That could be a diversion."

[Unlikely. The BHN blackout has stopped and they are no longer on the street. You'll never reach Flushing ahead of them, even if you got a taxi right now.]

Nick stopped walking down the sidewalk, his face numb from the betrayal. How else could he stop Lassiter and Borbola from fleeing? If Borbola managed to get Lassiter out of here, Nick had a strong feeling that he would never find the Stabilizer again.

"Tell the NYJPD to stop them at the airport. Text Pam and have her call the Burgess people, so they can contact their NYJ rep to back us up."

[What will you do?]

Nick said, "Chase them to the airport, I guess."

How much did Lassiter and the Stabbies now about what he was doing? Would Borbola have spilled everything or only select bits? Did he ever show all of his cards to anyone? Nick thought not because underneath the tough guy exterior, Borbola really didn't trust anyone. He could be running his own scam against the Stabilizers and he needed Lassiter free only for the moment. Anything was possible.

"Cross, send this to Borbola," Nick said. "'I almost nabbed Lassiter in Brooklyn, but was stopped by your drones. Convince me you didn't just hammerfucking betray me to the Alliance. All the best, Nick.'"

[Sent]

Nick walked another ten meters.

[Borbola responded by laughing and saying he wishes he could have seen the look on your face.]

Nick's face flushed with anger and he stopped walking. "How strong is our confirmation that Borbola is on Lassiter's side?"

[I have several minimal quality facial stills from them getting in the taxi. Why?]

"I want to profile Borbola. He's connected to Lassiter, and the Stabilizers, so he's covered by the Warrant now."

[He'll know the second you try to profile him on the BHN. Also, he probably has a first-class privacy block.]

Nick nodded. "Do it, anyway. So, he knows I'm not giving up." The BHN would be a dead end. What else could he use? He only had his own homegrown Kagent net covering Earth and the Kagent nets themselves.

[I have visual confirmation of Borbola and Lassiter in the taxi.] Cross posted a grainy video clip of the two of them inside the cab. Facial recognition metrics circled around them, showing the match. [This is from a bike messenger's headcam.]

"Well, shit." Nick stared at the viewer, not wanting to believe his eyes. "Send that to the Kagent Privacy Council, the Burgess Consortium, Pam, the NYJPD. Everyone needs to know that Borbola has betrayed us."

[I have the Radissons' profile of Borbola when he applied to be a Kagent from over ten years ago.]

"Hail a taxi," Nick said. "I want to be at the airport on the off-chance that the police can detain them."

A taxi zoomed up the street in less than twenty seconds and Nick climbed in. It took off north, heading west to Ocean Parkway. It would be a fight across the eastbound rush hour traffic coming out of Manhattan.

[The NYJPD says Borbola claims that Lassiter is a prisoner. They can't interfere.]

Nick frowned. The bounty hunter exemption had saved him tons of grief when he was one. So long as a bounty hunter wasn't violating local laws, the police were hands-off. Of course Borbola would use it as a shield.

Cross posted the other taxi's position on Nick's smartshades. They were already halfway to the Prospect Parkway with a three-minute lead. When his taxi reached the Gowanus Expressway, Nick accepted the fact that he wouldn't catch them. In an autodrive grid, there were no secret shortcuts, traffic jams, or accidents to shrink a lead.

"Where are they flying to?"

[Lassiter is on a Stabilizer Alliance chartered flight headed to a refueling in Vancouver. Beyond that, no flight plan has been filed.]

"Borbola?"

[He is scheduled to depart on three flights today, ten flights tomorrow from those destinations, and fifteen the day after that from the second destinations. He's also on eight returning flights back to NYJ.]

"Misdirection. He may not even leave the city."

[Could you take him right now if you did catch him?]

Nick shook his head. "No. I'm not ready. Can we track Borbola's offworld drones? We should be able to spot him wherever he pops up." Borbola always gave Nick shit about keeping a perimeter deployed, right? Nick would love to use that to catch him.

[We would need infrared modes on a sensing platform, preferably at ground level, to see them. Most feeds on the BHN lack the ability to detect offworld drones.]

"Let me see the Radissons' profile of him."

It was a tantalizing peek inside the life of the man who later became a bounty hunting legend. His early bounty hunting career had been stellar, which is what brought him to the attention of the Kagents. However, his Kagent psyche profile labelled him as having trust issues, and generally being a self-absorbed jerk who enjoyed showing off. It was surprising that Bridge took him on as a student, but hey, no one is perfect, right?

The Kagent profile included his actual family name. Borbola had grown up in southeastern Europe, and his parents were of African and Bosnian heritage. Nick wouldn't query the surname, because he didn't want to alert Borbola.

"We'll stick to the amoeba nets if we have to. There's no way he chases down every query by a 12-year-old fan of bounty hunters. Not without several Simons to do that work for him."

The taxi passed a sign for Giuliani-Sinatra. Cross posted a security cam feed of Lassiter hurrying to the chartered flight terminal. The feed cut out at that point.

Borbola's taxi rejoined traffic, with no destination listed on the taxi company database. Or, at least, none that was reported to the BHN. And then all BHN feeds in the area around the airport died.

"Borbola, I'm coming for your ass," Nick said between clenched teeth. "Right after I figure out where it is."

CHAPTER FORTY-THREE

PEARL RAPPED GENTLY ON THE double doors to Meredith's office. Meredith's lilting voice told her to come in and Pearl slipped between the doors as quiet as she could. She hoped the others working nearby weren't watching or paying attention, but she knew they were. Everyone was worried about Meredith.

Yesterday, Lisa had been shipped back to Earth for trial in several cities. She was facing multiple life terms in some maximum security prison. Meredith had a chance to visit her before she left Tessa forever, but she passed on the opportunity. And had been acting fine ever since.

Meredith sat at her desk, looking out the window at the orange horizon. A sandstorm was brewing out there, ready to wash over Concordia's beige city tent and to scour the side of the skyscraper.

"Pam should be online in a moment," Pearl said.

"Good. Sandstorms are mesmerizing, but soothing," Meredith said, nodding towards the window. "Especially when you're protected by all of these windows. They hit the building and the tent so hard, but they don't affect anything. I keep remembering that to maintain perspective. Harmless storms can happen."

"You're trying to tell me you're okay, when you can't be okay," Pearl said. Meredith had been suspended and even had to turn control of the firm over to Pearl while the Kagent Privacy Council investigated her. "Not after what's happened."

Meredith looked at her confused. "Oh, you're talking about Lisa."

Her expression sobered. "I was talking about the latest projections." She pointed at the viewers arrayed along the far wall, near the doors.

Pearl looked at the viewers, unsure how to handle the subject change. "Everyone is concerned about you. How you're taking Lisa leaving."

Meredith folded her hands together at her waist. "I'll know exactly where she is, if I ever change my mind about visiting her. But she and I have gone our separate ways, so I don't think that will happen. There's nothing more to say about it."

Pearl swallowed. Meredith didn't roll out her imperious tone very often. The tone strongly encouraged dropping the subject.

Another viewer flared to life and Pam Sullivan appeared from the neck up. "It's so good to see you both. How are you, Meredith?"

"I am focused on this project," Meredith said curtly. "I'm sorry. Let's not waste time talking about bygones when you're paying rates for emergency video chat."

"Borbola has joined the Stabilizers," Pam blurted. "Nick has proof. He's chasing after him."

To kill Borbola or be killed by him, Pearl mused. It sounded like the kind of stupid bounty hunter vendetta that made her hate her home planet. No matter how long she stayed away from Earth, she could never get away fully.

The most resourceful bounty hunter, with insider Kagent knowledge, joins the Alliance. And if the Alliance was working off of Lisa's Kagent access, too, they were twice as screwed as they had thought.

"For a long time, Borbola has thought of us as the enemy," Meredith said. "He must think the Alliance can oppose us. It's a vote of confidence in their capabilities."

"But what can he do for the Stabilizers?" Pam asked.

Pearl replied, "He's a bounty hunter. He's violent. Are they embracing violence?"

"Or he's changed. He could train them how to treat offworld

Kagents like the Dragoons," Meredith replied. "And that may be why these projections look so bad. And what's worse, so vague."

Pam added, "The question is: is Borbola just an operative, or does he influence the Alliance's strategy, too?"

Meredith shook her head. "Either way, he's dangerous. How much of the information that he gave Nick do you think is compromised?"

Pam turned a shade paler. "Nick hopes Borbola will tell him, once he's caught. It could be all of it."

Meredith paused and smiled sweetly at Pam's image. "Nick will be okay, I'm sure."

Pam nodded, but her jaw muscles worked to keep her composure in place. "Yes. Something else has happened that I should mention. The business sites are reporting that Cooper just stepped down as CEO of GoldLand Entertainment."

Pearl gasped. Old Uncle Coop was a fixture from her childhood. He must be over 75, now, if she had to guess. "What? He built that company. He's a living legend. Why?"

Pam looked at her netpad. "The company issued standard boilerplate about retirement, taking the company in a fresh direction. He is in his 80s and thought it was time for the next generation. His son Robert is taking over."

Pam continued, "We've suspected that Cooper Mangold was involved in the Alliance in some way. He wasn't on the donor list that Nick received from Borbola though. But GoldLand's approach to business adheres closely to the Stabilizer philosophy. GoldLand's headquarters are also in Orlando, very close to the Celebration headquarters."

Meredith bit her lower lip. "We've been concerned about the Alliance, with Craig Lassiter driving the ship. Now it looks like a possible ally of the Alliance is changing, and the Alliance has both Borbola and Lassiter on board. What do we know about Mangold's son?"

Pam looked at her netpad. "I have a dossier, but it's thin, mostly from press reports. I'll send it to you anyway. There's nothing about how he may feel about the Stabilizers, or offworld. But on the plus side, the transition to him could knock out any Stabilizer involvement from GoldLand for the next number of months."

"There could be an opportunity to affect the Alliance then, if its backers are distracted," Meredith said.

"That's what Nick is thinking," Pam replied. "I'm not so sure though. It depends on how tightly GoldLand and the Alliance are coordinating. The son could be a clone of his father on Stabilizer issues, or totally different. It may take a while for that to percolate down to affecting the Alliance. If there is any relationship at all."

Meredith waved at the numbers on the screen. "Perhaps that explains the projections looking dire."

Pam cleared her throat. "Um, Meredith, are you allowed to see those? You're still suspended."

"I am. Pearl has been feeding me projections like I'm a client."

Pam tilted her head. "I'm sorry, I had to ask. Nick and I have debated whether GoldLand is an Alliance supporter. GoldLand is heavily dependent upon offworld customers. Much more than those on the fundraising list that Nick obtained. I'll watch GoldLand closely. Things may get worse if they try to move away from profit centers that are reliant on offworlders."

"Good point," Meredith said. "Thanks, Pam. Give Nick my best." The call ended. She grew thoughtful in a cold, calculating way. Pearl had not seen her look like that before.

Meredith turned to her and said, "We're headed for a major battle with the Stabilizers. It may be peaceful, and fought in Pam's realm, or on the streets. We need to update our succession plans and prioritize workloads in case a number of us need to leave suddenly."

She turned to the projections. "Nearly all of the mutually beneficial paths have dropped to low probabilities. But our confidence on the tactical front is also low. The Stabilizers aren't holding protests, staging liftport takeovers, or anything like that. With Borbola joining, it's more unclear what the Stabilizers may do."

"I really don't want to go back to Earth," Pearl said, thinking she was picking up on a hint. "But I will if you think it's that important."

Meredith smiled a little and nodded. "No, I want you here. You're in charge."

Pearl frowned. "Do you think Borbola will come after you? Harm you?" Visions came to mind of assigning her a guard detail and drone defenses. Meredith was thinking something, or knew something, but she was holding it close.

"I don't know, dear. But you should also choose a backup. Develop a plan for the firm to continue even if something happens to any given member."

Pearl folded her arms. "You think the entire firm could be threatened?"

Meredith swallowed and looked at the floor, almost fatalistically. "We have to be ready for anything."

CHAPTER FORTY-FOUR

"GOOD WEATHER FOR AN OUTDOOR wedding reception," Nick said as he sipped a carbonated lemonade. He sat at a sidewalk cafe under the shade of a red-and-green umbrella. The hot late afternoon sun drenched northern Normandy in heat. For once, his smartshades were entirely appropriate to wear.

The cafe was on the Grande Rue of the Mont Saint-Michel abbey. Nick watched tourists tromp past the picturesque three-story stone buildings crowded together on either side of the narrow street. The happy tourists wore shades not much different than Nick's.

Nick liked Normandy. The ocean views were exquisite. The rising English Channel had made the abbey an island. What had already been a breath-taking cathedral on a hill, a walled abbey and fortress among mud flats, was now surrounded by crashing waves and salty spray.

Church bells clanged in a joyous melody. The wedding was over. The wedding party would be on the move soon. Nick checked the drone dashboard on his smartshades. Thousands of his drones were deployed across the ancient monastery, ready to be activated. He had drones hovering over the entire abbey, around the cathedral, and on each level down to the exit.

Nick pulled the white Panama hat snug and low on his head. You couldn't be too careful when you tried to take down Eldred Borbola. He flipped to the live feed from the drones hovering above the cathedral's highest tower. The wedding reception was in the lower part of the fortified town, at a private outdoor piazza with a gorgeous view of the Channel. The drones covering the reception site showed caterers scurrying from table to table, dispensing silverware and linen napkins.

The happy wedding couple led a procession down from the cathedral through the winding stone streets. The bride was a rising star in the micro-cobbler field and wore a highly refractive white gown that glowed in the sunshine. The groom was a commodities trader who wore a dark-green suit. He was also Borbola's cousin.

Cross highlighted the bounty hunter in the middle of the parade of relatives, well-wishers, and friends leaving the church. Borbola's mother was on his arm, walking with a small limp and talking with her sister, mother of the groom.

"What are we facing?" Nick asked Cross. Borbola was wearing a respectable gray suit and appeared unarmed.

[Standard personal drone perimeter. Nothing else.]

Cross highlighted the energy signatures of a dozen drones circling Borbola. There were no active drones anywhere else in the abbey other than Nick's.

The wedding guests began to trickle out onto the piazza. The wedding couple wasn't with them; they reappeared on a balcony with a photographer.

Timing the attack on Borbola was tough. Should Nick strike before the meal? After the toasts? During the dancing? Before the cake-cutting? The garter dance? Nick wasn't an expert on hybrid wedding traditions of two families that hailed from across Europe and South America.

He decided to wait until after the dinner and the toasts. He ordered a ham sandwich on a baguette and watched the reception. The sun was setting over the Channel when the toasts ended. He wiped the baguette crumbs off his hands, paid the bill, and started walking uphill towards the restaurant hosting the reception.

He called Borbola. The bounty hunter looked at his netpad and ignored the call. Nick called again and he could see Borbola walk to a quiet corner to take it.

"Nick," Borbola said. "I can't talk right now. I'll call you later tonight."

"I can tell when you're lying, remember?"

Borbola chuckled. "I'm not lying. I'm in the middle of something."

"Beautiful bridal couple. Did you plan on dancing? I figured you could slip away easier when the music started."

The look on Borbola's face was priceless.

Nick activated his drones. All over Mont Saint-Michel, his drones powered up. They rose off the cathedral's flying buttresses and out of ancient corners. On the smartshades, it looked as if a plague of glowing locusts rose up into the skies above the fortified monastery.

Nick could see Borbola watching the same thing on his netpad. The bounty hunter's body language snapped into a tense, defensive crouch.

"What the hell are you doing?" Borbola said. He jammed an earpiece in his ear and began swiping at his netpad. His mother noticed and looked apprehensive. Borbola waved her away and walked over to a quieter spot by the railing. "Why did you track me here?"

"Because you betrayed me," Nick said. "We had an agreement about the Stabilizers. But you joined them. You joined Lassiter. And you twisted me."

Nick's drones hovering high above the cathedral sensed thousands of drones pouring out of a hotel room window near the piazza. Shit. Borbola had come prepared, of course.

"Don't make a scene, just leave quietly," Nick said. Borbola had roughly 20,000 drones, about a third of Nick's number.

"How dare you, of all people, come after me and my family?" Borbola rumbled in a low tone.

"I'm not after your family," Nick replied. "I'm after you."

"Is that worth your family's safety? I would never go after them like this, Nick, never," Borbola spat. "Until now."

"Let's leave both our families out of this," Nick replied. He had never heard Borbola angry like this before. "My drones are only here for you."

Borbola hung up and stomped out of the reception.

Cross gathered Nick's drones like disparate strands of spider web. The web constricted over Borbola's drones.

Borbola's drones assembled themselves into a Flying Wedge and struck. They aimed straight upwards, into the darkening night sky, to break Nick's web before it fully coalesced. Borbola was not coming quietly.

Nick's superior drone force bent but didn't break. The count of dead and lost drones blurred upward for a full minute as Borbola's drones killed about one and a half drones for every one they lost.

But then the tide began to turn. Borbola's drone count began to drop faster than Nick's and the forward movement of Borbola's wedge tactic slowed and then halted.

Sentry drones that Nick had stationed outside of the piazza found and attacked Borbola's personal drone escort. But the bounty hunter had his drones in a defensive screen and they let him hurry across the stone streets.

Mont Saint-Michel sported a bustling night life for a monastery with a population of less than one hundred. Borbola melted into the teeming crowds. But on infrared, his halo of drone energy signatures gave him away.

Nick was walking uphill from the lowest level, near the entrance. If the bounty hunter even made it that far, Borbola would have to go through him. Nick expected that Borbola would be in custody before he physically reached him.

The battle in the air was winding down, with Borbola's surviving drones scattering with Nick's drones in pursuit. Borbola's personal drone escort also scattered, eliminating Nick's easy marker of the bounty hunter's location.

Cross highlighted Borbola's head, but the crosshairs flickered as he became lost in the crowd. Nick doubted that Borbola would hide and wait Nick out. He would try to sneak around and get away quickly. Or jump out and murder Nick.

Two-thirds of Nick's drones hunted down Borbola's remaining drones, while Cross directed the other third to search for the bounty hunter.

Cross posted a new video on Nick's smartshades. [He's doubling back, walking uphill against the crowd leaving the cathedral.]

"If he's heading for the catacombs and tombs inside the cathedral, block that off. Take him down the first chance you get," Nick said. He really preferred if the drones took Borbola down. He wasn't sure he could do it himself. And outside the church was better than inside, because, well, God.

[Affirmative.]

A woman tending flowers in a second-story window stopped when she saw Nick's drone swarm fly by on the street below, chasing down Borbola's drones. But the light had faded far past dusk and she wasn't sure. She shrugged and went back to watering her flowers.

[He jumped down to a lower level. He must have noticed the drones at the cathedral.]

Borbola was on the stucco roof of the building on the Mount's next level down. He dropped to the street on that level.

Nick bit his lip. "I'm coming up. Box him in."

[He just went inside this building.]

It was a small sweets shop, where the closed door made it unwelcoming for an incoming drone swarm. Nick's surveillance drones peeked through the door's window, but lost sight of Borbola among the shelves and other shoppers.

The shop was a level above Nick and a quarter of the way around the Mount. He hurried against the crowd, making slow progress. With night falling, the tourists were flooding towards the exit to return to the mainland.

"Don't let him get out the back," Nick said.

Cross parked the swarm above the shop, covering a side alley and the entrance to the street. They were poised to swoop down the second that Borbola popped out.

That was when Borbola's drones suddenly coalesced into a Flying Wedge formation and attacked Nick's drones. It was a feeble attack by an outnumbered force, but it was a distraction. The shop door opened and three people exited, followed by four more, none of them Borbola.

Nick began to run against the crowd. He couldn't let the Stabilizers' newest, most dangerous asset slip away. "Is there another way out of that shop?"

[I don't know. I'm tracking everyone who just left that shop, but the walking gait analyses are negative.]

Was Borbola still in the shop? Waiting for Nick? Or was there another way out?

The bounty hunter's remaining drones dispersed in the wind and powered down. They hid in downspouts, cracks in the mortar, tourist's shopping bags, everywhere. Nick hadn't expected to play cat-and-mouse this long with Borbola's drones. And it was tasking his swarms to hunt down each one.

The wind continued to increase, blowing his drones off course. There were dark storm clouds moving in on the remains of dusk.

Nick saw the shop entrance in the distance ahead of him. He checked his netpad for the trio of people who left the shop, who were coming toward him. None of them looked remotely like Borbola. Nick gulped in air and launched himself through the crowd towards the shop entrance as he powered up his three firearms. A close quarters firefight was not how he wanted this to turn out.

Cross posted a video feed of the crowd. [I found him, possibly, moving up towards the cathedral. He's wearing a light-blue t-shirt and has a sun hat on.]

"Thanks." Nick tried to cut across the crowd. A short, portly woman walked right into him while talking to her gangly friend. The woman lost her balance and began falling backwards.

"I'm sorry!" Nick yelled. He staggered forward, grabbing at her arm, and pulled her back on her feet. "*Excusez-moi!*"

The woman gave him a dirty look, but he didn't stick around. He rushed into the store and stopped to look around. The bright lights overhead forced him to squint. He sent his personal drone escort to reconnoiter the store while his eyes adjusted.

Shit.

"Cross, the candy shop connects to a souvenir clothes shop." The connection between the two shops was a hallway in the back. Nick saw the racks of t-shirts featuring the Mount and pithy sayings. Including a light-blue one. Really more of a powder-blue.

"Was this the shirt?" Nick asked, holding his netpad up to the powder-blue shirts.

[Yes. And I have a high probability match.] Cross displayed the path after Borbola with a green arrow on Nick's smartshades. Nick tossed the shirt back on the rack and raced back onto the Grande Rue.

Several tourists gave him strange looks. With the white Panama hat and wearing sunglasses at night, he looked nefarious, or at least odd.

[He just entered Saint-Pierre. He's probably trying to take the back stairs to the cathedral.]

Nick patted Slugger's reassuring bulge under his left armpit. Some part of him hoped that they wouldn't face off inside the cathedral or near the Borbola wedding reception. But the Mount was fresh out of abandoned warehouses where they set showdowns in those cheap bounty hunter action flicks.

"Stay on him." Nick doubled his drone escort. This was turning out to be much harder than he had expected.

[I have him.]

CHAPTER FORTY-FIVE

"SHOW ME. IS HE DOWN?" *God, I hope the drones get him,* Nick thought.

[Hold on.]

Cross displayed a composite feed from the drone swarm closing in on Borbola. He was jogging up the steps towards the cathedral in a powder-blue t-shirt. Nick couldn't make out his face in the dark.

Borbola knew how to throw off the walking gait software, but hiding his facial features was not something he probably planned to do when taking his mother to a wedding. Except, in the dark, Cross couldn't get a facial recognition match.

Borbola's escort drones began a series of futile dogfights against Nick's swarm. It would only be seconds before one of Nick's drones got through and knocked Borbola out.

But as Nick sprinted up Grande Rue, there was a sour feeling in his stomach. He split his attention between the video feed on his smartshades and the tourists hurtling at him like human asteroids.

Cross had a drone scan the target's face before zapping him. Nick's smartshades blinked red. He was not Eldred Borbola. Just a tourist wearing the same t-shirt.

"Find him!" Nick yelled. The crowds around him began to thin. He reached the first of several staircases leading up to the cathedral.

"Anyone wearing anything from that shop, or the shirt he had under his suit jacket. Wearing any hats and anyone limping or walking oddly."

Nick wondered if Borbola had doubled back through Saint-Pierre and had slipped by on the Grande Rue in the crowd. "Cover the exits."

[I am.]

Nick put a foot on the stairs, unsure what to do. If he wandered too far from the entrance, Borbola could escape. If he didn't head up to the cathedral, Borbola could hide there and disappear.

[He's ahead of you, to the right. Near the Tour du Nord.]

Nick had memorized the map of Mont Saint-Michel. The Tour du Nord was a tower once used to protect against invaders. There weren't any hiding places and it was highly exposed. But it did bypass the Grande Rue.

Nick leapt up the stairs two at a time. The ramparts along the top of the wall were lit with cheap organic lights that mimicked the feeble glow of wax candles. But he saw Borbola's body heat and drones clear as day on infrared.

The bounty hunter had stopped at the Tour du Nord tower. He was waiting for Nick as tourists milled about.

Nick stayed at the top of the stairs overlooking the lower ramparts, out of weapons range. "Send in the drones."

Borbola stared up at him from a hundred meters away, his arms folded confidently. A measly two-dozen drones circled him at shoulder height.

Nick called him again. "You're trapped! Come quietly or become unconscious."

Borbola replied. "I wasn't looking for a way out. I was buying time."

A massive wave of drones rose up from the ocean behind Borbola. The hostile drone count on Nick's smartshades rocketed from two dozen to thousands.

Cross drew all of Nick's drones into a massive swarm.

The two swarms flew straight into one another. On the smartshades, it looked like two flocks of differently-colored EM signatures clashed in the sky high over the abbey's eastern wall.

Lights flashed, and hundreds of drones winked out, falling into the ocean and the rampart.

Borbola backed up a step. He had no powered weapons on him.

Nick unholstered Slugger, and closed the distance between him and Borbola. "Surrender."

Borbola quirked a smile as he put his hands up. "Do you really think I'm the most dangerous person in the Stabilizer Alliance? You have no idea."

Nick kept Slugger loaded with tranquilizer rounds. One shot and Borbola could save his words for after his nap. But it would be easier to walk him out of here rather than carry him.

The wind off the Channel raked their faces with sea spray and the first drops of rain. Borbola backed his way down the rampart, staying out of Slugger's shortened effective range in the gusting wind.

The drone battle over their heads was blown laterally by the wind. A hazy flurry of dead drones blew into the abbey level above them, indistinguishable from the spray and grit in the wind.

Nick's drones were gaining the upper hand. Borbola wasn't using a Simon to operate his swarms. Ironic, because his stunt at Hamilton last year had caused a surge in offworld drone tech.

Nick just had to pen in Borbola until his drones broke through and zapped him. Nick had no interest in Kagent hand-to-hand combat.

Cross warned in blinking text, [Drones above you.]

Nick ducked and looked up. His smartshades showed fire-red drone signatures diving for him. He waved Slugger at them to bat them away. The wind blew them a meter away from his head, but some clung to Slugger.

The drones on Slugger each popped, followed by a fizzing noise. Then the drones died and fell off. Slugger was a non-metallic, non-electronic ammunition delivery platform that fit one hand. The drones had gouged holes in the barrel. He wasn't about to blow his hand off in a gory misfire.

Borbola's diversion had allowed him to run down the staircase behind him and put some distance between him and Nick.

Borbola's drones were flying some random mix of evasive patterns to delay their inevitable defeat. Nick would have to take Borbola himself. He holstered Slugger as he ran. From inside his jacket, he withdrew the object that security at Charles de Gaulle airport had so much joy examining: a stunstick that resembled a chrome penis.

Nick thumbed it on and heard a reassuring hum. Time to stick the bounty hunter with a stun dick.

Borbola hopped over another staircase and brushed past a couple strolling the narrow rampart. He pounded down a series of small staircases that led down to the Tour Boucle, a pointy fortification on the abbey's eastern wall.

Nick threw himself against the wall to dodge around the couple and came away with scrapes. He could see on the overhead map of the abbey on his smartshades that Cross was gathering drones at the Tour de l'Arcade to trap the bounty hunter.

Borbola's lead dwindled as his dress shoes lost ground versus Nick's combat moccasins on the rain-slicked cobblestone. Nick was only five meters behind when Borbola vaulted a gate that led to a staircase shortcut around the back side of the Tour Boucle. The ocean's waves pounded the Tour Boucle like an entire percussion section falling off a stage every three seconds.

Nick's attack swarm had broke through Borbola's drone defenses but were scattered by a sustained gust. Nick's swarm staggered through the shifting winds back toward Nick.

Borbola disappeared into a black pit of blindness in the staircase behind the Tour Boucle. The distance to Borbola indicator spiraled to zero as Nick vaulted the metal gate. He pounded down the stairs blindly. Borbola slammed him against the stone wall when he was in mid-step. Nick tumbled down the unforgiving concrete steps. He came to rest on his back in total darkness and pain. He lost his smartshades and stunstick and landed on his back.

Some darker shadow moved against the stormy night sky. It kicked him in the thigh with a glancing blow. Borbola was blind, too.

Another kick rapidly followed the first, this time in the shin. Nick moved before Borbola figured out where his vital organs were by process of elimination.

He rolled to his right. His butt, back, and an elbow strobed in pain.

Borbola kicked again, but hit the ground instead, emitting a surprised grunt.

Nick fixed on that grunt, ready to launch himself at the bounty hunter. He rose on his haunches like a track runner, and put his hand on the ground to steady himself.

But his hand touched cold metal rather than wet slate. Metal that crackled. The crackle was a charge from the chrome stunstick emptying into his hand.

Every muscle and neuron in his body screamed in pain, locked up, and shorted out. Blackness exploded and Nick knocked himself out.

CHAPTER FORTY-SIX

WHEN NICK CAME TO, SOMEONE was yelling. It was still dark but there was candlelight nearby. Weak, flickering, and orange. His vision swam in the feeble light.

He tasted salt on his lips and spray blew up his nose. The waves were still crashing below him but were louder, closer. He was a limp rag doll, unable to move a muscle. His nerve clusters snapped back on, one by one, each with an angry buzz. Pins and needles and pain.

But he was moving. Someone had a tight grip on the front of his shirt. His legs scraped against the stone wall.

The yelling, he realized, was in French, and it wasn't the person holding him. Nick had no idea what the pretty words meant. The little French he knew was locked away in some part of his brain that was not responding.

Someone hauled him back up, close to the stone wall. It was Borbola looking murderous and enraged, his face lit by the rampart's organic light. That was probably a bad thing.

Nick's head lolled back and he could see the foot-thick stone wall. Above him were purple-and-black clouds. And then the only thing beneath him were the waves crashing black-and-gray above him, reaching up for him. The waves threw themselves against the stone walls and then up them toward Nick. Slosh, explode, fizz, burst.

The wind knocked Nick against the rough stone wall, each point jutting into his back and legs. Thunker, Bruiser, and his drone backpack slid off and dropped into the ocean below like hi-tech tribute paid to appease an angry Poseidon.

His legs slid against the stone wall. The waves occupied his entire field of view. Borbola was dangling him over the side, holding on to his legs. Nick tried to sit up, to say something to the bounty hunter, but he was still a lifeless rag doll. The only sign of life in his body were nerves sizzling as feeling started coming back.

With an exasperated grunt, Borbola let go of his legs.

And Nick fell.

CHAPTER FORTY-SEVEN

THE BACKS OF NICK'S KNEES banged against the stone wall. The ocean roared against the rocks above him, nature's formidable grindstone, hungry to mangle his body. The wind scraped his face.

He jerked to a stop. Someone had his right leg. His shoulder blades and spine slapped against Mont Saint-Michel's thousand-year-old stone wall and pain enveloped his ribcage.

Bits of equipment broke free of his belt and dropped past his face into ocean. Among them he didn't see his netpad; if he had a working arm, he would have felt for it on his belt.

Whoever was holding his leg pulled him up. The wind shoved his body against the stone wall a couple of times, but the waves receded, and the night sky replaced it.

Someone was still yelling in French, very close by.

Nick's savior, a husky woman with a red face and short blond hair, helped him over the parapet and to the ground. Nick's head spun like a gyroscope. Slick, wet cobblestones, with rain falling on top of his head, felt like the safest spot in the world.

"Are you okay?" The man next to the woman asked with a heavy French accent.

Nick nodded and felt every limb was lit up with painful pins and needles as blood rushed in. "Where is the man?" he asked, out of breath, "who threw me over?"

The man patted his shoulder, reassuring him. "He is gone. He is gone."

"Ugh," Nick said, trying to stand. "I need to find him."

"Come over here," the man said, translating for his wife, who was speaking rapidly. "She does not like at the wall."

They helped him to the other side of the walkway. He pulled out his netpad and wiped water off the screen. There was no way he could catch Borbola, but Cross might still have a shot with the drones. He held the netpad up so the microphone could hear him. "Cross, where's Borbola?"

[He went down an alley to the Grande Rue.]

Nick staggered two steps and leaned against the wall. "Put every drone on the exits." A hundred drones spread out over the Grande Rue while the rest headed for the gates.

Lightning creased the sky. Everyone looked up, except for the security guard just reaching the scene. Thunder rolled through the heavens while the guard tried to hear the French woman's explanation of how she saved Nick's life.

The guard turned to Nick. "Are you okay, *monsieur*?"

Nick nodded. "*Oui.*"

Of course, the guard demanded a statement from Nick and the eyewitnesses. And he was in absolutely no rush. Nick would be tied up for a while.

[He's on his way out. I'm intercepting.]

The lightning split the clouds and a chilly rain of fat drops fell. Thunder cracked and echoed as the rain morphed into a downpour. Everyone around Nick broke out a poncho or umbrella. He looked down at his netpad, but he couldn't see anything on the screen.

"Shit," Nick muttered. Drones couldn't fly in conditions like this. Driving rain storms weren't something that offworld designers had to contend with when they configured the drones' flight capabilities.

[The drones are not pursuing. They are seeking shelter.]

In bad weather, the drones defaulted to programming that made them seek nooks and crannies to huddle inside while waiting for conditions to improve. Nick's drones went to ground, regardless of their current mission profile.

"Cross, override the default program. Don't let them lose Borbola!" He watched words get smeared by the water coursing over the netpad screen. "I can't read your texts."

Cross increased the font. [You'll just lose more drones, too. They can't see through this downpour. Borbola could walk right by without any of them noticing.]

The rain kept coming down.

Great, Nick figured, this would be up to him, or Borbola would get away. Nick tried to step away from the guard and the couple, but the guard stopped him with a curt hand motion.

"We have to catch this guy, right now!" Nick shouted over the thunder and tinny crash of the deluge hitting the stones. He pointed toward the Tour Basse and the exit beyond it.

The guard was in his fifties, and his sagging jowls looked unhappy to be standing out in the rain, arguing with this guy from Northam who had probably given someone a good reason to toss him over the wall. "Do you know who it was?"

"Yes," Nick said, ready for the guard to finally do something.

The guard shrugged. "Then he won't get away. But to catch him later, I need you to come with me."

The guard escorted Nick and the French couple to a guard station on the Grande Rue. When they stepped inside, the pounding rain dropped to a dull roar. The guard handed out blankets and asked Nick, "Are you hurt?"

Nick stretched his arms. "Nothing serious. But if it weren't for the *mademoiselle*, I would have died."

The guard activated his netpad and held it up to record Nick. "Can you describe the man to me?"

Nick gave him a detailed description of Borbola. The guard relayed it over his netpad. "We are looking for him now. Do you know him, *monsieur*?"

Nick shook his head helplessly. He didn't want them to know anything more than they had to. And without his smartshades or weapons, he actually did look like a tourist.

The guard said, "Have a seat, rest, and dry off. I will take statements from the others." He spoke to the woman and her husband in French.

Nick seriously considered bolting out of the station, but his body was having none of that. He had the adrenaline shakes and his nerves were all half-asleep and half on fire.

The guard and couple laughed about something and then the guard turned to Nick, "Is this yours?" He held out a chrome, penis-shaped stunstick. The French couple looked at Nick, trying not to giggle.

"We will notify you if we arrest this man," the guard said. "You are free to go. If you're up to it. You can stay here if not."

"You haven't found him, yet?" Nick asked as he stood. He headed for the door. His nerves still tingled but he was good to go. He stopped in mid-step, turned to the older couple and bowed his head. "Merci beaucoup."

They bowed in return, embarrassed.

Nick ran out into the rain. It felt like running outside in winter, wearing wet clothes and heavy boots.

"Any security cams here, Cross?" He said into the netpad.

[Only around the cathedral and they aren't on the BHN.]

The rampart walkway was a slippery, bumpy minefield for stumbling feet. Nick ran, slipped, and tripped his way toward the abbey's exit.

The guards there weren't even stopping people. One huddled under the covered drawbridge archway, letting every wet tourist by without a second glance. Another was assisting an old man who had fallen and turned his ankle.

The tourists' heads were down, covered by either umbrellas, ponchos, hoods, hats, or even shopping bags. Borbola could be anywhere or nowhere. Nick would need some extraordinary luck to pick the bounty hunter out of this crowd. If Borbola hadn't returned to the cathedral or returned to his hotel.

Nick stood there for 20 minutes, shivering under the archway, scanning faces. The guard asked him if he was waiting for family. He said he was supposed to meet someone here and she let him be.

The crowd thinned considerably, but the rain kept up a frantic pace.

"These storms," the guard said to him apologetically, "they get worse every year. Hopefully, the causeway will not be washed out again tonight."

Nick nodded. "I hope not, too. I'm in a hotel in town."

[Collect the drones before you leave,] he texted Cross.

She highlighted his drones' locations up and down the Grande Rue and the ramparts. [You have to collect them personally,] she replied. He couldn't afford to have them be washed away too, not after the battle casualties and all of his weapons were gone.

"I'm going to check for my friend, first," Nick said to the guard. He wouldn't mind getting stuck here, just in case Borbola had stayed behind.

"The drawbridge closes in 30 minutes," the guard said.

Nick marched uphill along the quaint shops and hostels of the Grande Rue, stopping to buy an umbrella and a glass jar. Then he worked his way up to the steps to the Tour du Nord, stopping every 20 meters to collect the drones in the jar.

By the time he rescued the last of the small swarms, it was clear that about a third of his drones had been either defeated by Borbola or swept away by the storm. The storm kept going, in great surges of rain lashing his legs.

He was one of the last people to leave Mont Saint-Michel for the night. He faced a long, wet, cold trek back to the Hotel De France in nearby Pontorson. Borbola had slipped away.

And Nick had no idea what to do about it.

CHAPTER FORTY-EIGHT

"WAKE UP," CROSS SAID, HER voice sounding distant on the netpad's small speaker.

Nick pried an eye open and noticed the gauzy white haze of daylight bleeding through his blanket. Shit, he had finally warmed up for the first time in 24 hours. "Go away, you awful, nasty, buggy algorithm."

"You need to get up now. You have to check out in 32 minutes. And you can't afford another night."

Nick pulled the pillow over his head. Pain shot through his arms, chest, and back from muscles that had stiffened after last night's injuries. "I'm not done sleeping. I still hurt."

"Checkout. Half-hour."

Nick moved again. Yeah, he was sore. He also had absolutely no desire to face the world. "Put some damn drones in the hallway and scare off the maid. If I get up, you'll just tell me exactly how bad things are. And I'll have to deal with it. So, fuck it all. I'm sleeping in."

Cross didn't respond. Nick closed his eyes and started to drift off again.

A ripping, piercing klaxon shot out from all directions. Nick's body went rigid. Pain shot through every limb and then converged in his head. "Cross!" Sore muscles flung sharp arrows of pain into his brainstem. He felt an all-day headache coming on. He threw off the covers and shuffled over to the shower cubby. "Not another word until I'm done, and dressed, and I tell you I am goddamn ready."

The events of last night swirled around in his mind like the water swirled around the shower drain. It was all an utter failure and he had just nearly avoided dying. Thank God for fat, nosy, French women.

His shirt, pants, and jacket were in a damp pile on the floor. He regretted not hanging them up last night. He knew from experience that there was nothing quite so self-defeating as having to put dirty, cold, wet clothes on over a fresh set of underwear. But by the time he got back to the hotel last night, he just had wanted to climb into bed.

He stood there, dried and naked, and scratched his head, trying to figure out a way to avoid the ruined clothes.

"Gun!" Cross yelled.

He dropped to the carpet as something thumped against the door.

Nick crawled to the night stand as a shot splintered the door and shattered the window behind him. He grabbed for Thunker and Bruiser, but neither one was there. They were sitting at the bottom of the English Channel, he remembered.

He dove behind the bed, the carpet scraping the skin of his back and bare ass.

The gunman fired again and then something heavy hit the floor in the hallway.

Nick stayed completely still. And then he snaked his hand up to the side table, feeling for the stunstick. It wouldn't be the most dignified way to die, but it was better than curling up in a ball.

"The drones knocked out the bounty hunter," Cross whispered. "One of Flail's."

Nick slumped against the bed. Did Borbola call them in? Maybe to remind Nick that he was even easier to track? Or was Flail still trying to get revenge and had waited until Nick was vulnerable?

He pulled his netpad off the nightstand and looked at the feed from his drones in the hallway. A big, ugly-looking Asian man was snoozing facedown along the wall.

"The police just arrived," Cross added.

Nick dressed in his icky, damp clothes, recovered his drones, and joined the crowd gawking at the snoozing bounty hunter.

When the police arrived on the floor, everyone had their story to tell and the police dutifully recorded them all.

And the witnesses looked to the police for an explanation of why this big man had decided to shoot up their hallway and then collapse. The cops fell back on the simplest, most obvious reason: The shooter was crazy or gelled and had shot up the hallway before conking out. People bought that and returned to their rooms or checked out instantly.

The policewoman who took Nick's name and statement looked at him skeptically. "You were assaulted at Mont Saint-Michel last night. Are you in some kind of trouble?"

Nick waved his hands. "No, I'm fine. Just bad luck."

The policewoman wasn't buying it. "Do you happen to be armed, *monsieur*?"

Nick shook his head. "No."

The thing of it was, he couldn't remember the last time he had used his lost firearms. He might have waved them around a few times, or intimidated people just by wearing them. The last time he had fired them, though? Months.

But letting them go felt like letting go of a crutch and finally walking free. He liked the idea. He was just afraid it wouldn't work out. Bridge had wanted him to unload his weapons during the Hamilton crashpoint. Kagents just didn't carry them.

"You should consider leaving the area to avoid trouble."

"Oh, I'm leaving this morning first thing," Nick said.

The police officer nodded, relieved. She scanned the bullet holes in his room and recorded where Nick claimed he was when the shooting started. Her partner verified that the shower cubby was indeed wet and recently used.

Nick thumbed through the hotel's checkout while the police packed up the bounty hunter. Flail's goon would sleep off his apparent gel binge in a jail cell.

Nick followed the police out of the hotel and quietly launched his drone patrol. No more getting caught with his pants down or off. Especially with Borbola supremely pissed off at him.

After he boarded a suborbital for home, he peeked at the projections. It was as bad as he had guessed. Catch Borbola; remove a dangerous Stabilizer threat. And maybe get to Lassiter, the bigger threat. Lose Borbola; lose Lassiter and any chance to twist the Stabilizer Alliance. He had hardcore enemies who seemed to be in control of the Alliance. There was a high probability that the Stabilizers would begin a bloody, messy fight that the Consortium may just win.

His netpad beeped. Pam's number. God, what was he going to tell her? He was standing in super-coach class and everyone but the pilot would hear him.

He found a pole to lean against and texted her instead of talking. [Failed. Broke. On suborbital hop home.]

[You okay?]

[Only sore. And humiliated.]

[Don't worry about it. Just come home.]

[Flail's people are still after me.]

[I know.]

Nick stood up straight in the cramped compartment, jostling the people around him. Fear clutched his bladder in a vise.

He typed furiously, [Did they attack you?]

[One was waiting for you outside our building when I came home. The police have him now. Threatening a city official is a bad idea here these days.]

Nick checked the BHN. [There's no contract out on the BHN for me or you.] But Borbola, Flail, any bounty hunter didn't need to advertise their personal grudges by posting them on the BHN.

[Never mind all that. Just come home, Nick. I love you.]

A portion of Nick's misery lifted. Maybe she really would stick with him in failure. It didn't change much about the Stabbies, but it made his aches, bruises, sprains, and cuts feel just a slight bit better.

[I love you too.]

CHAPTER FORTY-NINE

CRAIG HAD SEEN EVERY CORNER of Celebration at least twice. Even though the central Florida weather had swung towards spring, he had cabin fever.

Haruka was flying in today and that helped. They hadn't seen each other for over two weeks. He sat at the boardwalk cafe watching the sailboats tacking in the sun, the wind tugging at the open top of his button-down tropical shirt.

She had told him to meet her here. She didn't want him risking capture to greet her at the airport. It was mid-morning and he had nothing better to do than get there early and watch the boats out on the lake. So, he nursed a glass of fresh-squeezed orange juice while he waited.

She arrived dressed in high-end casual beach wear that emphasized her hips and bust. Her face lit up when she saw him and she gave him one of those knee to head hugs that pressed their waists together.

"How are you?" Craig asked.

"Jet-lagged. I need water, food, and sunlight," she declared and sat down. She poked at the menu for a few seconds, and then sat back and beamed at him. "How are you?"

"I'm hanging out," Craig said. "Spending the last of the expense account while I wait. The guy who fishes at the end of the boardwalk every day called me a beach bum, said I should get a job."

She nodded too fast, her eyes gleaming. She hadn't even heard him. She was waiting to speak. "Cooper resigned from the Board to make room for his son Bobby," she blurted. "The rumors about him working with offworlders were becoming a distraction, he told us, and it was time for new blood."

The waiter brought Haruka a baked potato. She sliced it into six equal-sized chunks. "The Board named you executive director," she said, her fork poised over the potato. "I abstained and Bobby wasn't there for the vote." She forked a fluffy white pile into her mouth. He loved that she ate with absolutely no grace at all.

He slapped his leg. "Well, hot damn. And Penny just fired me a month ago." He shook his head. "But what about us?"

Haruka chewed for a few seconds before saying, "I'm giving up my seat on the Board."

Craig reached across the table and held her hand. "You don't have to do that. Your family depends on you to handle its philanthropy. This isn't a government: We can make this work."

Were the two of them serious enough that they should be making career sacrifices for one another like this? Craig considered how little he had to show for the sacrifices he had made for work and decided yes, he would.

"That's sweet, but I decided this six months ago. It's time to move on. It's not you, Craig; it's my family."

"Your family?" he asked, concerned. He got pissed at the idea of them shoving her aside. Was it because of him?

She shook her head. "Joshua is taking over for my father. The family tradition is that when the next generation takes over the top, they take over the other positions soon after. They need to work together as a team. I was part of my father's team, not my brother's. If my uncle hadn't passed away at such a young age, I wouldn't have had the chance."

Craig squirmed in his seat. He had expected Haruka would be backing him up on the Board. "Who's taking your board seat?"

"My nephew Phillip, Kenji's oldest. He was a math major at the University of Manila. He's worked for a series of humanitarian places in Central Africa. He believes he can get a better return on the contributions using advanced metrics that I suspect are offworld ideas." She chuckled. "The only way to shut him up is to let him try."

Craig raised an eyebrow. "So, he's going to put the screws to me before I can really get started, huh? Can't wait for that." He sat back in his chair. "You're too young to hit the rocking chair and I don't have the energy for a full-time mistress. Shouldn't you go run part of the Gallardo empire?"

She patted his hand and smiled sadly. "When I was a girl, I was obsessed with the fashion subsidiary in Milan. The family has been holding the job for me for a couple of years now."

Milan? Oh, God. This was it. They were about to go their separate ways and try to hold up a romance on a series of suborbital contrails. She had to know this wouldn't work.

He held his breath and let it out in a sigh. "Screw it. Life's too short. I'll quit and go with you to Milan."

She pulled her hand away and all the warmth drained from her face. "You will not. You made a commitment to the Alliance. To my family. To my father."

"But I didn't think that meant losing you," he protested. "That changes everything."

She grinned evilly.

"You're shitting me, aren't you?"

Her grin broke wide open. "I not going to Milan. Ciebrian and Dave want me to overhaul Lobbying. Sal practically begged me; he told me the Communities need me and that he would pray for my acceptance. Pending your approval, of course, boss."

Craig laughed. "You total sexy bitch. I nearly had a heart attack!"

"Yes, you almost did. You looked so forlorn," she said and giggled.

He wanted to spank her on the ass, carry her back to his apartment and have a rough, raucous bang session. His cargo shorts shifted around under the table.

He shook his head, still not entirely believing it. "You would work for me. Huge conflict of interest, don't you think?"

She stuck out her tongue at him. "Oh, are you an ethics expert now, Mr. Shanghai? I'll be your most loyal subordinate."

"I'll bet. What makes you think, Ms. Gallardo, that you have what it takes to be the Alliance's next generation lobbyist?"

Haruka folded her hands. "I have wealthy, powerful, sympathetic contacts around the globe. Movers and shakers who can get things done. I have sweet-talked the worst and squeezed the best. Plus, my brother will be your boss."

He had been joking, but it sounded plausible. Recruiting rich socialites with superb networking skills made a lot more sense than training street protesters or cloak-and-dagger ops.

"You, my lady, are a genius," Craig said. "But I'm a horrible boss. Demanding, never satisfied, brash, kind of a jerk, plays mind games, and a very high chance of sexual harassment."

"Tell me something I don't know," she said, incredulous. The check arrived and when Craig made a grab for it, she scooped it up and gave him a disapproving look. Which was just as well, because he was barely solvent.

Craig held up his hands, defeated. "You just talked yourself into the job."

She gathered her things to go. Hopefully, back to his condo. "Anyone who wants to be a Lobbyist should have to."

Craig smiled. "Damn, I'm glad you're working for me."

Her icy demeanor didn't change. "You should be. My nephew has high standards. You'll need all the help you can get."

They walked out onto the Boardwalk. He turned towards the headquarters while she stepped towards the Boardwalk. She took his hand and pulled him close. "We need to discuss business in private in my suite." She leaned in and whispered. "My thighs itch."

Craig relented quite happily. The second they were inside the cream-colored double doors of her penthouse suit, Haruka pulled him into an embrace and kissed him deeply.

"Milan," he muttered, unbuttoning his shirt.

Haruka stepped out of her sandals and pulled her t-shirt off. She walked into the bedroom and found a hangar for it. Even horny, she abhorred messiness. Craig followed behind, hopping as his shorts snagged on his foot. She stepped out of her shorts and began folding them. Craig balled up his underwear and threw them at her bare back as he sat down to pull off his socks.

She shot a cold glance his way and undid her bra. Her breasts came free. Craig knew men who weren't turned on by a naked woman over fifty. He didn't understand them. Haruka sat down sideways on his lap, her small rear end on his left leg. Her thighs squeezed him fully erect as he kissed her deeply.

It struck him as funny that he once thought of trying to twist her, before he fell in love with her. Now, as they made their way down to the thickly carpeted floor, he bet she would have twisted him instead. She was twisting him right now, literally, pulling him down on top of her.

The carpet felt like a freshly dried towel on his knees. Haruka had her legs wrapped around his waist and wrapped her hand around him, guiding him in. The first time after being away from one another was always a quickie. The longer, slower, more exotic stuff would come later. And the way Haruka was bucking underneath him, this could be a record-setter for a quickie.

"Ah, Milan," Craig said, and felt himself let go.

CHAPTER FIFTY

ARRIVING HOME WAS A BLUR of images and sensations for Nick. The dry airline cabin, his throbbing muscles, the smell of the teriyaki dish they served onboard. Failed attempts to sleep standing up. The jerk of the plane as it hit the tarmac at Hamilton's airport after being cooped up in a nano-carbon tube for ten hours.

Cross deployed all Nick's remaining drones as Nick hurried to a taxi and again when he exited the taxi at the apartment building. It was dark already and he just wanted to kiss Pam and go to sleep.

Pam rushed into the glass mantrap to hold him. He buried his face in her hair. The familiar smells and humidity of the greenhouse transformed his exhaustion into sleepiness. Somehow, he made it to bed. He apologized for not being capable of saying much and went right out.

He woke up the next morning to find that his body was stiff but healing. The dire consequences of his misadventure in Normandy, however, hurt worse. He felt ashamed, broken, and defeated. With Borbola still out there, things were going to free fall into disaster.

He shuffled into the kitchen and tried not to make contact with his better half. But he nearly bumped into her as she rushed around the corner.

"You look like shit on an asteroid," she said. "Didn't you sleep last night?"

He nodded and fumbled in the cupboard for the breakfast bars. Grain, sugar and protein, not a vegetable in sight. Comfort food.

He found one but couldn't open the foil. Some muscles in his arms and chest hurt.

"Let me," Pam said.

Nick flopped into a chair and rested his head on his arm. She brought him the bar and a glass of water.

"Borbola escaped," Nick said, contemplating the first bite.

"I assumed," Pam said evenly.

"I lost my smartshades and guns," he said around a mouthful of cinnamon oat chunks.

"Oh, that's too bad," Pam said lightly, somewhat distracted. She would never say that. Maybe it was him losing his weapons. She, like Bridge and other Kagents belonged to the sacred church of drones and stunsticks. Kagents grudgingly accepted tranquilizer pistols. And now Nick was in the same boat but mainly through his own incompetence.

"I've failed to twist the Stabilizer Alliance."

She rubbed the back of his head. "Don't let the world fall on your shoulders. How bad is it really?"

Nick shuffled over to his workstation and leaned against the desk. "Cross, post the latest projections."

The viewer showed that the probability of the Stabilizer Alliance adopting a benign strategy had dropped to 11%. Which meant that there was about an 80% chance the Alliance would take the destructive path, whatever that path would be.

"You're going to ask if this is because of one model, or if I'm focusing too much on Craig Lassiter," Nick said to Pam. "Here's the answer."

He flipped through the various kinds of models to see if that was just a fluke of the macro model summary Cross had posted. The microsimulation, artificial agent, meta-model, and organizational models all showed the same thing. If Lassiter gave Borbola the resources to do to the Consortium members what he did to the Dragoons, the Consortium would find themselves facing a crisis beyond what they could handle.

"And this is what could happen." He had Cross display the worst outcomes. The Alliance could stir up antipathy towards the offworlders. It could shut down shipping, terrorize travelers, or commit small acts of nonviolent sabotage against cities with liftports.

The more extreme forecasts included the Stabilizers lashing out at the Kagents themselves, targeting Burgess Consortium members, or even detonating dirty bombs at liftports to slow or stop offworld trade, like Lassiter once tried in Shanghai.

"When they say to prepare for the worst, they mean this," Nick said. "But how do we prepare? We're deaf, dumb, and blind on the Alliance's moves. We can't spread ourselves thin protecting everything, or striking indiscriminately at the Alliance."

"What kind of early warning can we get about what the Alliance may try to do?" Pam asked. "We did stop it last time, when it had Kagent projections."

"Watch Alliance communications, physical locations, financial transactions," Cross said. "For example, if it stockpiles bathing suits and sunblock, we could expect it to hit someplace warm."

Nick drummed his fingers on the desk. "Pam's right; we need to create some kind of early warning system. If cities start seeing a lot of protests, or if city officials start being kidnapped, everyone in the Consortium should get an alert."

"Okay. Nick, I need to talk to you," Pam said, drinking one of her homemade juices. "Can you pull yourself away and turn off the Simon?"

[I'm off,] Cross texted, and deactivated the viewer.

Nick swallowed. This was it. Pam had given him extra time to straighten out his life, and twist the Stabilizers. He had blown it on every count. She was probably going to make him face reality about his business hitting bottom. She may even break up with him. Suddenly, he felt foolish, sitting there looking for some phantom Stabilizer plot, wasting time he could have spent shoring up the one relationship he cared about more than anything.

Pam sat him down on the couch and held his hand. "Nick, I love you."

He bit his lip, bracing for the emotional blow, feeling tears in the back of his throat. She had her business face on, the one she used during difficult negotiations.

"I love you too. What is it?"

She smiled. "I'm pregnant."

Nick opened his eyes, not realizing that he had closed them. His eyes kept opening until they bugged right out of their sockets. Or so it felt. But a smile parted his lips. "A baby?"

Pam nodded.

"Us?"

"Us. I didn't know how you would take it," Pam said.

"I love it. I thought you were going to dump me!"

"I probably should, but apparently, I had the poor judgement to let you impregnate me, so I'll just stick with it." She smiled in a way he hadn't seen her smile in a long time.

"I wish I could say I planned it that way," Nick said. He fell off the chair onto his knees and hugged her waist. Then he kissed her.

"How?" Nick said, feeling her abdomen. He didn't even have much of an idea where her uterus was. It didn't matter; there was a child in there somewhere. His child.

"I think you forgot to take your pill one time," Pam said.

No, could that be? He was conscientious about that. But there had been a couple of unexpected episodes they had on days he may have forgotten.

It didn't matter. They were having a child. They would be a family. As long as he didn't drive Pam away or get himself killed.

Nick held her by the shoulders. "I have never wanted anything so much that I didn't know I wanted before I had it, than this."

POST A REVIEW, GET KAGENT #3 FOR FREE!

Post a review of *Crashpoint* or *Twistpoint* on Amazon and/or Goodreads, email Mark (mark [dot] sarney [at] gmail [dot] com), and get a pre-release e-book of *Chokepoint (Kagent Series: #3)!* For free!

Note: It doesn't matter how you rate the book. Just be honest, and hopefully, entertaining.

GET MORE FREE STUFF!

Want special discounts, giveaways, and sneak peeks at upcoming titles from Mark Sarney?

Subscribe to his newsletter, The Scoop.

ABOUT THE AUTHOR

Mark Sarney has worn a Chuck E. Cheese costume, taken a phone call from Air Force One, and was the 6th grade dodgeball champion, but not in that order.

He is the author of the Kagent series. The third book in the series, *Chokepoint*, will be out soon.

He lives in Columbia, MD with his wife and two children.

You can follow him at marksarney.com and on twitter.com/marksarney or email him at mark [dot] sarney [at] gmail [dot] com

ACKNOWLEDGEMENTS

PATIENCE, TOLERANCE, SUPPORT:

Wendy Sarney
Karenna Sarney
Jaden Sarney

BETA READERS:

Nolan Smith-Kaprosy
Joni Lavery
Matt Lesko

EDITING:

Paula Stiles
http://thesnowleopard.net/

COVER, LAYOUT, DESIGN, AND PRODUCTION:

Glendon and Tabatha Haddix
http://www.streetlightgraphics.com/